Infernal Relations

By
P.S. Rover

FORTE BOOKS
Oxford

First published in Great Britain in 2022 by
Forte Books,
Oxford, England.

Cover design by Amanpreet Sohi

Discover more at
www.psrover.com
www.fortebooks.co.uk

A CIP catalogue record for this book is available from the British Library.

ISBN 978-1-9196492-0-7 (eBook)
ISBN 978-1-9196492-1-4 (Paperback)

Dedicated to my father

Chapter One

I was idling in my Cambridge retreat, away from all the strife that seems to originate in my world, watching a children's game of cricket and feeling that life couldn't have been any rosier when I had the first inkling that my present tranquillity would soon be upended. A sense of foreboding generally manifests itself whenever a return to the family home of Lockwood is brewing and, with a new term in the offing, I was in its thrall. This climactic upheaval rampages over my oasis like a monsoon. It haunts me every year, but little could I have known that these particular pangs were the harbingers of circumstances that would harrow the soul and boggle the mind at every turn.

It's not my usual practice to spectate when the standard of play is so pitiful and I was poised to turn away when something seemed to herald an intriguing shift in the dynamics. Until then I'd always assumed it was better to fasten a heavy object to a stout rod to really fling it, but here came clear evidence that it's far better, if you want to achieve more in the way of centrifugal force, if it's gripped and swung by something pathetically weedy. In this instance it was the bowling arm of a spindly boy with a floppy middle parting. Whether this unruliness was a deliberate ploy to appear more menacing was unclear, but after setting off in the direction of the pavilion and coming to a stop near the boundary line, this runt of the brood turned sharply and scrambled to the pitch and let loose what became, for a time, a new direction in the weaponisation of circular objects. The delayed release, when it came, carried such snap and velocity on the bounce that the batsman, an oversized and surly blighter, was a sitting duck when he was clattered roundly on the chin.

The viewing public recognised immediately that they had witnessed a once-in-a-generation breakthrough and were unreserved in their hoots of 'bravo' and 'I say!' Once the applause had petered out and all that could be heard was the bawling batsman, from out of the pavilion poked the bald dome of what I took to be the teacher responsible for these urchins. Rising to his full six foot four he strode intently across, covering ground quickly and, arriving at the snivelling mass, made a firm delivery of his own by landing a glancing blow above the boy's ear.

'Stop your whining!'

This display of sporting decency proved so popular with the viewers that pretty soon a standing ovation was acknowledging this blow for civilisation.

I was watching this triumphant spectacle through the window from my chaise longue and feeling an affinity for this hero of our times when I felt a full-on drowsiness come over me. I had noticed this tendency of late. You may have experienced it yourself perhaps. There you are in the middle of the afternoon thoroughly absorbed in something, actively taking part I mean, and your attention starts to ebb. This typically encourages others to repeat things you were glad you missed the first time. Setting things straight, you lay the problem squarely at your posture and explain that there's nothing physicians can do about it and, after shifting in your seat, you issue a polite 'do go on' before restoring the blindfold.

Truth be told, I had a longing for the licence that accompanies the time of life when it's dashed proper to be seen with mouth open and feet over the arm of the settee in the afternoon. Why, I wonder, should this practice be confined to the seniors? And I had it on good authority that I wasn't alone in my thinking. Inasmuch as there ever can be such a thing, there might be said to be public discussion under way at the time on the subject from all thinking quarters and I remember distinctly it was a chap from the British Medical Something Or Other who published a piece attributing the malaises of the day to the scourge of hurry and excitement of modern life. He didn't refer to it as a scourge, as I recall, but we seem to share opinions on the topic so I feel at liberty to paraphrase the fellow. I had also read about these hunter-gatherer types who, when they weren't slaying something, would be getting their full complement of forty winks. For these enlightened philosophers, it seemed there was nothing better than to put up a sign and turn out the light.

I became so curious about the subject that I added a few volumes to the library and made a point to digest them as soon as I found them again. Even so, the present inducement to clock out was particularly intoxicating. No sooner had I twanged the blindfold than I sank into a recurring dream that distresses me greatly at this time of year.

It begins with a brusque man with bristly mutton chops and a bushy moustache ordering me to go to a secluded spot surrounded by miles of forest. There I am greeted by a doddering old man who, while complaining of lumbago, leads me through the impressive grounds past a perfectly fine mansion towards a complex of decrepit dorms and outbuildings towards the place he calls my residence where he deposits my four cases before shuffling off. The purpose of my visit – to join the other jobwalas in the whole shabby enterprise.

I had got half-way through this harrowing torture of the subconscious when I felt a tickle in my right ear lobe and, suddenly, a rush of blinding light invaded my dulled senses triggering a bout of violent sneezes. Throughout this onslaught I discerned the sound of gleeful laughter. It was a man's voice. After the sound of furious scribbling came a sharp snap and a tiny projectile shot into my ear canal. With a heavy tut there came a mumbling about the sub-standard quality of utensils nowadays which revealed to me the identity of my molester – it was my cursed cousin, Monty. With his parents to thank for much of my upbringing, I bear something of a fraternal responsibility for this pestilential relation who can be relied upon to blot an otherwise peaceful existence. I was in such sporting bliss that I'd forgotten that he was visiting.

'Ah-ha, it lives!' he said as I struggled to lift my head. Trying desperately to shake off the lethargy, I felt like an opium enthusiast after a considerable dose.

'The creature rose in a fit of fury,' Monty gibbered excitedly, scrambling for another pencil. I lost no time in getting down to the nub.

'What the dickens are you doing?'

'No cause for alarm,' he said, 'it's what are referred to in the field as side-effects.'

He said this as though he were an eminent diagnostician on the frontier of a ground-breaking discovery.

'You know,' he continued, 'symptoms which stubbornly persist where they're not wanted. Like misfits at a soirée.'

'I know what fismits are, thank you, doctor,' I said, clouting my ear to dislodge the broken tip. 'But of what, exactly?'

'I'm testing the efficacy of this,' he said, handing me a semi-transparent vial. I squinted woozily in vain at the bizarre markings on the label. Nobody has been found who can interpret Monty's Palaeolithic scrawl.

'What is it?' I asked.

'Well, bromide, of course.'

'What!' I thundered.

Without waiting to hear any more I yanked the stethoscope from his neck and wedged the filthy earpieces firmly in my ears. Holding them tightly, I closed my eyes and tried to listen to my insides. It was appalling. I mean to say, I'd never stood on the precipice peering into a volcano, but I'd say the sound of gloopy bubbling molten lava would be the same in every particular. I felt myself becoming delirious and I was soon overwhelmed with visions of descending into a fiery pit. As I shook my head to stop myself plunging deeper into the inferno, I could hear Monty babbling away unintelligibly. While I wrestled with my slipping consciousness I was fixed by an inescapable feeling of pity that it was just my misfortune to be related to a sadist, when I opened my eyes to see he was still holding the chest-piece to his torso. By Jove! the relief was overwhelming.

I tottered to my feet and surveyed my surroundings. An assortment of pharmacological volumes from my bookshelves were strewn over the floor. It took a moment, but eventually I pieced it together. I'd seen this infestation take root in Monty before. Ever since taking on the role of the Danish prince in the blasted play that cannot be named, with its cackling witches and their potions, a feverish curiosity had been awakened in him. Entirely how it was that Monty had come to manifest a propensity for experimenting with solubles is a subject best unravelled by the field of psychotherapy, but I'd long come to the conclusion that probing into his subconscious would yield no answers, only questions.

Even so, little did I expect him to unleash his obsession on me in this ghastly way. Still shaky and with my throat parched, I was poised to confront the fellow when he raised a hand.

'No need to thank me, old man.'

I was stupefied.

'Thank you?'

'Really no need. I know how much you enjoy slipping into a bit of quiet time on the settee so I prepared a concoction.'

Lucky for me that he hadn't flipped to the pages on trepanning. This was Monty all over. What the Germans call an *Einfaltspinsel* – fascinated by everything, good at nothing. And yet here was this busy little Erasmus reworking the enlightenment for his own twisted ends. I mean, no one could argue that an injection of knowledge in Montgomery Fipps wouldn't be a welcome development on all sides. In fact, I'd be the last to fault his pursuit of it. If only it weren't the clambering, clodhopping kind. I was preparing to have it out with him when he said something which altered my outlook completely.

'I'll just finish this batch and you can keep it with you always.'

I felt the immediate outrage subsiding at these words.

'Hmm.'

Many deep breaths later, seeing that I was no worse for wear, I reflected on the upside of having the essence of nature's sweet restorer to hand. I imagined myself slipping into the land of nod on a whim and I found myself strangely more forgiving of Monty using me as a lab rat for his beastly experiments. The path of human advancement, I told myself, is often the story of the unlikeliest of persons stumbling upon something of utility.

So, in the interests of science I told him I was resolved to think it over. He rubbed his hands together, happy to have helped a friend get more pleasure in life, or rather in sleep.

'I think I missed my calling as an apothecary,' he said, reclining. He sat with his arms behind his head as if concluding a seminar at the Royal Institute. And this from the chump who should have been in our home town of Winsbrook attired in breeches and ruffs rehearsing for an amateur production of *Hamlet* as the eponymous brooding prince, of all things.

He'd posted me a tea-stained copy of the Winsbrook Repertory Bulletin some time ago, presumably so I might rejoice in the news of his casting, but truth be told, I was rather taken aback that he'd been selected to front it. I mean, this seemed a far cry from school productions which generally consisted of him dressing up as foliage, waving to his latest love interest in the audience during the quiet moments.

A few days later came his unexpected arrival at my residence, which shattered the solitude. He clattered my knocker like an outlaw ducking the imminent clasp of Scotland Yard.

'Monty?' I said, peering at the slovenly figure before me.

'Shh,' he said, pushing past me and ripping off the false beard.

'What the…'

He looked positively haunted.

'I've come to stay, Spencer. You don't mind, do you?'

I pondered this for a moment, but eventually relented. I often wonder if I should have been less hasty. I asked if he'd been given the boot from work again, but he pooh-poohed the idea. Then, no sooner had he sat down than he sprang up and wandered over to the window. After scanning the street thoroughly he seemed satisfied that the coast was clear and returned to his seat. He cut a perturbed figure and I could see that this was a time for drastic measures.

'Drink?' I said.

I poured two, but before I had time to take a seat, he'd snaffled his, so I placed the brandy bottle on the table.

'Don't mind if I top myself, do you?' he said, reaching for it.

'By all means.'

One learns to appreciate Monty's malapropisms. He glugged feverishly at the sort of measure usually reserved for a chap who's fallen overboard. As I examined the shambolic wretch before me I was reminded of something.

'Just a minute,' I said, after it eventually dawned on me, 'aren't you supposed to be in rehearsal?'

'Ha!' he exclaimed. 'Fat chance.'

I eyed him askance. There was something distinctly evasive in his manner. This could mean only one thing.

'You mean you've been kicked out of the play?'

'Certainly not!' he said, haughtily. He rose to his feet and began pacing the room. 'Certain creative differences have surfaced, that's all.'

'I see,' I said, playing along. 'You've parted brass rags.'

'Don't be absurd,' he said. 'The idea. I'm just—'

'Extricating oneself from a tight spot?'

He thought for a moment.

'You could say that.'

'By removing oneself from the production.'

'Exactly.'

'To lie low for a spell.'

'Quite so,' he said, fingering his collar.

'Staying at arm's length.'

'That's it, blast you.'

This lingered in the air for a moment. Then in an instant his expression soured and he crumpled.

'Oh,' he wailed, landing heavily on the chair, 'you've hit the nail on the crux of it, curse you.'

Monty's defences, such as they are, have a tendency to buckle under the slightest questioning and open up like a burst dam when sufficiently lubricated. And since I felt instinctively that we were getting to the essence, I pressed on with the zeal of a Spanish Inquisitor and lo and behold! the truth came tumbling out of him.

'It's all to do with this blasted Ophelia female.'

'I might've guessed,' I said at the inevitability of this. I popped on the blindfold. 'Do go on.'

'I was having an innocent chuckle with what's-his-name—'

'Whose name?'

'That gentleman I fall out with to the death.'

'Fall out with to the death…' I repeated, wondering which of the Bard's creations he was referring to. As I generally preferred the classics, I clutched a few straws.

'Duncan?'

'No.'

'Mercutio?'

He thought for a second.

'No.'

I shrugged in the end.

'Laertes!' he said, suddenly remembering.

'Oh, you mean Miles.'

'Who?'

'Miles Partington-Smythe. He's the chap you mean. Looks like—'

'Goliath. That's the chap. Anyway, we were getting along swimmingly until I said that if I didn't know better, I was convinced this Ophelia minx had been giving me the come on.'

I heard Monty pouring himself another moderate skinful.

'And?'

'Well, you could've knocked me down with a feather,' he said, taking a generous swig. 'Until then, he'd been a paragon of gentleness. Then that innocent little remark of mine seemed to unleash his inner beast.'

'Oh, how so?'

'The blighter threatened to savage me.'

'Go on,' I said. 'What else?'

'What *else*?' he said, aghast. 'Spencer, he wants to tear my ruddy limbs off.'

I stole a peek under the blinkers at his weedy extremities.

'Legs or arms?' I said, settling back under them. 'I'm trying to picture the scene.'

'Will you take that blasted thing off!' he snapped, whipping the blindfold off me.

An awkward lull ensued. I couldn't help feel that he was getting a bit hot under the collar over the whole business.

'Hang on,' I said, some of the story coming back to me, 'aren't fisticuffs part of the plot?'

He beamed in the manner of a mentor seeing his slow-witted protégé finally grasp the elementals.

'Glory be!' he said, throwing his hands in the air.

I humoured the fellow. It's the only way with Monty.

'I see,' I said, catching on. 'So, this playful badinage was your way of binding the company in ties of friendship, was it?'

'Exactly! But Miles didn't see it that way. He said I'd besmirched his good wife's name.'

I exercised my cousinly right and issued a disapproving tut.

'Had you?'

'Of course not,' said Monty indignantly. 'I said that I hadn't said a word against his good wife. But, beckoning him closer for a friendly word in his ear, I said, "But if I were you, old man, I'd stick closely to the *good* one".'

'Sounds friendly enough to me.'

'You'd think so,' he said in an aggrieved tone. 'But he didn't. He just turned purple in the cheeks and vented, "Ophelia *is* my good wife, you son of a—" something I won't repeat.'

'Crikey.'

The way Monty had set out the scene, it was all beginning to sound a bit Greek to me.

'Just a minute,' I said, revisiting an important detail. 'Exactly how many wives are there in this harem?'

'I don't care and I told him so. I said I couldn't remember how many merry wives he blasted well had, but, "Let's stick to the same play, shall we?"'

'Quite,' I said, suddenly needing a top-up. 'No good if he keeps changing the script. What's she got to do with it anyway?'

'Who?'

'This Osenia wench.'

'Ophelia.'

'That's the one.'

'She's his sister.'

Well, I mean to say, his wife *and* his sister! This was one beastly revelation too many for my delicate constitution. Frankly, this didn't surprise me in the least. I'd always had my doubts about Shakespeare. And fond as I am of the classics, I'd always hurriedly glossed over any suggestion of this sort of element in the ancient narratives. Anyway, that's where the matter rested for the nonce.

Two days later, during another maddening conversational tussle with Monty, the telephone sprang to life and a formidable female voice demanded to speak to him. Monty shuffled to the telephone and cautiously placed the receiver to his ear. After some stern-sounding one-way conversation pouring into him, I couldn't help notice his countenance undergo a marked change. By the time he'd replaced the receiver he'd taken on the stunned expression of a man who suddenly sees all.

'Oh,' he said, slapping his thighs and breaking into unrestrained mirth. 'Good heavens. You'll never guess.'

He was soon roaring like an imbecile and in the several minutes he took to gather himself I wondered if the day had arrived when the authorities would be called to take him away. Eventually, he put an end to his cackling and, I must say, it was a bit of a jolt to hear him resume this business of the play, loath as I was to hear any more about it, but he seemed intent to persevere deeper into the sordid details.

'I say, do you remember this rotten Ophelia business?'

'Now look here—'

'It's all been straightened out.'

I paused my wriggling.

'Oh,' I said, cheerily. 'With the other wives, you mean?'

I wondered if some sort of entente cordiale had been arranged, but as I studied Monty's demeanour, I noticed a distinct change come over the man. Forty-eight hours ago he had resembled an outcast who had been cruelly misjudged, but now he had the air of a juvenile in the dock confessing before his mother.

'It seems,' he said, suppressing a laugh, 'that it was all a misunderstanding. Ophelia *is* his good wife, but she's also his *only* wife.'

I was briefly nonplussed by this.

'So, he's not a profligate cad after all?'

'I know, surprising, isn't it?' confirmed Monty. 'Still, there it is.'

'And this business of Ophelia giving you the come on?'

'Oh, yes, she explained that. She *was* giving me the come on, but it's what happens in the play, apparently.'

'*Apparently*,' I repeated. 'So you haven't read it?'

'Of course not,' he scoffed. 'Imagine doing all that by rote. I glance over my lines before each wotsit…'

'Act?'

'Scene. And when others are looking at me expectantly, I know it's my next line.'

I understand this labour-saving method had enjoyed a brief spell of popularity at the Royal Academy of Dramatic Arts, but had come to an end, like all good things. Thinking back, Monty had always claimed he was destined for the limelight ever since his track record for raising Cain made him a shoo-in to play Pandora in our prep school. And here he was, front and centre this time, in similarly tragic vain. But there was still one burning question preying on my mind.

'So, does this mean you'll be returning forthwith?' I said, hopefully.

He sat bolt upright again, as if reminded of the gravity of the situation.

'No fear.'

'Why not?'

'Miles still wants to pulp me to a paste.'

I was fogged. I mean, I had started out wondering why on earth Miles would be after Monty's blood in the first place, but as the conversation had drawn on, as any conversation with Monty is apt do, I had begun to feel deeply for Miles. So much so, I'd started to wonder if the right and proper thing wouldn't be to hand Monty over and let the limbs fall where they may.

'It's better for all that I stay right here,' he said, ferreting in the liquor cabinet. 'Do you have any more brandy?'

And that was all there was to it. It didn't take long for Monty to put the incident behind him. It never does, of course, such is his carefree disposition. If there's one thing I admire about the old fruit, it's his natural ability to forget almost anything.

In the present circumstances, however, as I rose from the effects of being dosed and my eyes adjusted to the scene before me, I couldn't help feel a little miffed at how my modest, but decorous quarters had taken on a distinctly distressed appearance. Childlike drawings of an unfortunate-looking sleeping human subject appeared to have been flung about the floor, beakers of hellish fluids scattered the dining table and, for reasons that still escape me, a pair of knickerbockers poked out from under the chaise longue, as if it had all got too much and Monty had felt the need to air his lower half. An involuntary shudder ran through me at the grizzly prospect, but in doing so I was able to shake off the immediate signs of chaos and banish them from my mind. A few moments later, as I pondered the looming clouds on the horizon, I came to reflect that I ought to savour this time before the new term at Lockwood officially dawned.

My Cambridge abode is where you'll find me when my services are not required at the family estate in the town of Winsbrook. There doesn't seem to be much call for a co-bursar between the seasons, but lately my time away had become a sort of exile after the commandant – my father – had suggested I go and mind a lighthouse somewhere. So, in all but letter, those were the instructions I'd been carrying out.

Monty's arrival, on the other hand, is as predictable as the flight of the birds and his appearance is assured whenever he can wangle a spot of leave. This is on account of him being employed, if you can fathom such a thing, at Lockwood Institute in the admissions department.

You see, it's like this: we both put in some little time in the employ of my father and in season are resident at Lockwood Institute – a family-owned estate set deep in the heart of Suffolk. Billed as a premier retreat, this secluded nook specialises in the *appreciation* of humanities, international diplomacy, culture and languages, tailored for late developing youths whose well-meaning parents spend their days idling as civil servants, ministers, freemasons, industrialists, diplomats and dignitaries. Assuring its residents a path to society's most coveted positions, it is, some would say, a fallback option finishing school for the gentry who have failed to acquire the ways of their kith and kin and been denied entry everywhere else. For an establishment whose core mission is to carve out the seasoned men and women of tomorrow, to my mind, a fouler assembly of merry-making layabouts you'd be hard-pressed to find in all of creation. Since its inception, like a moth to a bulb, it has attracted a great many obnoxious upstarts on their grand tours. Recognised all over, Lockwood was seen as a byword for the training of men of affairs.

That is before it opened its doors to both sexes and gained notoriety for training men *in* affairs.

Be that as it may, this hive of activity is a kaleidoscopic mix and attracts visitors from all four corners, as it were. It might also be said that Lockwood is to the loafing offspring of dignitaries what a penal colony is to the skulking vagrant. My father maintains that just as the resemblance of Lockwood Institute to a correctional facility is not entirely without substance since it was formerly used in that capacity, when his thoughts turn to the sum total of my contribution, as he puts it, he is struck by how my admission to it seemed destined. And this is just the sort of cutting jibe that I have come to expect tumbling off his lips over the years.

'Chai!' exclaimed Monty as he re-entered hotfooting a tea tray and sloshing the beverage over the length of the carpet. Still under the effects of his latest creation, I was poised to decline, but I was parched and his other propensity for brewing concoctions is well known. By the by, Monty takes a particular pride in the art of tea-making and makes a point to consume this wholesome beverage far more than a man with an occupation ought. To him it is the elixir of health and wisdom. The medicine which breathes life into virtually any stone. He has thought this way ever since he was first sent to stay with his father, my Uncle Cedric, who was on a tour of duty in India. Seeing the young being weaned on it and the sick being healed by it, what other conclusion is there to be drawn? And since his return Monty has been an insatiable glugger of the stuff.

We were just about to settle into it when we heard something shatter. Then came another fracture and for a moment I wondered if it might not be Mrs Fanshaw's brutes next door slinging things. I dashed to the back window, but there was nothing amiss as far as I could see. I hurried to the front window. Ah-ha. There was the saboteur. A hideous black sedan of some description appeared to be clambering up the driveway and, in front of it on the gravel, lay the remains of a ceramic plant pot.

Monty joined me at the window and I wondered who this interloper was. The reprobate at the wheel, I mean, not Monty.

'Spencer, the pot.'

I thought this hardly the time to be concerned with the tea. Then he pointed to the heap of broken crockery.

'Never mind that,' I said, 'do you recognise the car?'

He shook his head and we stood watching. The front portion had scaled the drive, but the rear wheels spun endlessly on the gravel. In frustration, the driver floored the accelerator, which sent a spray of pebbles high into the air peppering a local septuagenarian with grit as he passed by. Now, I defy anyone to stand idly by at the sight of an elderly gentleman receiving a blast of gravel to the upper regions without giving some thought to action, so I reasoned pretty firmly as he floundered to scrape the muck from his eyes that if nobody else went to his aid sharpish, I might be forced to take it upon myself. But I hadn't advanced much further in my thinking when from my peripheral vision I noticed the approaching bus. Looking back to the drive, I couldn't help notice the car had begun sliding backwards and what with the old man stooping behind it to retrieve his fallen hat, I held my breath and closed my eyes to avoid the inevitable concatenation when there came a loud wrench and the handbrake took hold. The man shambled on, soiled, but unharmed.

In one final push, the driver gave everything until the wheels suddenly gripped and the car surged forward and butted the front wall with the force of a battering ram. It slid back down just enough to leave its rump jutting out, forcing pedestrians into the road.

Monty and I stood frozen in horror wondering which squadron of the local military had come to obliterate my ashram when the car began rocking violently, its springs straining under the apparent bulk contained within. After a struggle the driver's door swung open and sprang violently back on the fingers clasping the sides. In the months that followed neighbouring streets told of the bloodcurdling cry they had heard that day. A moment later a hefty boot stamped the gravel followed by an almost spherical bald dome. I recognised it immediately. It was my father's. Sons soon do well to recognise their fathers from all angles, especially such substantial figures as mine.

He rose to his stocky five foot nine and after inspecting his stubby bruised digits, kicked the wheel arch and muttered something which, reading from his lips, I took to be 'foreign junk'. Looking upwards, he squinted and popped his pipe – a comforter for all occasions – into his mouth to survey the surroundings of my suburban retreat. Chez Lockwood Junior consisted of the upper half of a tall terrace of late Victorian construction situated on a road of lively aspect and character. It was evident to me from the way he was squinting from house to house scratching his crown that he was of the mind that in all his puff, of all the hovels most abundantly in need of controlled explosion, mine was top of the list.

He stood for a moment shaking his head and inspecting his bruised hand. As he leaned back, the driver's door clunked shut. Instantly there came panicked knocking from the passenger side window and he began clodhopping round to the other side, his boots sliding on the gravel.

'Just a minute, my love. Let me just, Jesus!' he cried, whipping his hand away from the scalding bonnet. 'I'm moving as fast as I can, my love.'

I took it that this token of affection was intended for Kristina Aptula – odds-on favourite as my stepmother-in-waiting.

If you had said that the old commandant would pair up with one of the more mature inmates at Lockwood Institute, I'd have said the chances were remote but not outside the bounds of possibility. If, on the other hand, you'd said that he would take up with a Bulgarian duchess émigré who would become a permanent fixture in our lives, I'd have taken it as a sign of an irreversible mental condition. But, there in a nutshell, as Monty keeps reminding me, is why my streak at the card table is a losing one.

Sir Walter, as he insists on being called, stomped moodily across the gravel and rang the doorbell. You're familiar with the sort of ringer, I mean. Matrons use them on malingering patients during bed shortages. We didn't dare answer it. It rang again with more gusto this time.

'Spencer! I know Monty's in there,' thundered the voice through the letterbox. 'I can see his revolting breath steaming up the window.'

I'd always considered Monty's breathing the source of much trouble. Spurred on by guilt, I suppose, Monty broke the silence.

'You have the wrong house.'

'Monty?' boomed Sir Walter.

Monty gulped hard.

'I think he's onto you, Spence.'

The bell rang with more urgency.

'Monty,' I said, cursing him for the foundling he must have been, 'let's make a point to discuss this later, shall we?'

After taking a few deep breaths I answered the door.

'Wally,' I said, aiming for a son's radiant welcome.

'I told you not to call me that,' he said, tramping past. 'It's *father* so long as there are no strangers present and *Sir Walter* if there are.'

Try as I might, I had never got him to drop this absurd policy. After all, I couldn't help it if he was my father.

'Ah,' I said, feeling my geniality had been a trifle stymied.

In the time that I'd closed the door he'd stooped and risen quickly for a man of his deportment.

'Here,' he said, handing me his boots.

'Oh,' I said, grasping the beastly things. 'Throw them away?'

'Put them away, you imbecile.'

'Right you are,' I said, opening the door to the nearest cupboard. As I flung them inside there came the sound of breaking glass. I glanced within to see the remains of several smashed beakers. I'd evidently unearthed the storage den for Monty's life sciences lab.

'What was that?' asked Sir Walter.

'Pot fell off the windowsill, I expect,' I said, nonchalantly.

'Place is a death trap,' he muttered.

I was gearing up to ask to what I owed the pleasure when he stamped into the living room. I joined him and was pleased to find that Monty had made things look more presentable.

'Nose to the grindstone?' asked Sir Walter, lifting my blindfold from the chaise longue. 'Well, put the kettle on, man.'

It took but an instant for Monty to dash off into the kitchen. He never needs to be asked twice.

'New car?' I asked.

'Hmm? No. Well, yes. A gift from an attendee,' he said, fiddling with some loose threading on the settee, 'in lieu of payment.'

'Ah.'

'No wonder I didn't recognise it.'

'Hmm.'

I could feel the conversation beginning to sag somewhat, so I sought to touch on the purpose of his visit when something struck me.

'Good heavens! Kristina's still in the car.'

At these words Sir Walter appeared singularly unmoved.

'Well, isn't she coming in?' I asked, after a spell.

'No, I, er, shouldn't think so.'

'Well,' I said, 'perhaps she'd appreciate some tea. I'll take her some.'

'No, that won't be necessary.'

'It's no trouble,' I insisted.

'I would be deeply obliged,' he said, holding up a hand, 'if you would put an end to this drivel.'

As Monty re-entered, scattering biscuits on the floor, Sir Walter explained that he and Kristina were returning from a business event that would do wonders for putting the institute on the map, as it were. Roughly translated to you and me, this boils down to some festivities with embassy types – the sort of function in which Kristina is expected to pull her feather-light weight by working her charms on potential clientele.

'Ah, yes,' I said, still trying for a note of bonhomie, 'raise the profile, did it?'

'Yes, our reputation is once again rising. Looks like your extended purdah was just the ticket.'

'Kristina is a sweetheart for suggesting it,' I said.

'Still, why you insist on this clerk's cesspit is beyond me. Look at the state of it. You should be ashamed of yourself.'

Monty suppressed a giggle. We'd been expecting it and there it was – my father's favourite broadside, 'You should be ashamed of yourself.' When it concerned my best efforts in any capacity, my father's raison d'être was to be able to weave his favourite put-down into every conversation.

'Anyway, I hate to drag you away from your vocation, Spencer,' he said, sipping from the cup. 'Good lord, that's poison. But I must ask you to return at once.'

'Eh?'

This seemed to be anathema to everything I had heard so far. I was grappling with this unlikely plea when the penny dropped and his motives became clear to me. The ship must've sprung a leak somewhere and he'd evidently called on me to steer the vessel into calmer waters.

'Ah-ha,' I said, savouring this fatherly cry for help. 'The balloon has gone up, has it?'

'What?'

'Oh, come, come, this is no time to be coy,' I said, slurping Monty's hell-brew and holding back the tears. 'The war chest is no longer leaking. It's elementary. The coffers are being replenished and you want me to be your outright treasurer. Well, as you know, to me, refusing a plea for help is not unlike a Benedictine monk refusing a sip—'

'Francis Spencer Lockwood, it is owing to your prolonged absence that the institute's coffers are now flourishing. It is also the reason the job is no longer left solely in your hands. Nothing would compel me to ask you to return were it not an emergency. I have a special duty for you.'

I didn't like the sound of this at all.

'What sort of special—'

'Never mind that now.'

'You don't mean to say you want me to be your chief taster in sampling your cutlets and puddings again, do you? Nobody was trying to poison you—'

'Just return directly. And as for our tea aficionado here,' he said, turning towards the source of the slurping. 'Monty, your characteristic dereliction of duty has left me without my leading man and put the entire production in jeopardy.'

'Ah, yes,' began Monty, unfurling what he'd been rehearsing in his mind for several minutes. 'About that Ophelia and Laertes mix-up, I mean, that ghastly incest business was—'

'Spare me the bilge, Monty. I have no wish to know about your depravities, but lucky for you the way has been paved for you to rejoin the production without, you'll be glad to hear, any act of retribution by Partington-Smythe.'

Monty was so bucked by the news that he leapt to his feet and seized Sir Walter's hand and began vigorously shaking it.

'Yaow-ooh-ooh!' yelped Sir Walter, examining his bruise.

'Oh, I say,' said Monty, noticing the crushed digits. 'I had no idea.'

'The day you have an idea that will not strike terror into those around you, Monty, we shall all commemorate it.'

Monty flopped into the armchair with the relief of a man who discovers his terminal diagnosis had been meant for someone else.

'Good heavens.'

'Till after the play anyway. And, I can't say the same for Ophelia. Now, you will return with Spencer forthwith and assume your former responsibilities. Is that clear?'

'But—'

'But me no buts!' sneered Sir Walter.

And without waiting to hear any more, he stood up to leave.

'On the double!' he shouted, rattling the door in its frame.

So there it was. The writ had been served. I remained frozen in shock for some time. As I sat down reeling from this encounter, Monty yipped and, springing up, dashed towards the kitchen. It was only when smoke billowed into the hallway that I realised something must be ablaze in the kitchen, which is inclined to happen when Monty plays mother. Thank heavens father had already left.

Chapter Two

THE following morning at breakfast I brooded on the offensive from the senior regiment and sat staring at the table silverware. The face looking back had the aspect of a wrongly convicted fellow about him. In the space of a few days my solitude had been shattered, I'd harboured a fugitive and now I'd been lassoed back to the Gulag by the high command. If this stormy passage wasn't typical of the sort of misfortune that usually tugs on the heart strings in a Russian tragedy, it came dashed close.

From the corner of my eye I noticed Monty was a hive of activity. After scraping it clean, he was now staring at the bottom of the jam jar looking for meaning.

'Monty,' I said, trying my reflection in a spoon, plumbing the depths of nature itself, 'you'd say that I'm a man of the world, wouldn't you?'

He stopped to check if it was a trick question.

'What?'

'A man of the world. You know.'

'Erudite, you mean?'

'Precisely.'

'Learned?'

'Exactly.'

He was completely still.

'Go on,' he said.

'Well,' I said, thinking back along the Lockwood ancestral line, 'do you think I'll be the sort of chap who appears resembling some tsar at the citadel gates, forces entry and orders the underlings to hop to it?'

'Like Ivan the Terrible, you mean?' he said, chuckling to himself.

'If you please.'

He looked at me, sympathy bouncing off his features.

'Not a bit of it,' he said.

This cheered me a great deal.

'You loathe travelling, so you'd send someone else.'

And with that token of cousinly spirit, he resumed his quest for the jellied treasure. Eventually he decided that he'd extracted all there was and licked the knife, looking the epitome of boyish contentment. Now, call me petulant, but I couldn't help feeling somewhat pipped that he was completely untouched by the events of yesterday. Our respective fortunes had fared quite differently, that much was plain. While he'd been thrown a life line, I seem to have caught a noose.

'Here, old man,' he said, offering me a cup, 'something to raise your spirits.'

At this juncture most would've recoiled from this offering, but he'd said it with such a twinkle in his eye and so bleak did I feel at that moment that down the hatch it went. After yesterday's abuses this must seem the definition of folly, but you know how it is sometimes when you've been stung and a long-standing relative offers you a serum – you say, 'Make mine a double, barman.'

Well, it hadn't trickled far down the oesophagus before it was borne in upon me that what I'd imbibed must've been slop scooped from the drains.

The strain from keeping my left eyelid open would have been sufficiently diverting but for the marching band in my digestive tract which became my overriding concern. Thankfully, after a popping of the ears, this lifted. A moment later the burning smell in the sinuses faded and I came round. Throughout these spasms Monty, the great healer, had been eyeing me in the manner of a qualified doctor, and seeing my sudden turn of liveliness, clicked his fingers in showy triumph at this visible proof of his having saved a man from the brink of despair.

Then he moved jauntily to the living room with book in hand. From which twisted volume of Babylonian nostrums he'd excavated the recipe for this potion of darkness, I couldn't say, but I was resolved that this was the final straw. If the effect of this ooze, after bringing one's constitution to the brink, was to animate the subject then I can say it worked wonders. But it was also not without its side-effects of tingling in the fingers and an irresistible urge to wrap them around the throat of the chief brewer. Of this I had all the symptoms.

So, wiping my tears and straightening my back, I resolved to pounce on the blighter, but before I could unleash retribution my landlady, Mrs Prenderghast, entered.

'Will you be wanting any more, gentlemen?'

Of all the gormless questions!

'Destroy it!' I said, handing her my cup and its gloopy remnants.

As she cleared away she alluded to the very incident that had been preoccupying me.

'You won't believe this,' she said, 'but some plug-ugly has broke one of my garden plants with a motor car. Created an unsightly mess of the pots.'

'Has broken,' corrected Monty.

'Certainly he has,' she insisted. 'See for yourself.'

'No, thank you,' I said. 'I've seen all. Sheer vandalism, Mrs Prenderghast. Pure sabotage.'

Monty began fidgeting in his seat.

'What sort of man would do such a thing?' I continued, shaking my head sympathetically.

'I know precisely what sort of man.'

I bolted upright at once. Could she have known the saboteur was my father?

'Oh. Do you?'

'Certainly I do,' she insisted. 'A broad set and heavy-footed gentleman with cheeks like a squirrel preparing for winter. They says he was of some sixty years if I'm a day with a moustache.'

Monty became transfixed on her upper lip.

'How can you be sure of this?' I asked, nervously.

I mean to say, it was a vivid description.

'Mrs Montague from opposite saw him,' she replied. 'And Mr Kircaldy who was walking past had a very narrow escape. Rotten thing to do to a gentleman.'

This appeared all she had on the perpetrator, so I relaxed.

'I see,' I said. 'Well, he sounds a ghastly brute, if you ask me.'

By now Monty was looking increasingly pained. I suppose hearing a cousin turn in such an unfavourable character report of one's uncle to a stranger would make one wince, but to me this summation of the man was both accurate and well-drawn, so I was all for it. In any case, I had a specific reason to lampoon the fellow, besides it being quite fun, I mean. But Monty is so slow to see a ruse sometimes.

'Come now, Mrs Prenderghast,' he said, 'I'm sure Sir Walter didn't mean to destroy your plant pots. It was a new car, you see. What are you looking at me like that for?'

We both stared at him; she wanting him to say more and I wishing, as always, that he had never spoken at all. She shifted her eyes to me and a look of recognition came over her face as she suddenly remembered I had an unholy connection with someone by that name.

'Sir Walter... Lockwood.'

There was nothing else for it.

'Yes, I'm afraid,' I said, sniffling into a handkerchief, 'Mrs Prenderghast, alas, it's true. My dear father, who's been so poorly lately, popped in to see me after seeing a medical specialist. Of course, his coordination has never been the same since the diagnosis and you know these imported cars. I'm afraid the motor car quite got away from him.'

I'd hoped that the pathos of these words would invoke in her the maternal compassion to be found in every feeling woman, but the land-owning variety, letting rooms at an exorbitant three pounds five shillings a week, are a breed that defies classification. Seeing her expression not soften even slightly, there was no choice but to resort to her language.

'So that's why he instructed me to recompense you for the damage. Now, I know you'll refuse, but—'

'How much?'

Quite honestly, the crassness of the woman was beyond me.

'Shall we say a sovereign?'

She made no reply but there's something about a woman's glare that seems to convey so much more than a man's.

'OK, well, how about twenty shillings?'

She remained as stone-faced as a Greek bust and, in the face of this beastly assault on the purse strings, I buckled.

'Sorry. Of course, I meant pounds, twenty pounds.'

She gaped.

'Mr Lockwood!' she squealed.

'No, you're right, of course, twenty-five pounds.'

'What?' she said, incredulously, cupping her mouth and nose.

Sickening at her rasping nature, I grabbed my belongings and said somewhat testily, 'Thirty pounds and that's my final offer.'

'Very well. I accept,' she said, ending the tussle.

As Monty avoided my eye I thumbed through a wad of crinkly ones and slapped the lucre on the table. Mrs Prenderghast, meanwhile, beamed with the thrill of an unruly tot who's discovered her father's chest of spoils.

'Thank you,' she said, cooing over the booty. 'There we are. Five should cover it.'

I ceased wrestling with my jacket.

'Come again?'

'There's five,' she said, separating it.

'And the rest?' I asked.

'Is for me,' she said, whisking up the stash before resuming her ministrations. 'What a mess. Must run in the family.'

I stood there mouth agape and boggling. I mean, in all that's pure and holy!

This put me in mind of what happened to the verger in the churchyard of the parish of Winsbrook. Upon seeing my Aunt Beatrice, Monty's mother, rising unsteadily to her feet and assuming her to have taken a fall, he rushed from behind to assist and she, assuming herself to have been seized by an attacker, clubbed him with the cudgel that he'd urged her to carry for protection. I merely mention it because it just goes to show that these old matriarchs never lose the instinct for brutality. Still, concussions are easily forgotten. If only the same could be said for the lingering resentment of being swindled in this beastly fashion.

'Mrs Prenderghast,' said Monty sheepishly, as I vented silently, 'we'll be running along. We're riding the rails to—'

'Oh, I don't care, Mr Pip.'

'Fipps.'

'Just let me know if there's anything else you need. No? OK then.'

'Actually, there is one thing,' I offered.

'Oh?'

'Repair the fort, madam,' I said, rattling the door in its frame.

***

I'll mention nothing of the train journey to Winsbrook except to say that my lasting recollection is of the solitary traveller whose carriage we had the misfortune to join. He was a tall chap in his late fifties and dressed in a brown check suit with bow tie and reading gloves.

His whole aspect was of an official of the Transport Committee whose disapproving glare upon seeing us enter left little doubt that what he felt the world needed was significant reform on travel rights for the under thirty-fives.

This put an end to any thought Monty may have had for his usual prattle. So, we sat in silence trying to affect an air of decorum, which in itself is entirely self-defeating. The gentleman occasionally checked us with an authoritarian look over his spectacles when his suspicious nature became too much or when Monty peered over the man's shoulder to see what he was writing in his notebook.

'Do you mind?!' the man's face seemed to say.

Yet it didn't take long for the absurdity of the situation to dawn. There's something about being made to sit in silence opposite a chum that seems to taunt the inevitable.

After a while, seeing Monty's shoulders bouncing, lips twitching and eyes filling up, it was clear to me he was trying to keep the dam from bursting. The more I saw of him trying not to make a peep the more I felt the rapids surge within, too. Then up went his fingers to smother his mouth, but it was no good. A chuff escaped. A seep of air followed and, unable to contain it any longer, we erupted into the sort of raucous laughter that only two long-standing chums can. The man glared at us all the more until, eventually, realising there was no corking the bottle now, he collected his things and stomped out.

'You should,' said Monty, catching his breath, 'be ashamed of yourself.'

This seemed to stoke the fire. His peals went up an octave and we both roared even louder. You know you're in good company when the time can be passed in such a way. By the time we reached our stop our bellies ached.

Chapter Three

'AH, Quinton!' I said as we were greeted at the gates of Lockwood Institute. 'Splendid to see you, old man. How is the asylum?'

'I've prepared your usual room, sir,' said Quinton.

Head porter to Perceval House and one of the old guard at the Lockwood estate, Quinton Summerton Esq. had been a fixture of our youth and was a constantly reassuring presence.

'There we are,' said Monty cheerily, loading the luggage onto the fellow's back. Quinton shuffled off, dropping and recovering something every third step.

'It's this way, isn't it?' pointed Monty.

'So it is,' said Quinton, mumbling and changing course.

As we passed into the grounds and I surveyed the scene before me, I couldn't believe my eyes. I'd entirely forgotten the annual fête would be under way. The grounds were teeming and if the number of attendees in the grounds were anything to go by, it was indeed shaping up to be a bumper year. No expense had been spared. No wonder Sir Walter had been upbeat when discussing the institute largesse this year. The breadth of pageantry on display suggested the hardest job would be battening down the bulging coffers.

Immediately ahead the festivities consisted of sword-swallowers, fire-breathers and tattooed singers in a curious medley of cacophonous throat work, while in the distance, judging from the number of marquees, there was the usual mélange of book readings, food tastings and musical performances. Farther on the quad had become an amphitheatre while the croquet lawns were home to all manner of souvenir stalls. The whole effect on the eye was decidedly festive.

Except of course when you counted the long faces of the faculty who were routinely conscripted into making polite conversation with the inmates each year. Talking quietly on the side were Barnaby Allen-Winstable, Professor of Diplomatic Relations in Maltus House, and Cynthia Kendal, Professor of Linguistics.

I edged stealthily closer lest I discover a mutiny in the offing.

'Barny, you old goat, ready for another season?'

He blenched at the unholy suggestion. 'Heaven help us,' he said, swilling his claret.

'Oh, dear,' she said, frowning. 'Whatever's wrong?'

'Good god,' he said, slurping and wincing. 'Last crop were no use at all.'

'Why ever do you say that?'

If Barnaby had heard, he gave no indication of it.

'Do you know,' she continued, 'I was just thinking—'

'Most of them have never come across Milton or Paine so you can forget about the art of expression.'

'The philosopher fellow?' she said, pondering. 'Didn't he write *The Mortality of Sentiment*?'

'Seem more interested in drawing moustaches on girls in books than anything else.'

'Well, I gather Professor Stobridge from Literature is having similar difficulties with his female students. I think—'

'What's worse is they don't appear to listen to a word I'm saying,' he said.

'Must be trying,' she said with crisp bitterness. 'Well, perhaps, Barnaby dear, don't you think if you slowed down a bit they might stand a chance?'

'No, no. You're not following as usual!' he snapped. 'This has nothing to do with foreign languages. This rabble are mostly the offspring of the opposition benches. We're supposed to be weaning a class of thoroughbreds, leaders for the international stage, directors. Possessors of guile and acumen. The only thing this lot possess are acres of rolling hills from ma and pa.'

I knew that most of the faculty looked on Lockwood as a sort of menagerie for undesirables, so I turned to Monty for his tuppence worth as head of admissions and found that he'd done a bunk. I wouldn't have minded per se, it's just that his usual policy upon venturing anywhere on his own is to end up in the Lost and Found department. So, in the present moment, my feeling was that of a father who suddenly realises that the reason he's been so freewheeling this last hour is because little Geoffrey is still on the train. It was a few moments of frantic scanning until I eventually spotted the chump.

He was looking down quizzically at the chalk outline of a body while puffing effetely on an enormous pipe, which, in his hands, resembled an alpine horn. Unsettling, yes, but this didn't come as a complete surprise to me. Principally because amongst Monty's many unique qualities is his knack for acquiring objects. He takes after his father, my Uncle Cedric. Many's the time, after his returning from overseas, the custom officials would unearth worldly treasures in his jingling pockets.

'Good heavens,' he'd say, 'must've caught the sun, you know.'

He had to give it up when he became a vicar, of course.

At first I thought it was Monty's interest in human anatomy that attracted him to the oddly contoured outline. I'd never known him to be able to resist a murder reconstruction without treating the beak to a good sniff. After five minutes he usually declares the case unsolvable, but here, unlike the others studying the blackboard marked 'Clues', the object of Monty's fascination appeared to lie in the victim's beach ball-sized head.

I continued my ramble straight into what appeared to be a sprout-eating competition.

'Always room for one more spoonful,' joked Magda, standing on top of a crate luring them in. Though carrying the official title of head of alumni, Magdalena Emin was really the logistical brains behind the operation and delighted in being the grande dame of the events calendar. Here she was, in her milieu, responsible for the fête and, one felt looking at the semi-conscious striplings sitting with engorged bellies, responsible for their fate, too.

Invigilating this gastronomic feat of endurance was the redoubtable figure of the institute head cook, Mrs Caruthers. This babushka paced menacingly along the table ready to ladle more servings on the innocents who until then had only heard of English customs but could now appreciate how they had come to subdue entire continents.

The miasma had begun to set off my sinuses, so I began edging out, but Magda buttonholed me.

'Yoo-hoo, Spencer.'

Climbing hastily down and jangling a shawl with each step, she advanced towards me as if I were the last bus about to leave.

'I wondered when you'd be returning, you pustule,' she said, swatting me on the arm. 'I'm so glad to see you. I'll pull up a chair for you.'

I started. My constitution still hadn't recovered from Monty's sewer juice.

'Ah, well,' I said, 'I'd love to, old thing, but upset tummy you see.'

'Rahbish,' she said, 'you look no more rotter than usual.'

She meant rotten, of course, but despite having been part of the Lockwood family for some time, having arrived in tow with Kristina on the one-way express from Bulgaria, one still had to make allowances for the occasional slip-up. Even so, it did give me a moment's pause. She seemed to think me some slovenly Rasputin, as though I'd clothed myself by foraging wastelands. I gave her the head-to-toe and she became somewhat quizzical in demeanour.

'Do you like me in distress?' she said.

Well, of all the bombshells to throw at someone! It completely threw me. For a moment I simply gurgled, wondering what it was in her that always seemed to produce the unexpected and leave me unnerved.

'Gosh,' I said, fumbling for the reassuring note, 'I mean, no one wants that, old girl.'

She looked hurt.

'You don't think it's fetching?' she said, tugging on her bodice.

'Oh, this dress!' I said, catching the gist. 'Yes, well, it's very, as you say.'

'Fetching?'

'Florid.'

She furrowed the brow and appeared to be chewing this over rather too much, so I tried changing the subject.

'Well,' I said, as airily as I could, 'are you sure it's wise pitting these fine oiks against Mrs Caruthers' culinary delights? I mean, spoil them too early and there'll be hell to pay, what.'

More confusion seemed to suffuse her map.

'What is oiks?'

'Another word for delegates.'

'Pfft,' she said.

Filing it away firmly as the sort of bilge she'd come to expect from me, her attention returned to the contest, as did mine.

'Just a minute,' I said, 'isn't that little Fillip?'

Hunched bearishly over the table behind a number 'Two' plaque was Fillip Rossicky.

'Oh, yes,' she said. 'Holder of last year's crown.'

'Not this year it seems. He looks about ready to blow.'

Virtually on arrival this former winner had been scooped up and inducted into the rugger squad for Belling House and dubbed the 'Human Juggernaut' for the way he took to hurling aside defenders. And now he appeared for all the world as if he wished he'd crash-landed in France where things were easier on the digestion. Only Miles Partington-Smythe remained. He seemed to have the contest sewn up. This was unsurprising when I reflected. Seeing his eyes half-closed and bovine jaw action at work, I imagined that when he wasn't threatening to maul the likes of Monty, he was in his element grazing at pasture.

As for Fillip, well, I have to say I felt for the chap.

'Poor blighter,' I said. 'So far yet so close.'

'Don't pity him,' said Magda. 'It's the volunteer's lot to take what's coming.'

I found this a bit tough on the fellow, but to her mind if these masses of brawn couldn't tell from the miasma rising from the cauldrons that a case of dengue fever was preferable to the gaseous lumps they were shovelling down, well, they had only themselves to blame. I was pondering the runners-up, thinking it tragic that their fate now hung in the balance, when something seemed to tinkle Magda's memory.

'By the way,' she said, cracking her fingers like a pianist about to run amok, 'has Monty turned up?'

Monty was forever turning up in places, and usually sent back marked 'Unwanted', so I didn't immediately follow her drift.

'I absolutely must see him.'

'He was playing Eugène Valmont a moment ago,' I said, trying to locate the hound.

Pretty soon she joined in and, being somewhat on the tallish side, was able to unfold yards of neck and crane over the heads of much of the populace. I always seemed to find this telescopic searching quite disorienting.

'Why are you so interested in the blighter?'

I didn't think it was possible for anyone to look quite so disappointed in me as Sir Walter does, but having been his protégé for some time, Magda managed it all right. Being his lieutenant in the running of things, I suppose these things rub off.

'Haven't you noticed?' she said, pointing to the posters festooning the place. 'The play.'

They read:

'Winsbrook Repertory presents *Hamlet*.'

It's curious how one minute a chap can swear on his life that there were no signs whatever of the mystery object. Then someone draws your attention to the twenty instances of it yards away and you wonder how you missed it at all. It was as though a new world had come into view. I wondered why there were so many. Then I supposed that when it's a play whose name shall not be spoken, posters and flyers become of the essence in drumming up interest.

'Well, well, well,' I said. 'Opening night, eh?'

Then her interest in the fellow came to me. I imagine that Monty fleeing the production must have put the wind up her to no small extent. Being the events organiser and all.

And judging by the way her demeanour had changed in reference to him, I took it as confirmation that there was a growing anticipation building within her. She began clicking her knuckles one by one, premeditatedly like a soprano sharpening her fangs for the chap who'd jilted her in Act I.

Fortunately for Monty, he remained out of sight and this surge of bloodlust seemed to pass, more's the pity, and her interest returned to me.

'Come, I'll show you around,' she said, whisking my arm and beetling into the crowd.

Everything became a blur as I ricocheted from shoulder to shoulder. Being slung about in this fashion reminded me of when we had first met. Monty and I were journeying by train to Winsbrook for the start of another season and she entered the compartment where Monty and I were feeling the full force, you might say, of a fellow passenger.

I recall I was giving myself up to a restful doze when I was firmly socked in the ribs by an elbow.

'Didn't you sleep last night?' said a female voice.

I looked up, still blinking, at who it was with iron forelimbs. There stood a hefty-looking female dressed in pastels. She wore a cloche hat and drooping from the crook of her elbow was a pelt from something I guessed she'd probably just clubbed.

'Phew, what a day it's been. My word!'

About twenty cases landed on the floor.

'Aren't they heavy, these things? Oh, I must remember to put this in the right place because if I don't I'll worry and worry and worry about it all the way. Is anyone else like that? I've always been like that. You don't mind if I use that overhead space, do you?'

I was too flummoxed to reply so she sank a heavy heel onto the seat beside me and busied herself hurling case after case overhead. After flinging the last of them she came down hard and landed heavily.

'Oh, I'm sorry, did I catch your clogs, honey?'

The ensuing agony caused Monty to spring out of his seat and he fell face-first into this lady and got quite a mouthful.

'Whoah!' she said, shoving him single-handedly into the wall. 'You just sit back down there and control yourself, mister.'

With a thud Monty slid down the seat, eyes closed and limp.

'Madam,' I said, feeling sick from all the bobbing about.

'Now, you just keep an eye on your friend here. And we'll all just pass the time just fine.'

'Madam—'

'Oh I'm sorry, perhaps the fault was mine, I haven't introduced myself. I'm Cynthia. Omaha. How are ya? Move aside, move aside,' she said, flicking me in the bruised ribs. She casually threw her fur on the seat beside me, a leg of some description coming to rest on my lap.

'Madam—' I said, between sneezes.

I was given over so completely to this bombardment of the senses that I had barely noticed another passenger enter the carriage. She was a rangy woman in her mid-twenties dressed in navy blue attire sporting an unruly mane of wavy black hair, which when whisked to the side revealed what you might call classical features.

Naturally, she hesitated at first upon seeing the skunk lying limp in my lap, but after issuing a demure nod to all, she settled down with an economy of movement. I returned the gesture with interest by way of several sneezes, which Cynthia seemed to take as an affront to her furry accoutrement.

'Oh, here,' said the battle-axe, slamming the window shut. 'Let's close this, shall we. Seems to be getting to our friend here. Besides, we wouldn't want to catch our death, would we? There. Isn't this cosy?'

I struggled for voice in the stifling heat.

'Madam, are you quite sure you have the right carriage?' I managed to get out.

'Uh-hah, I asked the porter to check when I saw you two in here.'

She turned to Monty. He lay in a heap where he'd fallen, suit crumpled, hair ruffled and eyes still shut.

'Your friend seems much calmer now, see,' she said before turning to the new lady. 'Oh, don't worry, honey, he was just a little rambunctious at first.'

The new addition smiled gently and buried herself behind a broadsheet. And while she began her news briefing, Cynthia resumed her prattling. She'd been motoring for some minutes and I was wishing the almighty would just hurry up and take me when I decided to stir Monty back to the present. It didn't seem right that he should get to sail through the tempest blissfully unconscious, so I leaned gingerly forward and, choosing my moment, kicked him in the shin. He peeked an eye open and quickly closed it. The bounder! He was actually contemplating leaving me alone with her.

'Monty, wake up, you clot,' I uttered under my breath.

He just remained there, aping the wounded. Eventually, I could contain myself no longer.

'Forgive me, madam, but the thing is—'

'Cynthia, please.'

'Madam Cynthia, upon my doctor's orders, I must have absolute quiet. You could have asked him,' I said, indicating Monty, 'if he were conscious.'

'Oh, that's all right. You and Passepartout can sit back and get just what the doctor ordered. I'll just sit here quietly. You won't even know I'm here,' she said, wrinkling her nose and patting me on the thigh.

Glory be! and silence fell upon us. I closed my eyes and tried resuming my earlier repose, but it was soon clear that my nerves were still too shot to slip away.

Monty, on the other hand, seemed to have no such trouble. A minute or so later, I could hear the blighter snoring. This put the wind up me considerably. One could carpet bomb an entire area and in the one bedroom left standing Monty, blessed with his iron constitution, would be discovered in his long johns, slumbering and oblivious to it all.

As I slowly opened my eyes the new lady quickly grabbed my arm, put her finger to her lips and pointed to Monty. He was sitting perfectly motionless with beads of sweat trickling down his forehead. He gave a tiny shake of the head in the manner of a condemned man, as if one twitch from anyone would be curtains. And draped over him, resting her head on his shoulder, was Cynthia, snoring like a rhinoceros.

We savoured the bliss till Cynthia sputtered to life as the train approached her stop. After a similar rigmarole retrieving her things and a quick farewell, while the newcomer stood up and opened the door, our torturer squeezed out and clattered down the aisle like a giant pinball.

We waited anxiously to make sure she had left the platform before we all burst into laughter. Monty usually savours a moment of catharsis, but he soon became preoccupied and started patting himself all over. Then, after narrowing his eyes at me in a beastly suspicious way, he dropped to his knees and began scouring the floor like an opium fiend who'd dropped his pipe. I peered under the seats with him, without the foggiest idea why. And after a few moments of fruitless searching and looking totally outfoxed, he paused, muttering incomprehensibly as he often does at breakfast. An instant later a look of horror spread over his face. Suddenly rising he thrust his head out of the window and with the fortissimo of a naval captain seeing pirates absconding with his vessel, bellowed into the open, 'Stop her at once!'

Just as I was wondering what on earth had got into him I noticed our other travelling companion waving at us. Looking more closely, I saw there was something twinkly dangling from her hand.

'Yours, I believe?'

Gadzooks! It was Monty's pocket watch. Pilfered by our torturer and rescued by our guest.

'She was clumsy sneaking it from you,' she said.

She handed it to him, adding, 'Why do you have something this horrible?'

Monty accepted it as if it were holy communion and we both stood goggling, struggling to express our amazement. Monty held the watch out in front of him. She was right. It was a rotten-looking thing which had long ago stopped working. It was just an affectation of Monty's to be seen to check it.

'I... well, I mean... gosh,' he said.

'You're welcome,' she said, from behind her newspaper. She journeyed the rest of the way buried in the commodities section.

And so it was that Magda first entered our lives. Our jaws dropped when later that day Monty and I saw her flitting past a window in the manor. Later we were to learn that she'd joined the institute administration.

All could see, right out of the blocks, that here was rather a topper in every respect. A real crackerjack who goes into the board-room with a message for a chap and, seeing he isn't back from his round of golf, commandeers his seat to fill in. Sometime later he arrives to find not only the impasse breached but the cigars have broken out and everything has been buttoned up. A sort of business über-woman, if you will.

In due course we discovered, from Kristina since Magda avoids mention of her past trappings, that she came from a rich mining family. For Sir Walter, this unquestionably put the butter on the spinach. Soon afterwards Magda found herself at the helm. For many this came as a relief at first, but it wasn't long before we began to see the tiresome snap of the fingers accompanying the instructions. As a result some rather good eggs like Clifford Rainsby and Teddy Fothergue found themselves out on their ear, poor devils. I seemed to go largely unscathed, though it was not for want of trying.

'Spencer,' she said, once interrupting my lunchtime game of croquet with Aubrey Littleton. 'Do come with me. We must discuss your hours.'

I dropped the mallet and lost all feeling above the waist. Monty had already received his conscription notice and been asked to up his weekly stint to sixteen hours, and now the writing seemed on the wall for me, too. Having seen Monty end his shift and crawl for the sherry at two o'clock with the air of a desert nomad close to extinction, I quivered at the prospect. And here she was intent on inflicting the same drudgery on me. I was sweating profusely as I entered her lair, but before we could get into it we were interrupted by a representative demanding a refund for his delegation and she switched her attention to quell the rebellion. Fortunately, this was one in a series of storms that engulfed institute life that season so we never revisited the ghastly topic.

Becoming such a fixture round the place also meant quite a bit of time socialising and for a time she rather fell in with Monty and me, adding a pally sort of feminine perspective to life.

One afternoon during this period when I was submerged in the bath feeling at one with my primal self, a blurry face suddenly hove into view above me. It was Monty.

I came to the surface spluttering and with several fluid ounces draining out of my orifices while he rattled off some gobbledegook.

'Well?' he said.

He repeated the same, but it took an instant before my hearing returned.

'What the devil do you want?'

'I've just told you,' he said. 'Well, what do you make of it?'

He had the yapping, excited look of a spaniel seeing an approaching lake.

'I haven't the foggiest what you—'

'Listen.'

He read a note to me.

'My dearest blah-blah-blah, blah-blah-blah if only you could imagine how difficult this must be for me blah-blah-blah, but I wish you and Magda the best. Blah-blah-blah-blah. Lucille.'

'Eh?'

He checked me sternly.

'You're not asking me to read it again, I hope.'

'No,' I said, 'but what I want to know is why the deuce Lucille is writing to you.'

As far as I was concerned, Lucille was straight from seventh heaven and the absolute tops. I had rather hoped we might see more of each other.

'Why, you ignoramus,' he said, 'she's writing to *you*.'

'What!' I said, snatching the note.

I read it. It was true.

'But… but…' I gibbered.

It's always the case, I find, that straight after a hammer blow some blighter wants to quiz you.

'Well?' he said.

It was several seconds before the power of speech returned.

'Well, OK,' I said, slowly. 'Two things, Monty. First and foremost, why are you opening notes addressed to me? And secondly…'

I'd forgotten my second point, so I took up his deliberately sprinkled breadcrumbs to the inevitable question.

'What do you suppose this means?'

'Don't you think it odd that your last few entanglements have hit a brick wall?'

I pondered this. I may have been many things, but a stranger to female rejection, I was not.

'Not really,' I said, flatly.

It was crushingly dispiriting, of course, but not surprising.

'Just a minute,' I said, hitting on the salient point, 'why does it mention Magda?'

'Egg-zactly,' said Monty, emphatically. 'Thank you!'

There is a uniqueness to the way Monty can leave you feeling a mere beginner with the fundamentals of life.

'What are you blithering about now?'

He snatched the note and quoted from it again.

'"Wish you and Magda the best." Hark. Don't you see? They've all lost interest shortly after meeting Uncle Walter.'

'So?'

'Good God, it's like school again. Uncle Walter is trying to pair you off with Magda.'

I stared at the fellow for signs of mental collapse. Such ineffable hokum would usually have struck me as further evidence of the accelerating downward trajectory of Monty's processing regions that I had long suspected, but here he seemed lucid and convincing. So, giving the benefit of the doubt, I pressed on.

'But why?'

'Because she'd make the perfect daughter-in-law.'

I couldn't countenance that at any price.

'Would she?'

'Of course,' he said, assuredly. 'She's asset class. You've seen how the institute is humming now that she's at the helm.'

That much was certainly true. Monty is not without powers of persuasion and the more I listened, the more this became not only plausible, but downright likely.

'Bonds of convenience, you mean?'

He paused an instant. Then with the mystique of a sleuth revealing the most telling fact of all he leaned forward – 'A merger.'

While this possibility bedded into my consciousness all that could be heard was the gurgling sound of water draining away.

'I'd never imagined,' I said, stunned.

I clambered out of the bath.

'Egad!' said Monty, dashing out in horror.

The last of the water dribbled away.

'Just a minute,' I said, donning the robe. 'Which of us?'

'Huh?'

'Well, weren't your last few attachments snuffed out in the same way?'

'So?'

'I mean, it's beginning to look suspiciously like he's trying the same with you.'

He ruminated for a spell and the binary nature of the conundrum seemed to sink in. The jauntiness faded from his face. He left, a stricken man.

For the foreseeable future our existence became one of a state of perpetual dread. Don't let me mislead you, Magda remains a fine specimen of womanliness, but the thought of any union with a hard-nosed overachiever who insists on 'producing results' in all spheres of life put the fear of God into us. It was a ghastly prospect. I'd seen the ruinous effects that sort of thing can have on a chap's batting average and anyone contemplating such a life of purgatory has been bowled too many googlies.

In the days that followed, we avoided discussing this rather unsettling development in our lives. Then over breakfast one morning in the dining hall Monty accosted me.

'Spencer,' he said, gulping hard, 'I'd like you to know that I've been thinking very deeply.'

'Glad to hear it, old man.'

I always encourage this sort of thing in Monty.

'Yes. And I should like you to know that as only one of us can be blessed with the hand of Magda, I hope it will be you.'

The bounder. It was just the sort of degeneracy that I'd come to expect from the blackguard. When the chips are down, you can always rely on Monty to shove you under a bus.

'Oh, I couldn't come between the two who are clearly better matched,' I said. 'You are the far more deserving suitor.'

'No, you are,' he said.

'That's very kind, Monty, but you are.'

'No, you are.'

'Stop it!' I said.

We could have thrashed this out some more except many eyes had begun turning to us. And so it was that, without a further word spoken, we had come to a mutual understanding – it was each man for himself.

So, returning to the fête, it was with no little trepidation that I found myself arm-in-arm with Magda being ferried about the place. She wormed us towards the souvenir stalls. As we fetched up, there was a greying-bird holding a cartouche delivering a sort of sermon to the populace.

'Throughout the ages, ladies and gentlemen, all great civilisations have been born of trade. A very good choice, sir,' he said to the fellow inspecting a bit of tat. 'An ornament of such rarity. As I say, throughout millennia the story of bridging cultures has been one of mutual understanding and exchange…'

He'd started to rewind back to a history of the barter system when we ambled towards a sort of bazaar with sellers trussed as nomadic tribesmen for novelty's sake. All of a sudden, stirred by something shimmering in the distance, Magda headed for it, tightening her clasp on me. We lumbered towards it with all the grace of a sheriff and convict chained by the ankle.

'Oh,' she said, lifting up a string of beads, 'do you think these would suit me?'

'Oh, rather.'

'An alternative to these,' she said, revealing her anklet.

I must say she had exceptionally fine ankles.

'Is it possible to wear rosemary beads round the ankle?'

She discarded them and we continued on her way. Still lost in thought she absent-mindedly picked up a piece of fabric.

'Did you especially want a loincloth?' I said.

She dropped it immediately and, after wiping her hand on my arm, continued foraging. Her eyes lit up once more and she shoved me towards the jewellery section. After brushing aside various other uninspiring trinkets she began caressing some amulets and whatnot. How she could be so tender with one hand, and so firmly clamp her right one to stop me wriggling, beats me. I was just thinking of ways to get her mind off the swag when some cheers sounded in the distance, at the sponge-throwing stand I presumed. I was hoping to get my half-crown's worth if I could break free.

'Do you know,' I said, peering every which way, 'sounds pretty near to civil unrest in the offing to me. I'd look in if I were you.'

Usually she can hear a squirrel on tip-toe sneaking off with a cashew, but now, nothing. She seemed deaf to it. I tried again.

'Best nipped in the bud, you know, these things. I mean, before you know where you are the, er… well, the balloon has gone… out and the light has gone… Hasn't it? I mean, just ask Louis the… wot?'

The wheels had come off the vocal apparatus because we had arrived at a stall offering treasures from around the world and gleaming up at Magda's mesmerised face was a veritable trove of rings. She was fondling the goods with the air of a Roman empress inspecting the spoils from the provinces. They had a strong pull. It was some moments before she rose from under the spell.

'Were you saying something?'

'Me? Oh, well, I mean…'

The jollity had subsequently hushed, so I had to think quickly.

'I was asking your opinion.'

'On what?'

'You know, the claptrap that fellow was spouting earlier.'

'Which fellow?' she said.

'You know, Adam Smith there. Doing a publicity tour for the board of trade.'

She glanced over at the silver-maned orator.

'That's the History laureate.'

'Is it?' I said, stealing another look. 'I thought he'd retired.'

'He did,' she said, flatly. 'Too early. So, he's back.'

'Good heavens.'

'Oh, yes,' she said, as if explaining the facts of life to a freshman. 'It's amongst the main reasons people come to Lockwood.'

I was still thinking piteously of the erstwhile History laureate.

'Hmm? What is?'

'To master certain skills.'

'Such as?'

'Diplomacy. Negotiation.'

I was so pleased that we'd stumbled upon a distraction that it took me a few seconds to remember what I'd asked; and a few more to fathom what she was talking about. But then I examined it and there seemed much truth in what she had said. I suppose the art of how to put one over on the fellow on the opposite side of the negotiating table is a core skill and well worth mastering. This led me to reflect on my recent showing with Mrs Prenderghast that morning and I'd be lying if I said the business wasn't still rankling in my breast. Truth be told, it stung like a gaping wound. Yet here I stood in a veritable gymnasium where I might develop this muscle. And so it was in this way that, swept up in the moment, and vowing to secure my place as negotiator extraordinaire, I threw my hat into the ring.

'I'm going in,' I said. 'Is there anything you like the look of? I'll get it for you. How about those rosemary beads?'

She yipped with excitement and scanned everything there was to see.

'How about that signet ring?'

A sort of debilitating sensation stole over me.

'Spencer. Yoo-hoo. Are you OK?'

Woe betide any chap who grandly gestures to a lady her choice of anything her heart desires forgetting to add, 'from this section'. I daresay that the shape of history is the story of rulers who forgot to add that all-important detail. The unexpected request completely knocks the stuffing out of you. Still, what else can a chump do but sally forth?

So, I sidled up nonchalantly to the stall featuring 'Treasures from the Silk Road' and addressed the merchant directly. He appeared outfitted less by way of the Silk Road and more by way of the Old Kent Road, but authenticity isn't everything.

'Morning, squire,' I said, tossing a coin casually.

He had the aspect of a man who's been standing for eons without a sniff of trade and the last thing on his mind is a commercial tussle. This had to put me at an advantage, I felt.

'Yes?' he said, irritably.

I checked the blighter with a look. I wasn't standing for any nonsense, you know.

'How much for this brooch?'

'It is a signet ring.'

I looked again.

'Ah. So it is. Lucky for you,' I said, recovering, 'that it's just the thing I'm looking for, but I don't suppose this is worth very much, what?'

'Ten pounds,' he said.

I laughed derisively.

'Pffft. Ha! Oh, my word, good heavens.'

His face contorted with the suggestion that I had insulted his entire ancestry from the root and it was only when he stood up that I realised he'd been sitting down.

'Ah,' I gurgled. 'How much did you say again?'

'Ten pounds.'

'Here's twenty,' I said, scurrying back.

I slowed to a canter and handed Magda her blasted ring.

'There's nothing to it, really.'

'Spencer, my little cauliflower!' she said, giving me a peck on the cheek. 'How much was it? No. That's not important. Still, how much?'

'We agreed on a price of my choosing,' I said, clearing the throat.

'Well, it's wonderful,' she said. 'Is that rust?'

Just then came another loud cry from the sponge-throwing mob.

'Oh blast, what's that infernal noise?' she said. 'I'd better attend to it. Don't budge.'

With that she pocketed the loot and pushed off towards the din, leaving me to take a long, deep, life-affirming breath. Unshackled, I bade farewell to the loopiness of the fête for another year and scampered into hiding.

Chapter Four

AFTER ducking the order to stay put I closeted myself in my room for a while. Something about the barnyard jollity of the fête had sapped me of the pep I knew I would need for the evening's instalment of the Bard. It was gala night after all and something told me it would be a long one.

Whenever the tank seemed low in zing it had long been a self-prescribed remedy of mine to dunk the old frame and let the eucalyptus restore the vitality. I gather amphibians do much the same when slinking into the primordial soup, and it was with a touch of the primeval now that I slithered into the tub and cranked the lever. I don't know how long I'd been stewing in sin when there broke out a beastly knocking on the door.

'Spencer!' came the muffled voice.

More urgent knocking followed. Coming suddenly during a moment of peace and tranquillity, it catapulted me into a frightful funk. Quivering, I leapt out of the bath and, as the knocking became more insistent, without thinking I instinctively grabbed the talc and haphazardly began sloshing it over myself, which combined to produce a kind of mud-pack across the torso. After a momentary respite the relentless knocking started up again and in my haste I squelched to the door, leaving a soggy trail of footprints like a salamander yanked back to land for an emergency. Another heavy rap on the door followed and no sooner had I managed to drape a towel around the undercarriage than I opened the door. It was Magda.

'Omagod,' she said, averting her gaze. 'Why are you wearing aboriginal body paint?'

'Hmm?'

'No,' she said, flashing a hand. 'I don't care what you've been doing. Just come on. We need you to come.'

'We?' I said, mortified.

As she edged past I nervously poked the beak around the door to see who else she'd invited. No one, thank goodness.

'Trousers. Shirt,' she said, flinging some clothing on my head.

Throughout the years her comments on my presentation had been vivid and frequent. Now, apparently, she'd come to clothe me in person and had brought a selection with her. I was poised to raise the topic, but Magda has a sixth sense for stifling objections.

'First thing's first,' she said, pointing to the bathroom. 'Dress.'

A woman who comes knocking forcefully on the door and insists on dressing you is not easily turned and sent packing. So, resignedly, I whipped on the garms. No sooner had I returned than she took up the agenda.

'Thank goodness that hairy business is over,' she said. 'Spencer, we need you to act, God help us.'

'Come again,' I said.

She sighed, as if struggling to fathom how it had reached this point.

'We need you to be Polonius.'

I don't know if a woman has ever forced her way into your sleeping quarters asking you to be a Roman you've never heard of, but if you're anything like me, it comes over all Greek.

'Eh?'

'Our first choice refuses to take part in one scene.'

This additional morsel enabled me to discern a little more. Out of the primordial and into some other kind of soup seemed to be about the gist of it. The essence was, as I understood it, that there were a few last-minute snags in rehearsal that threatened to stand in the way of it becoming a riotous smash and, in the hour of need, my name had come up, as it were.

'Ah-ha,' I said, slipping my hands in my pockets, relishing the moment, 'you're facing a sticky wicket and need me to pull your chestnuts out of the inferno, is that it?'

She rolled her eyes, irritably.

'Stop that. Here, you'll need this.'

She handed me a floppy, mangy beard, of the sort Monty wears to avoid being disembowelled. It was just the sort of chafing accoutrement she might spring on a chap.

'Just a minute—'

'Shh. No fiddle-faddle. Just come to the games room instanter. Understood? God, I need a drink!'

'Well, old girl, you've come to the right place. I know just where we can—'

She slammed the door, having swiped my single lowland malt on her way out. Whether to confiscate it from me or to soothe her own pre-performance jitters, I couldn't say. In the case of the latter, she certainly had the right idea.

It had been some time since I'd last seen her this rattled, so I thought I'd better institute steps to rise to the challenge. And first on the prescription sheet was my own snort of the malted stuff, so I decided to pass by the commandant's lair for a quick swig of his private stash. He maintained a strict stranglehold on the better vintages but the momentousness of the occasion seemed to call for something extra.

Whizzing along the corridors I bounded up the lobby stairway before silently creeping into Sir Walter's chambers. I was somewhat out of breath as I tip-toed in, but I was caught even more on the hop when something grabbed me by the neck from behind.

'Whorra-aarghgh,' I said. Or it may have been 'Horrha-aarghgh'.

It's difficult to tell the difference when a giant hand is constricting the airways. It was only after it relented and a goodish bit of coughing and spluttering from my side that I recognised my assailant.

'Sir Walter?' I said, gasping.

'Spencer?' he said, tugging at my beard.

He'd shaved his mutton chops and was wearing full regalia for his part in the play. This was fast becoming a family production.

'I saw some suspicious blighter creeping about,' he whispered agitatedly. 'For a moment, I thought your safe-cracker friend was back. Why are you shuffling about shiftily? Are you looting the place? And why are you wearing this revolting shrubbery?'

I caught a glimpse of myself in a mirror and started at the likeness to a young, irascible Sir Walter.

'Magda asked me to be Bolonius.'

'She didn't!' he said, reflectively. 'Oh, sweet lord. We're sunk.'

The shock seemed to pass and he returned to the here and now.

'How does this explain your presence? Keep your voice down.'

'Ah, I thought I'd lubricate the old vocal cords. Only proper before going on stage and all that.'

He narrowed his eyes and his bushy moustache twitched.

'If you're bootlegging my finest again, you little heathen—'

'Absolutely not. Never again,' I said. 'Still, time is pressing, old wise one. Disclose the whereabouts of the hooch and we'll say no more about it.'

'I told you to whisper, you fiend!'

I switched to a whisper and asked him why he was insisting on this cloak and dagger stuff, but his manner remained furtive. Slippery even.

'Uh, it's a delicate matter between Kristina and I, which needn't concern you.'

I was still wrestling with this titbit of yet another quarrel when there emanated the low rumble of a contralto gargling a fixer before going on stage.

'Shh!' he said, freezing on the spot.

We stood motionless to the sound of someone retching. At first I thought the old commandant had baited the trap by lacing the scotch again, but he put a finger to his lips and pointed to the dressing table. Only then did I notice Kristina's clothes strewn about the place.

'She's getting dressed,' he whispered.

I was stumped by this googly, not least because her room was some way along the corridor. Then as I scrutinised him more closely and detected a certain sheepishness in his demeanour, the penny dropped. I'd got the wrong end of the stick in supposing a rift. In fact, relations were closer than ever.

Just then we heard the key to the bathroom door.

'Behind the curtains!' he hissed, frantically.

Shooting in the air with a startled leap, I landed balletically behind the drapes and as I steadied the netting nothing could have prepared me for what manifested itself before my eyes. What I had supposed to be Kristina was evidently something else. A pale, cadaverous, hunched figure emerged holding a candelabra, paused momentarily at the threshold, and then scuttled towards the centre of the room, its bare feet slapping on the hard floor as it moved. It was such a bone-chilling presence that I became convinced at that moment we had come face-to-face with the restless phantasm of the Ivory Lady herself. Her spirit had been rumoured to haunt these grounds for years. Coming to a stop in the centre of the room, she sniffed hard and emitted a long unearthly hiss before beetling back to the bathroom. The door remained ajar. An instant later the sound of running water could be heard. My instinct was to race like billy-o, but with the bathroom adjacent to the entrance, I daren't move.

Suddenly I felt something seize my shoulder and I emitted a startled cry. The running water stopped instantly. What followed was one of the longest moments I can remember. After a while the water resumed. Turning to my left I saw the drapes flap and from behind them emerged Sir Walter.

'What the dickens!' I whispered. 'Why are *you* hiding?'

He seemed confused and reflected.

'Habit, I suppose,' he said. 'Now look—'

My hand shot up, instinctively.

'No, thank you,' I insisted. 'I've just seen a ruddy banshee.'

'What are you drivelling about?'

'The Ivory Lady, I tell you. She's here!'

He began studying me, looking for the tell-tale glazed eye and flushed cheeks of one who is one over the eight, but seeing my febrile, quivering form and bloodless face seemed to give him pause for thought and he took on an unsettled air. He'd heard about the Ivory Lady, of course, but had always dismissed any notion of the supernatural as claptrap. He sniffed a few times to be sure I hadn't already been at the tipple.

'Well, what did she look like, this Madame Bovary?'

I was stunned. Surely to goodness he had the evidence of his own eyes.

'Eh?' I said. 'Didn't you see her?'

'No,' he said, sheepishly, 'I always turn my back when she's dressing.'

I gave a gibbering description as best I could.

'It was a terrifying sight. A bony figure, cold blue lips, sunken cheeks, powdery white complexion, dry, flaky skin, dark eyes, arched eyebrows.'

I saw in him the familiar fatherly disapproval that what I needed was to sleep it off and buck up my ideas.

'And I suppose she was wearing an ivory dress, too.'

'No, but she was wearing a head ornament of some sort.'

'What?'

He suddenly became attentive.

'A garland, you mean?'

'I suppose so.'

'Just a minute,' he said. 'Like a crown?'

'Exactly!'

He paused, running the rest back in his mind. A light seemed to come on.

'That's Kristina, you nincompoop.'

'It couldn't be.'

'It is. Take my word.'

He was absolutely adamant. I paused a moment to reflect. I had to admit, this grotesque creature of the night cut an even more ghoulish figure than Kristina with the lights off.

'It couldn't be,' I said, shaking my head, 'this was far more haunting.'

'Well, of course,' he said, 'she's playing the ghost of Hamlet's father. Someone else is doing the lines from backstage, but she's the haunting presence. She couldn't be more delighted. I'm Claudius.'

'Oh, thank heavens!' I said, placing a jovial hand on his shoulder.

The relief pouring over me was nothing short of a deluge. Sanity was with me again. I was still marvelling at Everyman's capacity for delusion when a stern disapproval came over him once more.

'Anyway, you shouldn't be here. She already thinks you're consumed with lust for her.'

'What!'

'It's why she refrained from entering your sty in Cambridge.'

My surprise at this disquieting revelation had given us away.

'Is someone there?' she said, peering round the bathroom door. 'Is that you, Jolly-Wally?'

She returned to her den after receiving no reply. I turned to the man with, I have to confess, a broad grin.

'If you ever repeat that to anyone…'

I held up a reassuring hand.

'Your growing number of secrets are safe with me,' I said. 'Just one thing – bravo on the ghost, but you've picked the wrong Claudius. When it comes to pouring cursed potions on the unsuspecting, Monty is your man. Take *my* word.'

I pushed off, hearing him pop a cork as I turned the corner. Fetching up shortly afterwards at the games room I peered in to see a cluster of morose thespians shrugging haplessly about something. I was lingering on the fringes when Magda's keen instincts spotted me.

‘There you are, Spencer,’ she called, advancing towards me and leading me to the centre. She straightened my beard after my tug of war with Sir Walter.

‘There. Now, there’s no time to lose. Everybody, this is our stand-in.’

She thrust into my hand what appeared to be someone’s scalp.

‘Hurry up,’ she demanded. ‘Put on the wig and get behind that curtain.’

She began hustling me behind the drapes.

‘Steady on,’ I said. ‘What for?’

I’d spent as much time behind the netting as I cared for, frankly.

‘Hop to it, Spencer. Don’t dally,’ boomed the voice of Aunt Beatrice. She was standing at the far side of the room beside Monty and was scolding him for carelessly resting his sword on her dress, which had resulted in a most unseemly rip up the back. Two years older than Sir Walter, some might say that she was rather long in the tooth to be playing Gertrude, but heaven help anyone who dared hint at such a thing.

Magda set about filling me in on the details.

‘What do you know about Polonius?’

She ploughed on after seeing no spark of recognition in my face.

‘He is Ophelia’s father and the man who Monty, sorry, Hamlet accidentally bumps off with a dagger.’

‘Bumps off?’ I said. ‘You mean that old fool who gets it in the gizzard?’

‘Yes, that’s right.’

This reminded me of the septuagenarian I’d seen rehearsing in the amphitheatre earlier, squirming on the floor in the throes of death.

‘Well, what happened to your original Polonius? Age caught up with him?’

‘Monty’s aim,’ she said, looking askance at our eponymous front man, ‘being what it is, Polonius has been rushed to the infirmary.’

‘What!’

'He's OK. He's returning as we speak for the rest of it. He just refuses to do this scene, that's all. Doesn't trust Monty.'

Leaving aside the possibility that I'd got the wrong end of the script, there was one overriding conclusion I'd come to.

'So, you want me to stand behind the curtain and be knifed?'

'Yes, now hurry,' said Aunt Beatrice, holding the drapes open.

I looked at Magda to see if she was quite sane and she nodded encouragingly.

'The other Polonius will deliver the lines from backstage, you just need to play the shrouded man and fall to your death.'

'We don't need a Dying Swan act,' said Aunt Beatrice, 'just a simple fall will do.'

'Exactly,' said Monty, practising a few thrusts into thin air.

I stood there goggle-eyed, flummoxed by the whole thing.

'Well,' I said, 'I've been on the receiving end of some stinkers in my time, but this plumbs the depths.'

'Well, that's why it must be you, don't you see?' implored Aunt Beatrice. 'An intimate trust has built up between you and Monty over the years. Like a chap who, over a lifetime, has been bitten by so many snakes that he's acquired a sort of immunity.'

Monty, who had begun combining a lunging action with his striking motion, reassured me that the previous confusion, when it came to where to thrust the dagger, had arisen from distinguishing *his* right from *Polonius's* right, but all was now clear.

'Now, I've got it, you see,' he said, with a sharp jab at waist height. 'It's adagio to the right. No, wait, left.'

I took that as the clincher. With Monty's long history of calamities racing through my mind, I sounded my final word.

'Well, if you think I'm about to slot behind another curtain after only moments ago being glued to the spot behind the curtain while Kristina was getting undressed...'

As my words tailed off I noticed a change in their expressions that could have but one meaning.

'Oh,' I said, sighing deeply at the inevitable.

***

By some miracle Monty managed to avoid the main arteries and we somehow made it to the inaugural event. The stage lights of the amphitheatre shimmered in the darkness and an expectant mood hung in the atmosphere amongst the throng of spectators who'd waited for final rehearsals to conclude. This made the occasion all the more ripe.

Conditions outdoors couldn't have fared much better. Below a starry transcendent sky, the stage became the focus. A hush descended and out clomped our compere to introduce the season-opening performance, only it was not Magda who appeared from the shadows, as we might have expected, but Sir Walter. Swinging his arms with a boyish elasticity and stumbling as he came to a halt, he settled at the centre with a gentle swaying motion like a Jack Tar who was three sheets to the wind.

'*Bienvenue*, ladies and madames. May I welcome you on this 'spicious occasion. It gives me great pleasure to present Winsbrook Reptilory's inaugural performance of everyone's favourite tragedy of William Shakespeare from Hamlet himself. So, please slump back under this midnight summer's air… on this midslummer's night… on this crisp evening. And please do stay for the duration. Particularly members of the cast. And another thing—'

Fortunately, his oratory was abruptly ended when in the hazy distance he noticed what he eventually realised was the arm of Magda discreetly beckoning him offstage.

Chapter Five

EVEN stage neophytes like me know that it behoves one not to dwell too much on opening night snags and a certain latitude must be given. So, when Monty was delivering his favourite 'If you prick us, do we not bleed?' speech and Yorick's skull slipped from his fingers and rolled into the audience, I assumed from their open-mouthed surprise that they were a benign, forgiving bunch. But when some scenes later the skull reappeared and struck Claudius on the head and a pipped member cried out, 'If you wrong us, shall we not revenge?', all the indications were that this dictate was beginning to wear thin amongst the viewing gentry. So, after four acts of similarly improvised mayhem, it was round about this time that I decided to cut my budding theatrical career short. Exiting offstage in the manner of a defector creeping past the border guards, I hared round the amphitheatre and dived indoors to safety.

I couldn't help reflect on a bit of inspired thinking while I was painstakingly shedding the outer layer. No further trace of Polonius remained by the time I decamped to the post-production soirée in the lobby.

I was pleased to find on arrival that I blended in amongst the Savile Row set. There were a few chaps still clad in the fashion of merchants from the Old Kent Road, but most had gone for something more top-button. The ladies were gliding about mostly in Parisian couture, I seem to remember. Add to this mêlée the eclectic professor class, serving staff and a musical duo mangling the gut strings with piano accompaniment and you have the end-to-end.

'Would you please show your appreciation for the Sabauri Chamber Ensemble,' announced Magda, clapping to start things off.

She waited an instant, but the audience's readiness for applause had taken something of a knock and the populace turned their backs.

Craning my neck to peer over the feathered head-dresses, I spotted Monty. He was still clad as the Danish prince, standing by his brethren, garnering all the attention he could. Naturally, I thought to join him when I paused to consider whether it was wise to associate with such a visible target. It was only by discerning from the stunned faces of the populace that I came to realise that far from being consumed with bloodlust, as I'd imagined, they were still contending with shock and befuddlement, which are the preliminaries before rage and barbarism. So, I wandered across to see how the land lay. He was in discussion with some of the newest inmates, by the looks of it. A clique consisting of two petite young women in cocktail dresses, Sofia and Eva of Greece and Switzerland respectively, who, like many Anglophiles before them, had stopped in at Lockwood to brush up their already impressive linguistic prowess before touring South America, apparently where they felt it would best be put to use. Beside them was Ludovic, a tubby, supercilious-looking blighter from London with slick hair and a pencil moustache.

I nestled up just behind Monty trying to eke my way into the ebb and flow. He blenched, as if a short-range assassin had snuck into striking range.

'Sweet Mary,' he said, clutching his chest. 'For a minute, I thought that ape was back.'

He meant Miles, of course, after their unusually protracted and brutal tussle on stage in the final act.

'Anyway, what kept you, blast it? Now that you're here, you can help me with these two. I've been flailing for the past ten minutes.'

He returned to the cluster and placed a forefinger on my chest.

'Here's a Lockwood, if you'd care to know.'

By their expressions they didn't particularly appear to be in the market for one, but eventually both ladies extended a gloved hand.

Catching me in two minds, I dithered too long and they snatched them back. Ludo, meanwhile, regarded me as if I were a back-street financier come to sully the name of the arts.

Naturally, this had chastened me a tad, so, content to merely loiter, I made myself all ears and settled alongside to listen to them raving about something. Whatever it was seemed to have moved them deeply.

'Fascinating,' said Sofia, pinching a cocktail glass from a passing waiter and taking a snootful. 'I can't remember when a production employed lines from so many plays.'

'Or playwrights,' said Eva. 'This is clearly an institute with a difference. How do you account for it?'

'Well...' said Monty, gulping and looking pleadingly at me.

Feeling just as flummoxed, I shook my head. After all, I was a last-minute addition who knew nothing about the Bard, except what I'd recently learned of his debauched sensibilities, of course.

'One must never allow oneself to become a slave to the written word, you know,' said Monty. 'Only by unlocking the emotion of the moment can one hope to liberate the arts.'

Monty's powers of expression can usually be relied upon to desert him when most in need, but judging from the way the ladies' eyes ballooned and their lips parted, he appeared to have struck the right note with this inspired effort. It caused me to revise my opinion of him briefly, too.

'I totally agree,' said Sofia, snaking an arm into the crook of Monty's elbow. 'Shows inspired thinking.'

I was stunned. Nobody had ever accused Monty of this before.

'So brave,' agreed Eva, staking her claim too.

Not everyone was so taken with it, of course. Ludo began to bray rather violently. I thought briefly that he'd choked on a walnut when I realised he was laughing.

'What! Never seen anything so ham-fisted in all my puff. Can you imagine that at Covent Garden? Well, *you* probably couldn't,' he said, sneering at me.

The Danish prince and I exchanged glances over this scathing heretic while the ladies regarded Monty and me with expectant eyes. I couldn't remember the last time I had provoked such strong feeling in a stranger and it left me all of a twitter. Monty, also flustered and shocked at the man's brass, appeared momentarily dumbstruck. But very few women I've known stand idly by while the object of her interest is being roasted by a bystander and it seemed that, for Sofia, this incivility had overstepped the bounds of polite discourse.

'Yes, Ludo, we have a thirst for new experiences. You, on the other hand, seem to hunger for the familiar and, clearly, have the appetite of a whale.'

I have nothing to prove it, but I rather thought Monty was gazing devotedly into her soul with a hint of reverence. It seemed to galvanise him.

'Here, here,' he said, sounding more like himself. 'I'm always thirsty. Never satisfied, me.'

Then he appeared to lose the thread of his point.

'Did I mention Polonius is also here? Newcomer to the stage, but what a natural, what?'

He gave me a hefty pat on the back and chortled like a hog. A moment's silence ensued before I realised I was expected to lend something to this oratory, and I was running through all the hackneyed phrases I'd heard in theatrical circles when I felt an arm slip into mine which whipped the words from me.

'If I could just make one suggestion,' said Eva, taking me into her confidence, 'if you could fall *after* the knife goes in rather than before, that would be better.'

She wore the mischievous look of a leading light of varsity life who'd skewered her next lame-brain. Typical of the breed, I thought. By now I had, of course, come to the view that she wasn't my type at all. Then she handed me a gin and winked.

'Love to,' I said, clinking away.

It's a small thing, but sometimes that's all it takes. This insignificant gesture set me on a train of thought and got me reflecting on my life choices. I mean to say, I was just wondering if my milieu might, in fact, be distinctly brighter were it to contain more of these dainty, artistic types when it became clear that the true devotee in our midst was still finding this too much to stomach.

'Now look here,' he said, insistently, 'in no other acting guild will you see Laertes bashing Hamlet's head repeatedly on the ground gibbering "How dare you slur my wife's name." Nor does a fatally poisoned Gertrude spring back to life after croaking it to pull Laertes off by the ear.'

All technically correct, of course, but as often happens to the minority view, it was snuffed out, unequivocally. He was rebuffed with a combined effort from us, which rested in no small way on the unspoken female kinship that forms the basis of such intrigue.

'Ludo, you really are such a…' began Sofia, the telling phrase eluding her.

As ever when these unfinished thoughts hang inviting in the air, one must do the decent thing.

'Stickler?' I offered, striving to quell the awkwardness.

Sofia rolled her eyes and tutted in irritation.

'Fascist?' suggested the Swiss.

She received a kindly embrace for her effort. Then, misreading the general direction, Monty provided his tuppence worth.

'Militant ass?'

'Extremist blighter?' I said, following his lead.

'Potato head!' exclaimed Sofia, finally, exuding satisfaction at finding the mot juste.

'Exactly!' agreed Eva. 'It was on the tip of my tongue. A gnarly, useless potato head.'

Monty and I exchanged a glance at how, lacking this sort of female telepathy, we were fools to even try. Still, it seemed to meet the case so we didn't quibble.

It's a wise man who, seeing the majority position harden, decides against useless countering, and Ludo, feeling that there wasn't much else to do except issue a 'Pah!' and take the high road, buzzed off into the crowd leaving us evenly balanced.

Quite a bit more clinking of glasses ensued between our foursome after this. Giving myself over to this jollity, there was no two ways about it, I was beginning to sink into the most topping free-flowing revelry I'd experienced since my arrival. I was beginning to feel, particularly after the third gin, that I'd been needlessly apprehensive about returning to the institute early or taking to the stage. Admittedly, my homecoming had been somewhat bracing and required some deft footwork to avoid being speared by a relative on stage, but in every other respect this season was shaping up to be one without the usual rancour I'd come to expect. Certainly, the present circumstances were nothing if not decidedly promising. I was thinking along such lines when my thoughts were interrupted by a tap on the shoulder. Well, you know how it is after about the third gin. It rather caught me on the hop.

'Magda!' I said, embracing her in a hug. Then for reasons that escape me, I began rubbing her back, as if to help her digestion.

After clamping hold of my arms like pincers and dropping them by her side, she began pulling me away when she realised I'd become caught on something. On inspection she noticed that what I was attached to was one half of the duo of females, still giggling at my exuberance. Also attached to the other end of this human chain appeared to be Monty.

'Everyone,' said Magda, nodding agreeably to Sofia and Eva, 'there's to be an announcement and I must ask Spencer and Monty to join me.'

Monty looked stricken by this blow and it echoed my own thoughts on the matter.

'What for?'

'There are some people Sir Walter would like you to meet,' she said through clenched jaw.

I didn't like the sound of this one bit. In the past Sir Walter had coerced me to mingle with some frightful upstarts in the vain hope that it would transform me into 'a man of worth'. Given he hadn't tried this gambit for some time, I imagined he had long resigned himself to this impossibility.

With promises we'd be back in a jiffy, Monty and I threaded our way through the multitude.

'What's the meaning of this?' he asked me.

'I haven't the dickens.'

'Who's the towering old beak in regimental uniform?'

He pointed to some rather imposing blighter approaching his third flush of youth, attired in military insignia. He was standing by the piano.

'How should I know?'

As we neared I could see Sir Walter was enjoying a raucously pleasant time with a duo of his own. One half of which was a well-proportioned and impeccably attired cove who had the air of a public speaker about him – well-fitting tuxedo and not a tuft of hair out of place – a born hobnobber he appeared to me. There was much reciprocal back-slapping going on between them. And standing beside him was a nattily dressed but stumpy female with feral eyebrows and piercing green eyes.

Just as we arrived to stand sheepishly beside them without the foggiest clue why, the military bird seated himself at the piano and broke into a thunderous fanfare. Sir Walter immediately rapped on the instrument and gave a throat-slashing gesture. It had the desired effect for the populace were roused to attention. From the pageantry of it, I took it that we might be in for a speech from Magda and that Monty and I had been beckoned there to form part of an impressive backdrop, like unwilling courtiers, but before she could take the reins, Sir Walter began his own blaring.

'Well what!' he barked at the populace.

After a penetrating echo, a murmur of expectation spread amongst the confused mob. Sir Walter swayed on his heels, trying to focus on the hundreds of eyes goggling back at him. Magda quickly slotted in beside me and by the way she leaned forward frowning, I gathered she was just as perplexed by Claudius's animated stage revival as we were. Like all of us, I suppose, she had assumed that the unscripted stage work was over and this was her moment. The crowd ceased shuffling and a hush descended just in time for Sir Walter to clear his throat down the microphone, causing a deafeningly high-pitched peal to ring out across the lobby.

'Well,' he said, 'everybody, I'd like you all to welcome the Saudi Chamber Music—'

'Sabauri,' said his friend, bowing humbly.

'Hmm? Oh. The Shabauri Chamber Onslaught—'

'Ensemble,' said Magda.

'The Sharabi Chamber Music – oh, perhaps you'd better do the introductions.'

Defeated by the inconsiderately titled trio, he waved Magda in. She scooted over and he came to lean heavily against me, exhaling pipe smoke into my sinuses.

'I'd like to introduce you all to our resident musicians and guests of honour this season. Nikola Mintoff, lead violinist for the ensemble and ambassador for the Chamber Music Society in his native Malta.'

Hurrah. I knew he was the type to inveigle his way into society functions.

'We also have Brigadier Valeri Sabauri on piano, a highly decorated officer of the Georgian infantry, and his delightful daughter Natalia, on violin and also a patron of the Chamber Musicians' Association in Tbilisi. And as a special token of appreciation in honour of our new patron, henceforth, Pitts House is to be renamed Sabauri-Pitts.'

Gripping his pipe between his teeth, Sir Walter began clapping boisterously and egging us on to do likewise. The populace obliged like the child whose ear is twisted by its mother and told to enjoy itself. As the restrained applause died away, Nikola, setting out on an address of his own, gestured grandly to stem the adoring masses. I suppose he imagined he was at the Royal Albert Hall giving a dry discourse before a rapt audience.

'And may I say what a pleasure it is to be residents to this prestigious institute and to meet you all. Natalia and Valeri will now treat you to a piece specially composed for the occasion. I'll step out of their hair. If anyone has requests, please don't hesitate to ask me as I join you. Thank you.'

And for the next few moments the ensemble advanced a tuneless farrago of ear-piercing screeches and deafening dissonance. You know the sort of thing that has horses neighing and kicking stable doors in distress and is loosely described by loonies as 'experimental'. To right-thinking ears, on the other hand, the overall effect is a cluttered medley of miserable discordance. What the evening needed, to my mind, was something more in the way of boogie-woogie. I felt strongly on the subject.

'I say, Spence,' said Monty, thinking along similar lines, 'do you not feel by the way the pianist is bashing the keys that he might be able to unleash more aggression on the bass drum?'

But I was too preoccupied for Monty's misfiring bon mot. I'd noticed that Nikola, after oiling into the crowd and shaking hands like a returning emperor, had struck up a deep discussion with Eva and Sofia, but especially Eva. Neither had this gone unnoticed by Monty.

'Spencer, do you see what I see?' he said.

'I do, old chum.'

The last note finally died amid a spattering of claps, mostly from those who recognised a return to the good times. This included Monty and I, and we were poised to bolt off-the-line for our former positions when we felt a pull from behind. Sir Walter had a hold on our jackets and with a flick of the head he beckoned the torturers over.

'Natalia and Valerie, I'd like you to meet our graceful hostess this evening and my chief aide, Magda.'

'Oh, I've met Va-*leri*,' said Magda, laughing infectiously and making a pig's breakfast of the man's moniker. 'So nice to see you again.'

She extended a business-like hand, but the towering Brigadier leaned forward as if taking a chomp and deposited a kiss on Magda's cheek.

Of course, most attendees meet Magda as part of the induction, particularly since it's no longer in Monty's hands after he found the excitement of being surrounded by so many females too intoxicating.

Magda turned to introduce me.

'Oh, I know who this is,' said Natalia, springing forward and threading her arm into mine. 'Our plucky guide in the wilderness. It's an honour to meet you, Spencer. We've been so looking forward to it, haven't we, Valeri?'

The Brigadier took my other hand and began shaking it vigorously.

'Indeed, we have. How exciting. Thrilling.'

'Ah,' I said.

I suppose some chaps' chests might puff out at such a reception, but I was positively stumped; mainly at how this contrasted so exactly with Ludo's initial impression of me. How odd, I thought, that to some you are a blight on the environment, and for others you're nothing short of a human marvel.

Sir Walter also seemed mystified by their admiration.

'Anyway,' he said, eager to move things on and embracing Monty like a proud father, 'this, of course, is Monty, tonight's leading man and Lockwood's favourite son.'

Upon hearing this Natalia unhanded me instantly and shifted her attentions to Monty.

'Oh, yes, of course. Lockwood's stage improvisor. And if I'm not mistaken, a virtuoso and man of science. A pleasure to meet a man of so many talents.'

She began smothering him with kisses and only stopped when the Brigadier wanted to express his unswerving fealty, too.

'Bravo. Splendid range.'

And this, if you can believe it, in deference to Monty. By the rush of red to his cheeks I thought he was having an allergic reaction to Natalia's lipstick.

'Well, gosh,' he said. 'How embarrassing.'

Extraordinary. I was at a loss to remember when our stock was so high. They seemed to regard me as one of life's great outdoorsmen who sets out across crocodile-infested swamps and sneaks past cannibals across ravines to settle a bet against Clifton at the club; when in fact my career-topper in this field had been acquiring three scouting badges before I was expelled for forgery. Scarcely worthy of this level of devoted fandom.

As for Monty, nobody could deny that he is one of life's strivers, but a clearer example of slipshod scholarship you will not find in the civilised world. From my recollection, the one time he's entered the realm of the standout few is when he fell out of a rowing boat during the Marlow Regatta one year, which was only discovered when the boat moored and the team was declared illegal. And yet to this Georgian pair, he was an intellectual colossus who, when he wasn't receiving the Royal Medal, unwound as a titan of the stage.

The conversation with Monty naturally inclined to just the three of them, so I turned to Magda and Sir Walter for answers. This needed fleshing out.

'Sir Walter, these chums of yours. Are they the full biscuit?'

'Huh?'

I repeated the question in his ear, only louder.

'Lord sake!'

He wedged a gherkin-sized finger in his ear and began wiggling it about.

'Damned filled my ear with saliva!'

I turned instead to Magda, but she seemed fogged.

'What do you mean?'

'Well,' I said, 'they seem to think that I'm descended from Shackleton and Monty is one of the illuminati. How do you account for it?'

This only seemed to confuse her further.

'Altitude sickness, I expect,' scoffed Sir Walter. 'Comes from living in the Balkans.'

'Not the Balkans, Sir Walter,' said Magda, respectfully, trying to avoid a diplomatic incident, 'the Caucasus.'

'What?'

She returned to the matter at hand and a second later a spark of recognition flashed across her face.

'Oh, I think I know. They probably got it from this.'

She darted across to the reception desk and returned with what I'd seen people poring over. I'd thought it was a programme for the Danish play.

'The Pre-Season Handbook,' she said.

'What?'

'I'll say what!' snorted Sir Walter. 'Damned expensive waste of money.'

'Here,' she said, flicking through it. 'It contains a short biography taken from attendees given during the admission process. And a few words on staff and faculty. It was Monty's idea.'

She saw that she'd lost me. Monty was a font of ideas. All stinkers.

'As an ice-breaker for the first week, to get to know each other, you know.'

I had no recollection of this.

'Did I write mine?'

'You were in exile.'

'So, I take it mine's blank?'

'No,' she said, waving at a friend in the distance. 'Monty wrote it.'

I immediately whizzed through the booklet to find my entry. The introduction to Francis Spencer Lockwood Esq. read, 'Spencer Lockwood. Co-bursar.'

Factually correct, of course, but a little sparse, you'd have to say. No artistic licence by the great man there. Interestingly, no mention of my being the great wanderer either. Scratching my head, I turned to Monty's and my jaw fell open. I read it to Magda and Sir Walter.

'"Montgomery Fipps Esq. – two tours of duty in India, thespian, art critic, experimental physician, botanist, chemist, draftsman and musician."'

Sir Walter roared so loudly that his ears popped and he could hear again.

'Tours of duty?' asked Magda.

'Beatrice took him when he was a tot,' said Sir Walter. 'And when he was sixteen when Cedric had that trouble, you know, with that memsahib.'

Consigning that episode to the pages of history, I moved swiftly on.

'Draftsman?'

'Cleric,' said Magda, tittering. 'Musician?'

'Accordion,' I said. 'Never got beyond first principles.'

This seemed to stir a memory for Magda.

'Ah, that explains that beastly racket from Belling House. I thought someone was performing an exorcism.'

Sir Walter roared again and the three of us hit upon a rare, to-be-treasured moment of unanimity, for this was no mere embroidery. Together the thought that was encircling our minds was whether we had in our midst the finest spinner of whoppers in the northern hemisphere. He was so deep in discussion with the Georgian duo that he hadn't the foggiest he was giving us so much joy. More of Monty's chequered history passed between us and for some time you could not have found a livelier group of people enjoying themselves more thoroughly than we three. If a chap should have predicted, at the outset of this soirée, that there would be this much bonhomie between me, Magda and Sir Walter, I would have taken it as a sign of something malignant in his cerebellum.

The jocularity paused briefly when Quinton, who was standing in for a servant, thrust a tray at us.

'Coup d'état?'

Magda hurried him away to fetch his dentures lest attendees from the more volatile regions become startled by a mix-up over crudités. Chalk it up to Magda for another incident avoided – another area in which she had established an impressive tally.

This reminded me how it was that most learning happens outside the classroom. Sir Walter was at odds with this thinking, for no sooner had they gone than he began reminding me of that ghastly assignment he'd mentioned when summoning me back. Fortunately, over the chirping masses I didn't catch the detail. My attention returned to Eva and Sofia. Particularly at how Nikola had now taken to whispering in Eva's ear.

More often than not, a laugh and a girlish tap on the chest would result followed by a gradual reddening of her cheeks. I was envisioning the life of a travelling musician-cum-ambassador and imagining how it was bound to produce a trove of anecdotes to appeal to the opposite sex when the fallacy of my train of thought was brought home to me. The scales, you might say, fell from my eyes when Eva whipped her hand back and jerked her drink in his eye before storming off. I was speechless. Even Sir Walter broke off mid-flow.

Sofia quickly followed but in pursuit bumped the arm of the attendee who had been giving us a waltz on the piano. This mangling of the remaining bars brought everything to a screeching halt. In the midst of this general confusion stood Nikola, mopping the visage.

'Did you see that?' I said, pawing at the arm of Lockwood Senior. 'Lucky she didn't swipe the blighter.'

He shook his head and tutted. Again I had proved a disappointment. Even on the subject of female outrage, on which we are all lifelong students, to him, I was a mere beginner.

'Why would a woman smack a sticky, wet cheek which she had just made so by her last effort? Ridiculous.'

I had to admit this seemed to contain a kernel of logic.

'You think she should've gone for the other cheek?'

'No, no, no,' he said, impatiently. 'The rules of engagement are clear. Have been since time immemorial. It's a swift palm across the cheek or a sling. Never both.'

'A fling?'

'Sling, man. Sling, sling, sling!' he said with a raised voice.

We weren't able to debate the merits and shortcomings much further because the pianist, as if touched by the hand of inspiration, broke into the most deliciously lively swing number. Finally! Something with a bit of zing. The hall became instantly swept up by the jubilant rhythm. The less inhibited coves were already shaking their tails to it and it wasn't long before the eyes of the lobby seemed to shift to the centre of attention – Monty and Natalia who had found their own school of rhythm.

On a quick point of order, most people, when they set eyes on Monty's weedy frame, assume he's recently escaped across steep mountain slopes from a labour camp where he was only fed once a week. But those who have settled down with him for his standard five courses and seen him demolish second helpings, or seen the last crumb disappear into that bottomless tract, tell me they've been changed for life. Never again will they be so easily fooled. For every great conjurer has a trick, and Monty's piéce de rèsistance is his metabolism. This internal perpetual motion machine has helped keep the man's frame feather-light, his limbs bendy and his joints elastic.

All of which Natalia put to excellent use when flinging and flipping him about the place. It was thanks to this lightness of chassis that enabled her to lock onto his arms as he faced the wrong way and flip him onto her back where he rolled off carried by the momentum. He was still seeing double when she scooped him up and jacked him over her shoulder one minute, both legs cartwheeling over her head, and whisking him out from under her legs the next. Things slowed while she reverted to basic Charleston footwork if only to catch her breath, but it wasn't long before a determined look came into her eye. You see it in gymnasts before a tricky dismount. Once sufficiently oxygenated, she gambolled towards him and hurled herself at his midriff with forked legs either side of his chest.

Now, it's one of those universal truths that when females do this, they expect you to catch them. What's less well known is that most males would rather they didn't in the first place. So, naturally, when it came for Natalia to fling herself at the stationary target, she had every right to expect hands to come from below to support her undercarriage. What she hadn't expected was for Monty to freeze in terror, lock his arms to his sides, close his eyes and hope for the best. The overall result being that, having clamped his arms to his side, no such support came and she slid all the way down for a soft landing. Whether it was this finale that brought about the end to the music, I do not know, but suffice to say that an end had been brought to things.

The onlookers, who'd long stepped away for fear of losing an eye, were standing with mouths agape, stunned by the frenzy of motion they'd just witnessed. Anyone marvelling at Monty's windswept aspect and side-to-side rocking would have seen not only a pupil of Life, but that rarest of things – a survivor. I mean to say, the sort of chap who is blown overboard by gale-force winds in the swells of Cape Horn and, guided by Providence, washes up on the beaches of Tahiti.

For her part, Natalia slowly rose to her feet with wrath shooting from her eyes. Her whole aspect was that of a woman who finds herself at the centre of a public humiliation and can't decide if raining black fire is sufficient reckoning for the man responsible.

The pianist, having sworn an oath never to get above himself again, returned to a waltz and this allowed everyone to assume their former positions. All this and I could've told Monty he'd be much happier with the foxtrot. Just then a hand landed on my shoulder. It was Magda's.

'Well, shall we?' she said, offering a shapely hand.

For an instant, I didn't grasp what she meant. And then, as the realisation set in, terror gripped me. I consider myself an obliging chap when it comes to the other sex, but my natural instinct seemed to forewarn an ill wind.

'Pffft,' I said. 'You know, I think I'd rather… That's to say…'

A thought struck me.

'I'm sure Monty would be only too pleased.'

I craned my neck to spot him, but he was probably receiving medical attention somewhere.

'Oh, come on. Don't be such a bore,' she said, exuding a gleam. 'I have something to tell you, my little scout master.'

'Well,' interrupted Sir Walter, joining my hand with Magda's. 'What are you waiting for?'

Polite excuses tumbled out of me at a rate of a hundred knots a second, but he was adamant. I'd often seen this effect take root in him when he was on his way to becoming blotto. The subtle hint becomes a shove in the back.

'Nonsense. Go on,' he said, winking at Magda.

To me this was clear evidence that Monty's suppositions had been right – Sir Walter was indeed trying to pair us off. And I was still examining the seemingly irreconcilable fact that Monty had hit the nail on the head with the equally daunting realisation that I appeared to be in the frame, wondering which position was the more disquieting, when Magda took hold and began hustling me into a sweeping dance.

'That's it,' she said, twirling me around.

And there, in one fell swoop I had become the chap who hears the heavy clanging of all the exits being closed while a veiled figure approaches menacingly from behind.

'What are you doing?' she said, interrupting my trance. 'It's counter-clockwise.'

She pointed vaguely at the directionless mass and began counting our steps.

'One-two-three, one-two-three.'

But it was impossible to concentrate on the tedium of this while my mind was running amok. Visions of possible home life assailed me. I imagined myself pitching up at the breakfast table, still prising the eyelids open only to find breakfast now concludes at 10am, the daily crossword has been filled in and there is a note carrying the day's instructions: 'Morning, darling, the most extraordinary thing keeps happening. Herbert called mentioning some silly game. Golf, I think. Anyway I've cancelled it because your financial report on the new Haslemere site is needed by 4pm. Also, we're giving the Bensons dinner tonight.'

And if that doesn't dash the colour from a fellow's cheeks, I dread to think what would. I shuddered at the ghastliness of it. Not that I'm against enterprise, you understand, but at least Faust extracted something in return for his soul.

No sooner had my feet kicked into some semblance of rhythm than Magda shifted my focus yet again.

'OK, upsy-daisy, look at me. That's better. Now, your father asked me to put you in the picture. Are you listening?'

'What?'

'Good. Now, did Sir Walter mention why he asked you back to Lockwood early?'

I couldn't remember him *asking* anything.

'He ordered us back, if that's what you mean. Forthwith.'

'Forth what?'

'Right speedily.'

'*Et voilà*. Well, he has an assignment for you. A sort of special duty.'

She smiled in an earnest sort of way, as if it were an honour entrusted to few.

'Oh, yes?' I said. 'What sort of duty?'

'To escort our guests of honour.'

She tipped her head towards the musical trio.

'Escort them?' I said. 'Off the premises?'

Considering the nuisance they were already making of themselves, here, I thought, was a task I could put my back into. But she corrected herself.

'He means that you will be their host. Do whatever they want to do during their short stay at the institute.'

In every particular this proposition struck me as beyond the pale.

'But what do I know about hosting musical ensembles comprising Georgians and the Maltese?'

'Oh pish. You're an excellent host. There isn't a game you don't play, a hobby or pastime that you don't fritter your time on.'

'Yes, but—'

She rattled off several that make up the typical roster in the more clement months.

'Croquet, tennis, swimming, horse riding, watercolour. All you need to do is see to their every whim.'

'Watercolour?'

'Or roller skates. I hear they're quite à la mode.'

I ignored this preposterous suggestion and put to her the burning question of the moment.

'Why?'

'Hmm?'

'Why are we laying out the special china for these tone-deaf blighters?'

'Spencer!' she said, checking if anyone overheard me. 'They are benefactors and will be making a generous donation to the institute.'

No use arguing in the face of Mammon, I thought. And then, just like the pianist earlier, inspiration struck and Monty's musical inclinations came to mind. He'd already made a splash with the trio. Surely there could be no one better than the man of the hour.

'Why not ask Monty?'

She paused and thought for an instant, evaluating the proposal thoroughly. The present musical number came to a finish and we hopped back amongst the minglers when she finally spoke.

'OK.'

'Huzzah!' I said, waves of relief gushing over me.

'A fine idea.'

'Spiffing,' I said.

'Both of you can do it.'

'What!'

Before I knew it we were standing in the shadow of the Brigadier, beside Sir Walter and Nikola who, I imagined, were probably discussing the finish on the new name plaque for Sabauri-Pitts House.

'Ah, here comes our host,' said Nikola, slapping me on the back. 'Your father has just told us. I do hope we won't be an inconvenience.'

I smiled wanly, but my heart sank at this. I had long ago discovered that when someone promises not to be a nuisance, that's precisely what they will be.

'Not at all,' said Magda, offering my civilities for me. 'I'm sure you'll find the salubrious surroundings to your satisfaction.'

'I'm sure we will,' said the Brigadier.

'And now, if you will permit me the pleasure of this dance,' said Nikola, escorting her away.

She acquiesced graciously and left me with Sir Walter and the towering old beak in regimental uniform.

'And whether it's gameplay or horseplay, you're in stellar company with Monty and Spencer,' said Sir Walter. 'Right, Spence?'

'Hmm?' I said, looking after Magda. 'Oh, absolutely.'

'Excellent,' said the Brigadier. 'I like people who're fond of the outdoors. Shows a daring spirit.'

'And,' I added, striking the diplomatic note in front of Sir Walter, 'of course, if I can be of service, don't hesitate to ask.'

'You're too kind.'

'Incidentally, how long will you be staying?'

'Ha!' he guffawed.

Sir Walter gave off a hoot of laughter, too.

I thought this an odd reply and couldn't help notice a distinct gleam come into the Brigadier's eye. I gave a short nervous laugh of my own. The Brigadier leaned forward conspiratorially.

'Just long enough to capture the beast,' he said, winking and reverting to his towering height.

He bore the aspect of a man who was as chuffed as it was possible to be. I hadn't the foggiest what to make of this tommyrot, of course, but then again idioms seldom travel well, I thought. And since it seemed inevitable that I'd be feigning understanding for much of their stay, I glossed over it.

'Absolutely topping,' I said, cheerily.

'That's the spirit,' added Sir Walter.

And then, something happened which seemed to defy all worldly understanding. From nowhere an arm snaked round my waist and a hand took hold of my head and pulled me into a tight embrace, my face thrust firmly into the chest of the Brigadier.

'Spencer Lockwood, I like you. We will catch it together.'

Well, words failed me. With my head resting on the Brigadier's bosom, the mind raced for explanations to this most unseemly conduct. Could I bear a likeness to a long-lost son or nephew perhaps? Did I remind him of his younger self? Looking back, what I should have done is express outrage like Eva and exclaim, 'Unhand me, you wretch!' and storm off for sympathy from a close friend. But so much for hindsight.

'Well, I like you, too,' I said, floundering for the proper etiquette.

If only I'd known this would simply encourage him.

'You see,' he continued, 'it's the old ritual. Think of it as an ancient dance between man and beast. Don't worry if you have never done so before. I will lead.'

'A dance?' I asked, horrified.

'The hunt, Mr Lockwood.'

'Hunt?'

'I know it's out of season, but Sir Lockwood Senior has already granted me permission to shoot.'

'Shoot?' I blurted. 'Shoot what?'

My family's propensity to use me as fodder appeared to be taking another turn. The Brigadier appeared at a loss for an instant.

'The beast in Winsbrook forest, of course. Mr Lockwood, I feel an excitement I have not felt in quite some time.'

I blenched.

'Would you excuse us a moment, please, Brigadier?' I said, gulping deeply. 'I need a word with Sir Walter.'

With a respectful nod and courtly wave, the Brigadier bade us *à bientôt* and left us just as Nikola and Magda seemed to have ended their clinch. They seemed as snug as any two could be dancing a waltz, but that was not germane. There were more pressing matters at hand. She joined us and I lost no time getting down to it.

'This ghastly Brigadier wants to murder someone.'

'Not murder,' scoffed Sir Walter. 'Hunt.'

I couldn't see that there was much in it either way.

'OK, he wants to hunt someone.'

'Some*thing*, you imbecile. Some*thing*.'

The stack of unpleasant surprises earlier had rather left me abaft on the details. I tried to recollect his words and after a second it came back to me.

'That's right,' I recalled. '"Some beast," he said.'

'And what is wrong with that?' asked Sir Walter, puffing on his pipe.

By my reckoning there was no game, fowl or fauna nearby that couldn't be found elsewhere. I observed Sir Walter's manner and he seemed as proud as a peacock. I froze in dismay.

'Don't tell me you've sold a worthless stack of hunting licences again.'

'Of course not,' he said. 'No stack this time.'

Monty, the oracle of the age, had also joined us by this stage and his ears had pricked at this talk of a beast. Content just to listen so far, his excitement now piqued.

'What sort of creature?'

'Finally, a sensible question,' said Magda. 'Sir Walter has entered into an arrangement with the Brigadier to hunt a creature which the Brigadier believes to exist in Winsbrook forest. Something unusual, he says. Something he's seen with his own eyes.'

'That's right,' said Sir Walter. 'Natalia mentioned he hunts trophies. Heads apparently. So, I had an idea.'

He relit his pipe.

'And you've arranged that the Brigadier should bag it?' I asked.

'Sold the exclusive rights,' he said, smiling with the pipe clamped between his teeth. He had the air of a chap nominated in the Honours list again.

It took a few moments, but the pieces to this diabolical arrangement came together in my mind and there was no two ways about it – a foul deal had been threshed out. In exchange for a chest of glittering silver, Sir Walter had agreed to rename a house, sold a licence for a pointless jaunt in the woods and saddled Monty and I into the bargain. I was completely dumbfounded. I mean, what a way to earn the honest day's salt! The bottom lip drooped and time seemed to stand still. Perhaps concocting a wheeze of this sort is what is meant after all by having the *fibre* to excel at this dark mercantile art.

I was briefly carried away imagining what sort of beast the Brigadier might have witnessed and hoped for all the world that it wasn't Cerberus – the three-headed dog that guards the gates of hell and mangles those who try to escape – when, fortunately, my reverie was cut short.

'Now, both of you,' said Sir Walter, putting his arms around Monty's shoulder and mine while lowering his voice, 'you will oblige the Brigadier on this expedition.'

'These two seem to be a real hit,' said Magda.

With Monty and Natalia's gyrating earlier and my being swept up in an emotional embrace by the Brigadier, Magda obviously thought we were just the two for the job. Delighted to hear this, Sir Walter began rubbing his hands together in ecstasy.

'Good show. That's settled.'

He tooled off, shaking hands and slapping backs, spreading the bonhomie.

'But what do I know about enchanted forests?' I protested.

'Which of them is going on this hunt?' asked Monty.

Magda explained that it would just be the Brigadier and Natalia. While I despaired at the gloomy prospect ahead, I could see from his expression that Monty was anything but disheartened at our assignment. Rather, he appeared upbeat and seemed to view this journey into the wilds of Winsbrook as a jolly escapade.

I heaved a heavy sigh.

'Look,' said Magda at her most conciliatory, 'what's the worst that can happen? You go walking in the lovely fresh air and return after a day or two. Just think of how pipped Sir Walter will be.'

'You must see the silver lining, old fruit,' said Monty.

'Exactly.'

There are times when Magda's pragmatism and Monty's buoyancy become a little wearisome, but I had to concede that there was something in that.

'But we don't know the first thing about shooting or surviving in the wilderness,' I said.

'There's nothing to it, old man,' said Monty, cheerily. 'Fear not, Magda, I'll look after the young scout.'

'Even so,' she said, unconvinced. 'I'll have the staff bring you a short practical guide to the outdoors. I'll arrange for you to set off tomorrow afternoon. You'll enjoy it.'

'Chin, chin,' said Monty, clinking her glass to round things off.

That was the abominable last straw. I plodded straight off to bed.

Chapter Six

GENERALLY speaking, a carefree mind sees to it that I have no need for Monty's fetid swamp goo to get a spot of restful shuteye. More often than not I emerge raring to put wrongs to rights and restore order to the world on the tennis lawn or on the crease gripping the willow, seeing the whites of the eyes of the bowler, but as I flipped the blindfold up this particular morning, there was none of this characteristic effervescence of spirit.

As I saw it, when it came to summoning us down early for this ghastly assignment, dirty work had been perpetrated by Sir Walter and Magda, his dutiful right-hand man. As it stood, the dilemma that faced me this grim morning was choosing between ending up in the slavering jaws of an abominable beast or winding up in the slithering hands of a Brigadier. Even Hercules hadn't faced anything *this* grim in his Order of Labours.

And in spite of what Magda had said, flicking through *Scouting for Boys* before sleep hadn't helped in the slightest. On the contrary, it seemed to bring on one of those out-of-body experiences where, from above, I pictured myself sitting in the forest swatting flies, all the while situated just behind me over the shrubs stalking me with a gleaming iris was a nine foot pelican.

As I lay in bed, the mind boggled at how I was arm-in-arm with a toothsome filly one minute, and the next, I was in almost the opposite predicament. As I put it all together, it seemed that my forebodings on the morning of my return had proven well founded after all.

Nevertheless, making work of the ablutions, I set off to crown the day. Peeking my head beyond the threshold first to check for trophy hunters, I was down by the buffet cart in a jiffy. I arrived to see a chap with a pippin of a black eye gnawing on some bacon gristle and it was only on closer inspection that I noticed that it was Monty.

The pummelling he'd taken at the hands of Miles had developed into a real peach. I joined him.

'Here comes my companion in arms,' he said, chomping away. 'Beautiful morning, wouldn't you say?'

'Nonsense,' I said, banishing outright this pop-eyed cheeriness. 'Dark clouds loom. Can you not see them? Try looking with the good eye.'

'Cheer up, old man,' he said, radiating brightness, totally oblivious that he cut the figure of Goliath's sparring partner. 'You mean you're not looking forward to it?'

'No, I'm jolly well not,' I said, indignantly. 'The old timer has placed me squarely in it.'

I sat with arms crossed, but right away I could see that he was on a different plane altogether. Discussions with Monty are apt to take sharp turns for the perpendicular and he made a screeching turn now towards the subject that was evidently uppermost in his mind.

'Did you meet Natalia last night?' he said, egg dangling from his lips.

'Of course I did, you dolt. We were introduced together.'

Contrary to what you might think, Monty straining to recall this moment from last night came as no surprise to me. I had seen it countless times before. He'd been caught in the glare of those wild eyes of Natalia's and this had induced a sort of seizure in the lobes. It came back to him.

'Oh, good heavens,' he said, sloshing tea into the saucer. 'So you did.'

I paused a moment to see if any other flashbacks from the night might occur to him. None did. Eventually I relented with a pressing question or two of my own.

'I hate to bring it up straight away, old man,' I said, 'but do you recall a promising exchange with anyone else last night? Besides this Georgian Terpsichore, I mean.'

He stopped chewing to think all the better and after a moment the lips began smacking again as he shovelled forkful after forkful of scrambled egg.

'Oh, you mean that Swedish number,' he said, slurping the tea. 'Sandra, what?'

'Sofia,' I corrected, 'and she's Greek. What I'm getting at, my lad, is how you happen to have transferred your fascination from this absolutely topping lover of the dramatic arts to this other Terpsichorean she-devil who, on her best days, raises the dead playing second fiddle.'

His eyes twinkled with excitement and, swallowing a spadeful, he put down the cutlery.

'Isn't she a knockout?' he exclaimed. 'I tell you, Spence, until you've been spun, flipped and whisked around at the hands of this divine corker, you don't know the first thing about exhilaration. I'll admit I had to wait a goodish while for my nerves to stop jangling, but when they did and I came back on the scene, I was ready for round two. Only for some reason, she'd stalked off and the pianist had gone lame. No stamina, these youngsters.'

I was aghast.

'You really think that a girl capable of an exhibition like that should be moved to top billing?'

'Absolutely!'

'Someone who flamboyantly tosses you base over apex is just what the doctor ordered?'

'Positively she is,' he said, resuming his quaffing.

He began humming the piece from last night, his body shaking and gripped in the throes of rapture. It was so clear that any tomfool could diagnose it. This gibbering was unequivocally the first symptom of onset mania; the delirium before the sweats. It was an appalling display. I mean, breakfast with Monty usually is, but first and foremost I was perturbed at how he could consider last night's spectacle as anything other than an affair to forget. Still, even the most slapdash of observers, seeing the man jigging and jiving at the table this morning, would have taken it as evidence of one thing, and one thing only – the man was unwell. Every fibre of his being seemed to shout the fact. Like a chap with cloudy eyes going for an early morning dip in the Congo River, he had no idea what he was doing or saying.

'Incidentally,' he said, tea cup half-way to his lips, 'what were you doing canoodling with the Brigadier?'

'We were not canoodling! The man was rather overwrought, that's all. Just let his paternal instinct get the better of him.'

After *his* cavorting antics the man had the immortal rind to look at me as if I were the one in need of a hot compress on the head, blast him. I was shaking my head in disdain and pouring the breakfast blend when Aunt Beatrice and Uncle Cedric – virtually my surrogate parents – entered. Seeing us laying waste to the fare, they joined us.

Always pleasant company, I could not imagine two more sprightly souls with whom to chew the cud in the morning.

'Tea, mother?' said Monty, lifting the pot.

'Pour on, shipmate,' she said, evidently in jovial mood. 'Spencer,' she bellowed, 'I've just been speaking to Magda. So, it's tally ho, is it? Ha!'

Blessed with enough fortissimo to shake the chandeliers, she saw me groan and chortled all the more. Uncle Cedric, on the other hand, wore the hangdog expression of one who's received a court summons. He nestled in amongst us.

'Spencer, some bottles of communion wine have gone missing from the chapel. Was it you?'

Aunt Beatrice choked on a sip. I'd never before met anyone who could choke and glare at a chap at the same time.

'Eh?' I said.

While Uncle Cedric rubbed her back, much as I'd done to Magda's last night, he unfurled more of the allegation.

'Walter was just telling me that you were intent on snaffling his wares last night.'

'Spencer,' said the aunt, having recovered, 'you godawful reprobate. If I discover it was you, it'll take a ruddy miracle to save your hide.'

Egad! For Aunt Beatrice, who was a renowned prankster herself, if there was one thing she wouldn't abide, it was looking lightly on the holy orders. Fortunately, I had a watertight alibi for this one.

'If you must know, I returned from my purdah yesterday morning, so I hate to break it to you, but your snaffler is another.'

Accepting this, she turned her penetrating eye on Monty, who, having just loaded another heap into his mouth, made his denial through panic-stricken eyes and a dizzying shake of the head.

'We returned together,' I said.

She studied our faces and appeared content, for now, at least, to just simmer.

'OK,' said Uncle Cedric, 'but when I find out who is responsible I shall report them to the highest authority.'

I was still wondering exactly which authority he meant when Aunt Beatrice brought things back to earth.

'Anyway,' she said, spotting Kristina creeping about the opposite end of the hall, 'must dash. Bag a big one, boys!'

She tottered off, leaving us to mill about with Uncle Cedric. His glasses had steamed up while blowing on his tea.

'Where is she?' he asked, squinting around the room.

Monty pointed towards the tête-à-tête unfolding between Kristina and Aunt Beatrice. Satisfied, Uncle Cedric returned to us and leaned in, speaking in hushed tones.

'Now listen, boys, I don't want you to think I'm accusing you of anything. I just said that because I thought she might be listening.'

I looked nervously around.

'Who?'

'Your sainted aunt, of course,' he said. 'That business about the bottles going missing, I mean.'

'You mean,' asked Monty, echoing our mutual thoughts, 'they're not missing?'

'Well, that's the problem, you see. When you drink the wine, you're left with the empties. I refilled them with blackcurrant water but she became suspicious and sniffed one. Then she took a sip and spat it over me as if I were a spittoon at a wine tasting. When I walked past the parishioners they thought I'd been in a knife attack. Well, you know all about that, Spencer. Anyway, I had to think on my feet, you see, so I told her some scallywags had got to it again.'

And there in a nutshell is why nothing could extinguish my love for my Uncle Cedric. He was in every way a corking chap.

I placed a well-earned arm round his shoulder and reassured him his secret was safe with us when I received a thwack on the shoulder from behind. I swivelled round to see that it was the Brigadier. Natalia stood behind him. They had no doubt come to haul us out into the dreaded forest.

'Good mourning, Spencer, Montgomery, and to you, Mr Fipps. I have tracked your whereabouts.'

'Morning, Val. A-hunting we will go,' sang Monty, 'a-hunting we will go.'

Just when I thought he'd forgotten the rest, he substituted the remaining tune with the versatile 'lah-lah's.

'Good morning,' I said, uneasily. 'Ah, will you excuse me? I—'

'A capital idea,' said the Brigadier, pulling back my seat and tipping me onto the table. 'Let us waste no time.'

And before I knew what had happened, his eight inch fingers nestled on my shoulder and yanked me upright.

'My Lockwood – or may I call you Spencer?'

'Certainly,' I said.

After all, the Lockwood clan may be many things, but petty is not one of them.

'I think it is vital that we beggin.'

'Come again?'

'The hunt. We discussed it yesterday evening. Magdalena has kindly provided us with rifles, but we will need two camels.'

Sharing the job of bursar, I occasionally miss the odd thing, but unless we'd moved into a lucrative new sideline of which I was unaware, I had to break it to him that the institute coffers, when measured in camels, was nil. A distinct shortage.

'Ah,' I said, gulping a bit. 'Now, we may encounter some difficulty on that score.'

A heavy heel stamped the floor. He seemed thunderstruck.

'But why?'

'Nobody pays us in camels anymore.'

I observed his countenance to see if he'd caught my drift. Every host knows the importance at the outset of making clear the boundaries of requests that are acceptable and those which are the brainchild of an unsound mind. And this was clearly the latter.

'Oh, that is a shame,' he said morosely. 'Marvellous creatures, you know.'

'Majestic,' agreed Natalia.

'Enchanting,' chimed in Monty.

He beckoned Natalia to join him, which she did. The Brigadier, meanwhile, knitted the brow and for a while it seemed to me that all of Mother Nature's oddities were traipsing through his mind two-by-two and at any moment he might demand a troop of baboons to handle the luggage, so I did a quick recap at the menagerie adjoining the institute, care of Arkdale's farm:

Horses – a dozen or so
Sheep – an abundance
Pigs – well stocked
Donkeys – a small herd

'No matter,' he said, finally. 'Four horses will do. And two mules for the provisions.'

'Provisions?'

He seemed taken aback by the question and stood there blinking at me.

'Perhaps Spencer has never been hunting before, father,' suggested Natalia, helpfully.

'Ah,' said the Brigadier, bowing the beak. 'That would explain it. Perhaps, Montgomery, you will be kind enough to arrange the provisions. Fear not, Mr Spencer. You are in good hands.'

Last night he had made that abundantly clear. On the whole, I am forced to admit that he was beginning to strike me as a pertinacious blighter. In fact, the whole ruse was beginning to give me the absolute pip. The thrill of gripping onto a stallion's mane mid-chukker as it surges in pursuit of the ball is one thing, but trotting around the forest with a bloodthirsty field marshal salivating at the prospect of putting one in from afar was another.

Largely up to this point Natalia had been goggling and cooing at the structure that Monty had been playfully building using sugar cubes and slices of toast, but now she joined in to get the third floor going.

'Are you sure you wouldn't prefer to leave it a day or so?' I asked, with a final throw of the dice.

But he was adamant to the last.

'Absolutely not. There's not a moment to waste.'

'Or lose,' said Monty.

'Precisely. We don't want to lose. If we delay, we may lose our quarry to someone else.'

The imposing stature of the man, which shared more than a passing resemblance to an oversized heron, held me fixed firmly on the spot.

'Come, Natalia,' he said. 'We will meet you both at the east gate after a change of clothes.'

As he clapped his hands and Monty's toast tower collapsed on the table, he and Natalia disappeared through a corridor, he with enormous strides, she scampering furiously to keep up.

'Well,' I said to Uncle Cedric, resigning myself to the inevitable, 'say a prayer for us, won't you?'

'I'll say!' beamed Monty, insufferably.

After several minutes flicking forlornly through the wardrobe it was apparent that I was woefully lacking in the appropriate get-up for this sort of binge, and I was just about to pop across to Monty to see what he had in store when a brainwave swept over me. Having donned the apparel I deemed best I buzzed off, and no sooner had I stepped out of the main entrance for some fresh air than a hoarse, guttural cry rang out across the grounds. Seeing the birds taking flight and squirrels scurrying away for dear life I was impelled to the possibility that something might indeed be prowling in our midst. Perhaps, while snaking through Winsbrook, a poorly loaded crate had toppled out of a passing transportation procession, smashed and released a wild creature.

It came again. Only this time I discerned from its throaty articulation that it was some other lanky abomination. I peered over the hedge and standing beside an Equus entourage was the Brigadier. He waved an arm to beckon me over.

I zipped along the east wing and emerged onto a scene for which none of my senses were prepared. As I came to a stop, my mouth drooped open. Attired in red jacket, gold braid, cream jodhpurs, pith helmet and military insignia was the Brigadier, resembling the godson to Tsar Nicholas II with free rein to massacre at will.

Just as I was wondering what sort of dodo wouldn't notice this bejewelled figure creeping towards it, there came from behind me a sharp utterance which caused me to leap out of my skin.

'Spencer!'

Standing with his arms akimbo was Monty proudly donning a sola topi and a linen shirt with a drinks canister strapped over his shoulder. And rounding off this affront to the eyes was a pair of knee-length shorts from which sprouted two stalks which, only in Monty's parlance, could pass for legs.

'Like it?'

I was at a loss and he divined as much from my expression.

'Found it lying about from father's tours in India. Worn by all the sahibs, don't you know.'

I was just musing that if only we could drape a sarong around his underpinnings we might all find the jaunt more bearable, when there came another sudden high-pitched blast of noise.

'Attention!'

From the wings, pointing a rifle at my torso, stepped Natalia, and from the way she started slapping her thigh and cackling, my panic-stricken visage must have been just the sort of larkiness she felt we needed on this expedition.

At one time I would've chortled heartily with her, but my views on this sort of tomfooling whoopee had changed considerably one clay-pigeon shooting weekend when the disc, evidently taking umbrage at my chum Archie's slipshod method of loading, twanged sharply and thwacked him so firmly on the temple that he fainted from the impact; and it was only thanks to lightning reflexes on the part of the lady pulling the trigger that catastrophe was averted. Archie lost part of his ear, of course, and when the breeze picks up, it's best to stand upwind of him because of the whistling, but let this serve as a useful reminder to us all, I maintain.

Needless to say then, at the sight of this diminutive figure pointing that beastly thing at me, I quivered some. In her ensemble of camel shirt, neckerchief, khaki shorts and enormous black boots, she cut the figure of a junior member of some women's militia. I contrasted the father and daughter duo, she primed to sweep across the Serengeti spreading destruction and he dressed for a tsar's homecoming, and I couldn't help draw parallels between myself and Lockwood Senior, wondering if we were also birds of a feather. She rested the rifle on her shoulder and her chortling died away when something grabbed her attention.

'Good heavens, Spencer, why are you wearing a kilt?'

'What?' I said. 'Oh, I see. No, these are tweed shorts. Ventilation to the legs and all that. I don't know how Sir Walter fits into them, personally.'

She seemed captivated by the bare Lockwood limbs. The Brigadier appeared a good deal unnerved, too.

'*Mister* Lockwood,' he said, dropping a few registers, 'I agree. Your attire is most uncommon for our purposes.'

He pointed at the dome.

'Ah, the hat, yes, well, I think you military commanders have missed a bit of a trick, you see, because—'

'It is a chauffeur's cap?'

'Golf actually. And more of a hat, really. The rest of my belongings are up in Cambridge—'

I broke off, having noticed something.

'Excuse me, but has anyone noticed we appear to have none of the required number of horses and twice the order of donkeys?'

'Ah, yes, the Brigadier and I were just discussing the situation,' said Monty, motioning me for a word in my ear.

The two of us trudged a few steps away and it transpired that he'd been collared by Magda earlier. Apparently she'd kiboshed our plans to use steeds, claiming their need by other residents, so had doubled the number of donkeys instead.

'Mr Lockwood,' barked the military senior. 'These will not do. We may need to give chase. I specifically asked for horses.'

'Not to be a stickler, Brigadier,' I said, 'but if memory serves, the noble horse was an afterthought. Anyhow, it's no good, I'm afraid. I have received word that I cannot deprive the estate of its essential resources. I see that you and Natalia each have gaming rifles so we shall simply have to make do.'

He looked away in disgust, snorting like a jilted buffalo. For a short while this was all that could be heard, but in the end he accepted the fait accompli with the grace of Emperor Nero himself.

'Very well,' he said in an aggrieved tone.

'Oh, come now,' Monty said, irrepressibly, 'courage mounteth with occasion. These are hardy, noble creatures with a sort of rugged appeal, don't you think? Or did you have your eye on something with particular *ass*thetics?'

Monty chortled at his own effort.

'Don't fret,' I said, 'they're every bit as *ass*letic.'

I never could resist a bit of wordplay. I eyed the Brigadier expectantly, but nothing. Not a glimmer of a smile. No mirth seemed to penetrate the hide. I couldn't help feel that it's at moments like these that one appreciates the badinage of one's everyday companions.

'Come, Mr Lockwood. We must not delay any longer,' he said, eager for his next trophy.

We each claimed a trusty mule and Monty, never one to let a chivalrous opportunity pass, sprang to Natalia's aid to hoist her up. And after a valiant third heave she landed with a bump, but anyone with a modicum of the right stuff would have surmised immediately from her grimaced expression that she didn't think much of being hoisted side-saddle. The viewing angle was anathema to her. She fidgeted and chafed, feeling blindsided. This detail, however, had passed over the Monty sensory apparatus and only came to him belatedly when he, delighting in a job well done, gave a courtly bow just at the moment she flipped a stout leg over and booted him on the eye socket with considerable force.

I'd be hard-pressed to provide an exact count of the times Monty had been given the boot. More than records permit, I'm sure, but none to my knowledge had done so quite this literally. I imagine it's manoeuvres such as these that have led many a noble knight across the ages to quiver at the thought of committing such a gesture. And if it comes at this price, who could blame them? Still, I thought philosophically, some would say that this was comeuppance for letting Natalia down so badly in her running jump sequence.

Monty staggered for several moments until, having stabilised himself somewhat, he locked eyes on his topi, which had flown off on the moment of impact. He lurched to retrieve it and, after missing twice, finally grasped it. Then he steadied himself before plodding gingerly back to tackle the trickier business of negotiating his own mount. Pausing to breathe deeply and after the third attempt at clambering onto a braying donkey, he slung a leg over its back and slumped into the saddle.

Natalia had long since adjusted herself astride and now had the air of one who has taken the reins of Pegasus himself.

'Thanks God!' said the Brigadier, shaking his head with disdain at this rigmarole.

With this as our merry fanfare our intrepid dragoon set off ready to smite the enemy. The Brigadier led the charge with me in tow, followed by Natalia and Monty bringing up the rear.

Chapter Seven

AFTER a few minutes in silence we crossed the frontier of the cultivated grounds and passed into the dense undergrowth of the forest. I hadn't quite appreciated how close the wilderness really was to the institute grounds.

And I must confess that until this outing my view on donkey excursions was that they were about as pleasurable as swimming in a mangrove swamp during monsoon season, but after a few minutes of plodding along quixotically on my mount, you'd be hard-pressed to find anyone more in favour and I soon came to think that the experience should be open to all for the greater good. What's more, it appears that I was not alone. It was a spell that brought about a much-needed oasis of calm for us all. I even felt a thrill of swashbuckling adventure passing over me.

After some time, having judged that we'd all settled and our earlier friction had lifted, it seemed to me an opportune moment to learn more about the mission.

'Tell me, Brigadier,' I said, casually, 'what exactly is the strategy of our offensive? I mean, giving chase is now out of the question, so are we to lure the creature into an ambush? Sneak up from behind with a rock or land one from afar when its back is turned? Or did you have something more devious in mind?'

He threw back a sour and unpleasant look.

'I realise that you are a novice, Mr Lockwood,' he said, emphasising the mister, 'but an experienced hunter doesn't concern oneself with needless fretting. Since you ask, however, we will scour the ends of the forest and flush it out. It will become alarmed at our presence and reveal itself.'

Not being one for laying waste to wildlife myself, I was content to accept this stratagem from a seasoned hand. If this sort of tactic had worked in the past, who was I to question it? But question it, I did.

'Then should we split up for some sort of cross-fire and regroup?'

'And what if we do that, Mr Lockwood? What if the target is between us and each of us is concealed from view, will we not risk shooting each other? No,' he said, tutting. 'How much you still have to learn.'

A lesser man would perhaps have taken umbrage at being chided this way, but all too visible to me were those gilded robes, glinting in the sun. They served as a sobering reminder that here was a man who'd seen active service and whose favourite pastime now lay in letting the fauna have it with both barrels. So, in the end I decided that diplomacy was the best policy and I met this frostiness with the sangfroid for the occasion. (Incidentally, Sir Walter is always quick to distinguish between sangfroid for the occasion and the occasional sangfroid; the latter being a fortuitous happenstance on the part of any Philistine.)

'Of course,' I said, amiably. 'As you think fit.'

He nodded agreeably and I was pleased to see an affable side to the fellow. It became him well. Monty and Natalia had dropped back and throughout much of the afternoon, this being how we were paired, the air was punctuated by their howling laughter and giggles. Not that I minded, of course. I was content to just saunter along following the Brigadier. And I was in the act of doing precisely that when he came to a sudden halt with the realisation that the person guiding us should be Monty.

I sat up directly, flabbergasted. Why the dickens he wanted him to lead I couldn't fathom. My mind raced back to Monty's scroll of infinite merit in this year's handbook, which you'll remember had listed everything in the gamut of human accomplishments except being a member of the Knights Templar. It was just conceivable that this bushy-moustached Brigadier had inferred from that diabolical sham that what our platoon needed on this trail was a born leader with command over nature; and that such would be child's play to a man of Monty's broad depths.

I sought an exchange with his eminence as we entered open woodland.

'Monty, did you know that Valerie considers you to be a safari ace?'

'Yes,' he said, clearing his throat, 'I'd gathered that he'd come away with that impression.'

'What gave him that idea?'

'I did.'

'What!'

If the Brigadier's hosiery wasn't a loud signal to all living creatures of our arrival then this exclamation of mine certainly was. My conjecture had proved correct. The Brigadier was operating under the wildly deluded misapprehension that when Monty wasn't studying the human condition or capturing it with stage portrayal, he was traipsing through the Brazilian rainforest on his way to the Andes.

'But, Monty, you don't know the first thing about ensnaring creatures. What could possibly come…'

And there I ran aground. For in this moment of lucidity I began to suspect what Monty had in mind. I braced myself for it.

'Don't you see,' he said, 'the only way to make a hit with Natalia, she being daughter to this spiky field marshal, is to show that I belong to the same tribe.'

I won't deny that at times I have wondered whether Monty belonged to a different stratum altogether, but now was not the time to dwell on past indiscretions.

'And how do you intend to prove that?' I asked. 'Have us go in concentric circles until we're dizzy or pounced on by a mythical beast?'

'Who says it's mythical?' he said, thrusting his chin upward.

Monty's tendency to argue does become a trifle wearing at times.

'I do.'

'Well, that's all to the good,' he said, 'but we're straying from the point.'

'Yes, I'm glad you brought it up. What *is* our point?'

'I'm coming to that, blast you. Now, the way I see it,' he continued, 'is that it doesn't matter if we go round in circles. In fact, top-hole idea, Spence. Concentric circles it shall be. I just need time to... cast my spell. Now, Spencer, we haven't got to your part in proceedings yet.'

I uttered a cry of disbelief. There was one thing I'd been hoping he wouldn't say and that was it.

'You mean you're roping me in?'

'Of course! You're vital to the mission. You just keep the Brigadier entertained long enough for me to work my charms on Natalia. Just as you've been doing so far.'

Until this last clarification, I had feared the worst, but it appears that I'd jumped the gun. What he'd envisaged was something quite benign after all.

'Engage the fellow in idle chit-chat, you mean?'

'Exactly.'

'Just small talk?'

'That's it.'

'Nothing more?'

'Unless you'd care to pass the time cuddling each other again.'

I didn't deign to rise to that.

'Splendid man,' he said, patting me on the shoulder.

Oh, the long-suffering friend. I set about rejoining the Brigadier at the rear when Monty grabbed my arm. He was gazing dreamily at Natalia, his eyes now twice the size.

'Doesn't she remind you of Lady Godiva?'

I left him to his sordid fantasies and returned to the Brigadier. It took some time to flush the image from my mind.

Smiling as I joined him, he was pleased to hear that Monty was in the driving seat, so to speak. He returned the smile warmly. Half a mile or so later, when I sensed instinctively that those thorny spikes had softened, to encourage more of this mateyness, I decided to ask the Brigadier some well-chosen questions apropos our quest.

'So, Valerie, what is this creature?' I asked lightly. 'Some sort of stag?'

'Call me Brigadier,' he growled.

Well, it just goes to show how wrong a man can be, doesn't it? A formal footing it was to be.

'Since you ask, it walks on four legs.'

'Four appendages, eh,' I said, in the manner of a learned man. 'Mammalian, reptilian, amphibian, marsupial?'

He frowned, much like Sir Walter does when he perceives I'm deliberately bamboozling him with gobbledegook.

'What?'

'You know. What classification of animal is it?'

'I could not say.'

I listed the aforementioned groupings again and to each he gave the same reply. Then he shook his head peevishly and tutted loudly. It was quite vexing. Here I was compiling the facts to improve our odds and yet this seemed contrary to everything he felt important in the world. His answers were clipped, evasive. Almost as though he'd sworn an oath never to reveal the solemn truth. Still, with the tenacity of a reporter sniffing something lurid for the front page, I pressed on.

'Is it tall?'

'Define tall.'

'OK,' I said, patiently. 'Did it have antlers perhaps?'

'Maybe.'

It seemed to me that he'd stopped listening, so I decided to test him.

'Did it have three heads?'

'Perhaps.'

I was beginning to feel a strong empathy with those Spanish Inquisitors who felt it their divine duty to strap chaps to the rack for cross-examination. How I could use such a device now. It seemed only fair if he was going to be this tight-lipped.

Changing approach, I put something to him that was not only critical to our success but our survival, too.

'Well, how will we recognise it?'

He threw a hand in the air and mumbled something frothy in his native Georgian. Needless to say the precise translation went over my head, but in its similarity to a confab I once had with a Spaniard who gesticulated in almost exactly the same way, I'd say it roughly translated as, 'Save me, Mother of God.'

'It looks between a cow and a moose,' he said, exasperatedly.

Finally a breakthrough! It was still a morsel, but a juicy nugget at that.

'Any distinguishing features?' I continued, boldly.

'It had large, flat feet. I saw the creature myself not two days ago.'

Huzzah. Now, finally, we were getting somewhere. Tally ho for perseverance, I thought.

'May I ask where?'

'I saw it from a distance, but it was virtually on the grounds of the institute. It stepped between the trees and disappeared. Ah, now I remember. It had a brown coat. And long skinny legs.'

'How long?' I asked.

'As tall as Natalia.'

'How thin were its legs?'

'Feeble. Like yours.'

I pondered this description deeply for some moments. I'd seen some extraordinary misfits in *National Geographic* in my time, but anything with such an assortment of features had to be the most unflattering creature. The next thing the Brigadier's overactive imagination would be telling me was that this chimera had been put here to bear the sins of local amoralists. Perseverance only takes you so far. I had to sieve the facts from the slop.

'Do you know when it was last seen?'

'I told you,' he snapped. 'I saw it just before nightfall, two days ago.'

There was something distinctly unsettling about this whole affair, but I couldn't quite fathom precisely what. The more I strained the nut, the farther the answer seemed to dance. An unease stirred within me.

As to our anatomical chattering, I was getting pretty fed up extracting morsels of fact from this detail-averse blighter. What I had established was that if such a creature existed it was probably an ungulate. And if this were true, to find only one tottering about would be almost unheard of. Possibly, it was a layabout who'd woken to the fact that while it slept the colony had moved without leaving a forwarding address. Or it was a loathsome specimen that had been expelled for polluting the atmosphere and gone to Lockwood for like-minded company. Failing either of those two possibilities, we were on the wrong track altogether.

The other point on which I had now become staunchly fixed was that if on this foray we happened across a ragtag band of cannibals looking for something to go with their vegetables, the Brigadier would feel a firm shove in the back with my compliments.

I was dreaming of this when his hand shot up and he called us to a halt. He gathered us round and sought discussion with our navigation supremo.

'Montgomery—'

'Monty, please,' he said, affably.

'Very well. Monty, you are familiar with the topography of these woods. Would you propose the next step?'

'Topography?' repeated Monty.

He took on the aspect of a goat that'd been asked its thoughts on the cosmos.

'A course of action,' said Natalia, looking up into his eyes trustingly.

'Certainly, Natalia, love,' he said, his ears turning a delicate pink.

He began muttering to himself.

'A course of action, course of action...'

Monty is not often given to thinking on the spur of the moment, and for the most part, he takes on the look of an elderly village squire who's been woken before the innings is over. After jiggling the eyebrows a few times and sticking his finger in his ear to clear the cobwebs, he gazed skyward for divine intervention. After nothing came, he pursed his lips ruefully and lowered his head to eye level. At which point he caught sight of me, his eyes lit up and I knew immediately that I was in the wrong spot.

'Just a minute, Brigadier,' he said, hustling me to the side. 'Spencer, here's your chance to help me, old man. You just climb up a tree to—'

'Just a minute—'

'Don't interrupt or you'll miss the salient bits. Now, a hundred yards or so into the undergrowth you'll climb up the tallest tree you can find to get a good lookout. Once in position, shout back at me that you've seen something other-worldly moving near you and you're in mortal danger. And remember to put some soul into it. None of this wooden performance we saw with Polonius. There's a good fellow.'

Here he patted me on the arm and jiggled his eyebrows again as if nothing could be simpler. In fact, he'd lost me from the start. Particularly this wretched business about trees. I replayed what I thought he'd said.

'You want me to climb up a tree, claim to have spotted the beast and call upon you for rescue. Is that it or have I missed a slab of this tomfoolery?'

'No, that's it.'

I guffawed heartily. How he could entertain the wildest hopes that I'd ever countenance such a proposal was beyond me.

'Balderdash, man.'

'Don't worry, I'll come surging like the dickens. Man of the moment and all that. Brave. Fearless.'

'How does this help our mission?'

‘Blast our mission, it’s *my* mission that I’m concerned with.’

Here, you might say, the shilling dropped and I understood the essence of Monty’s eureka moment. It was, not to put too fine a point on it, another helping of amateur dramatics, only this time the derring-do was set against the backdrop of the woods with a come-to-the-rescue ploy. I was to be the bait, he was to be my saviour and the danger element was a figment of Natalia’s imagination. Only, blockhead that he is, he hadn’t considered Act II. Would we return empty handed and without a carcass trailing from our grasp? Would that not rank as abject failure and put him at deficit? Is the couch not shown to the man who returns without the daily catch?

I pointed out these obvious flaws in his plan of operation and was glad to see my well-reasoned objection penetrate. He fell into deep thought, mumbling incoherently, searching for the sequel.

‘I’ve got it!’ he said, an instant later. ‘We’ll fire a couple of shots into thin air and stomp back disappointed. Yes, that’s it. I’ll say, “It advanced towards me with its slobbering jaws and in the heat of the moment I fired, but it fled.” Yes, that’s the ticket.’

I scrutinised the man’s features to see if he was serious, and he was. Eyes blazing and as steadfast as those early aeronauts who had strapped planks to their arms, toasted victory and jumped off the precipice hoping for the best.

As I reflected on this ghastly wheeze, I was gripped by a paralysing thought. I would, for some indeterminate time, become separated from our coalition and therefore become prey for anything that happened to be lurking beyond. Already I’d been having misgivings about what might actually be at large, so this was the most ghastly aspect of the whole proposition.

‘OK. Well, what if there is something out there? Have you considered that?’ I said. ‘I don’t much fancy being the sacrificial lamb, I can tell you. A lab rat? If I must. A septuagenarian who takes one in the tum and rolls around squirming? At a stretch. But hitching the skirt and flashing some leg for a frothing cow to sink its teeth into? I draw the line.’

‘I thought there was no mythical beast,’ he said. ‘Unequivocal you were on the subject.’

‘Yes, well…’

‘And even if there is, you’ll be up a tree. Anyway, besides their many admirable qualities, cows aren’t especially renowned for their climbing ability.’

‘How about goats?’ I asked.

He looked perplexed.

‘Are we chasing a goat?’

‘Maybe,’ I said. ‘The point is they climb. The more fleet-footed even scramble along cliff-faces. Oh my word, yes.’

The self-appointed savant in our troupe furrowed his brow deeper still.

‘Cows climb cliff-faces?’

‘Give me strength,’ I said. ‘Goats!’

‘Everything OK?’ enquired Natalia.

Our bickering had not gone unnoticed and the Brigadier had begun fidgeting with impatience.

‘Just be a minute,’ said Monty. ‘Now, park the zoological rambling, Spence. Time is a wasting.’

It was true that I’d categorically pooh-poohed any suggestion of a beast earlier, but since my subsequent anatomy quiz with the Brigadier, some doubt had crept in and had been gnawing away at me steadily. Having discounted all likely contenders to be roaming the woods, we had narrowed the field of possibility considerably to either some sort of flicker of the eyes or, more worryingly, some Frankenstein’s monster assembled from the scrapheap of different animal parts. And it was along these lines that my imagination was now galloping. And, it just shows my state of mind that I now found myself not entirely dismissive of the idea of its existence. No longer could I discount outright the Brigadier’s sighting as some ludicrous fancy. So, now that these convictions had been stirred, I tried again to make Monty come round, along different lines.

‘OK. Do you remember last year’s intake of residents?’

'I do.'

'Does the right honourable member recall saying it was as if they'd escaped from the innermost crevices of Germany's Black Forest?'

'I certainly do. A more despicable concentration you could not find at this latitude. Your point is?'

'My point is,' I said, 'that something has drawn them, as if guided by a lodestar, to the bedlam of Lockwood. Why Lockwood is such a Mecca to the unbalanced and warped of mind is a mystery. But who knows what they've been getting up to in these woods or what unspeakable forces they've unleashed in that time.'

'Spencer, your imagination is running away with itself and it's putting you into a dreadful funk,' he said, placing a hand sympathetically on my shoulder. 'Now, hop to it, my man.'

Until the last moment, I thought he might come round, but no. Stubborn to the last.

'I'm not climbing up any blasted tree,' I said. 'Why don't you climb it? Perhaps your ape-like climbing will impress.'

This was laced with more zip than I'd intended, admittedly, but I was beginning to feel strongly that what he was asking was an imposition. The whole ruse struck me as the woolly-minded dippy imaginings of a brain made light-headed by infatuation. Beyond the giddy limit, from every angle.

He began imploring me again, but I checked him with a hand to stem the bilge. We had reached an impasse. I'd hoped that a few moments of forest air would give him time for this episode of deliriousness to pass. After all, it behoves a man to think deeply before sending cousins up trees.

I was gazing up at the forest canopy estimating how many bones I'd break in the event of a fall when Monty spun round to address the Brigadier.

'OK, Spencer will take a position at altitude. Once we've confirmed our whereabouts we'll decide our next steps. Right, Spence. On my command. On the double.'

Then, turning to me, he joined palms together at waist-height and contorted his face into a sickening grovelling expression. I was stunned. The blighter had ruddy hoodwinked me. I felt a rush of unity with Natalia and Miles in our shared desire to pummel the blighter. And I was just preparing to add my contribution to his facial bruising when the Brigadier barked.

'That's an order, man!'

Natalia simply shrugged her shoulders at me, which just about summed things up, in a nutshell. There it was. I'd been dispatched. What else could I do except storm off into the woods to climb a tree?

So, anxious and vigilant for slobbering ungulates, I set off and some moments later I was beyond view. I was scanning around for something with an easy ascent when by Jove! it hit me. An idea that is. I don't know why it hadn't occurred to me before. This wheeze didn't require me to climb a tree at all. When examined closely, all Monty required from me was a bellowing cry by way of a cue to come charging in. This was something I could do perfectly ably from terra firma. After a moment delighting in the perspicacity of this, I drew myself up, inflated my lungs and gave all.

'Monty!' I bellowed. 'I see it moving towards me. Help!'

I waited. We're told that time feels longer when we're engulfed in peril and I can confirm beyond any doubt the veracity of this statement. After what felt like several moments of complete silence, Monty was nowhere to be seen. Another moment passed and I began to wonder if the blighters had abandoned me altogether. I hollered again with more fortissimo this time. Anyone carrying a tea tray within twenty miles of me would have seen frightened tea spoons leap for their lives at this supreme effort. And it had an instant effect, but hardly what we'd intended. The sound of a shot reverberated in the woods and was followed by an urgent cry, which I took to be Monty's. The words weren't in range, but there was something inimitable about his panic-stricken falsetto that convinced me he was at large.

'Someone, please help. Monty!' I cried again.

Again, another shot rang out followed by more indecipherable articulations from him. His cackling, manic cries seemed to come from one direction and then drifted towards another before returning to originate from somewhere in between.

I issued my loudest cry yet. Still more shots rang out and if Monty's cries were agitated before, they sounded downright petrified now. His erratic peals took another turn of direction, this time towards our entourage, and then they suddenly stopped, as if a plug had been inserted.

Just as abruptly as it had begun, the commotion ended. I sat down on a fallen tree to catch my breath. For some minutes I just sat filling up the lungs until my pulse stopped dancing. As a calm descended, I reflected on the recent scene. You hear of fellows – family men usually – going berserk in woodlands. 'Be back for supper, darling,' he says, only to be discovered at evenfall up a tree trying to spot icebergs. And with Monty being predisposed to flights of fancy, it seemed almost inevitable that we'd see something akin to this from him at some point. Perhaps by some osmosis he had made the leap into a bloodthirsty huntsman and was obliterating everything in sight in a rampaging frenzy. But, rather than dwell on these possibilities, putting the needs of yours truly firmly to the fore, I sat down for a little time to myself.

I was given over so completely to the peace that I was loath to return to our babbling troop just yet, so I lingered, savouring the array of chirping, tweeting and cawing engulfing me. Having emptied my thoughts in this pleasant stillness, my attention soon became drawn to a sharp buzzing beside my ear. A bee was taking an interlude away from the clan, just as I was. It seemed fascinated with me.

As a rule, bees belong to that group of animals with which one tries to maintain a quasi-harmonious relationship, along with alligators and such like – any pest that can spoil a summer picnic, I mean. And since I was still contending with onset tinnitus from

Natalia's recent efforts with the violin, I'd had my fill of high-pitched ringing in the ear, so I issued a casual swipe. A moment later it cropped up by my other ear, completely unaware that its company had worn thin. So, putting my feelings into the universal language, I flapped and flailed my arms furiously and in this flurry I managed to land one on the back of its thorax. Dazed, it buzzed off into the undergrowth leaving me in peace.

I was basking in quiet triumph in the ensuing calm when at once the whole forest was abuzz and in the distance a dark cloud loomed like a floating shadow. Immediately I saw what had happened. Its pride having been somewhat bruised, this little blighter had whizzed round to the hive with his tragic story, with the result that a squadron of reinforcements had been unleashed and were now advancing towards me at a rate of thirty knots a second.

I bolted with the lightning reflexes of a commuter seeing the train doors closing and after covering three hundred yards in a blur, I shot out onto our trail just behind the entourage. As I landed there came an ear-piercing cry from Natalia, and the Brigadier spun round rifle first. It was now my thorax facing the treatment.

Thankfully his fingers fumbled or else the next gormless head to be mounted would've been mine.

'Mr Lockwood! Did you see it?' he frothed.

He drew back the weapon.

'Mr Lockwood!'

But my faculties had seized up and I was unable to parley with the man just yet. Not least because the loyalist regiment of the bee colony I'd offended could materialise at any moment and let loose its retribution on me, but mainly because my attention had been drawn to something else. Monty lay spreadeagled on the ground with his head in Natalia's arms.

'Mr Spencer!' said the Brigadier, shaking me by the shoulders.

I don't know if a pal has ever perpetrated on you the sort of jiggery-pokery that Monty had on me, but it leaves you feeling a trifle miffed and uppermost in my mind had been the chance to have it out with him at the earliest possible juncture, but seeing the man sprawled on the canvas took the wind from my sails completely.

All I could do was point at him. Natalia, who had been caressing his head in a tender fashion, was now gently tapping him on the cheek trying to revive the blighter back to consciousness. She saw me fumbling for expression.

'I rifled him on the head,' she said, matter-of-factly.

Gadzooks! And they say a picture can tell a thousand words. This illustrated superbly how misleading the image on one's retinas can be. For some reason not yet understood, she'd rammed the butt of her rifle sharply on the top of his head. Of the dozens of reasons someone might want to do this, by my reckoning that made two superb efforts by Natalia this day alone, which put her leagues ahead of Monty's other recent love interests. The upshot of this was that she had effected just the sort of action on the blighter that I thought was coming to him. As a result, my own yearning to throttle him seemed to evaporate. Consequently, I'd have to say, she'd shot up in my estimation considerably. I mean, setting aside her propensity to inflict torture on the masses with the gut strings and her gyrating motions on the dance floor, when I pondered her *net contribution*, to use Sir Walter's parlance, already it was considerable and weighty. Firstly, she had succeeded Violet, Jasmine and Heather and had therefore broken the theme of girls named after flowers. This was a welcome change for all in Monty's inner circle who felt that they had more in common with scorpions than flowers, but she had also, to her infinite credit, not only landed a thumping boot to the Monty eye socket, but had sloshed him over the crown in the same day. And as far as I'm concerned, anyone who does that has done their duty for mankind.

I was wondering if she might take it amiss if I gave her a peck on the cheek, by way of thanks and all that, when the Brigadier began shaking me by the shoulders again. It snapped me out of my stupor.

'I assure you Mr Fipps is quite fine. Now, did you see the beast?' he said, agog.

His face was flushed and feverish, his eyes wild with excitement. You know how it is with these ex-servicemen with a rifle in their hands – the urge to relive past action becomes overpowering. I was desperately trying to remember Monty's script.

'I definitely saw something.'

'Well, what was it? Was it as I described?'

It seemed to me that virtually anything on land might be mistaken for the thing he'd described, but this was no time for pedantry.

'Oh, my word, yes.'

'Yes!' he roared. 'It exists, it exists.'

Then he seemed to deflate instantly.

'And we let it get away.'

He became sullen and downcast. I may not have thought much of trophy hunting as a way to pass the idle hour, but seldom had I seen a man more crestfallen, and in spite of our maddening dialogue earlier, my heart went out to the man. So, standing on tip-toe, I placed a sympathetic hand on his shoulder. He eyed me askance, but I kept it there.

'You mustn't blame yourself.'

'I blame you!' he snarled.

I couldn't follow the logic of this, but by the way he frantically began scanning the woods, I took it that he was a man who cared little for semantics. Or, for that matter, my sympathy. Meanwhile, Monty had begun to stir back to life, moaning and blinking groggily.

'Look, he's waking up,' said Natalia.

'What?' said the Brigadier.

'Father, he's awake.'

'Who?'

This was as far as their sympathy seemed to stretch.

'What were you doing lunging at me like that?' she said, shaking Monty.

Then she turned to me.

'Jumping out as you did, you're lucky my father didn't shoot you.'

I'd been thinking the same thing. Given the chronology of events, things could have ended quite differently. Sometime after disappearing from view I'd sounded the warning that the beast was in our midst. This must have left father and daughter not a little rattled. Then, all of a sudden, something springs at them from the bushes.

'Oh,' I said, combining explanation with a lightness of touch, 'I was being pursued, don't you know. Pesky things.'

She gasped in a pop-eyed sort of way.

'Was it the creature?'

'Several hundred creatures.'

She gave a sort of squeal, which I judged to be excitement, but may also have been searing pain in the frontal cortex.

'Several hundred? Did you hear that, father?'

She beckoned him over and he was with us again in a flash. He lent his ear while she rattled off a few words in Georgian and almost immediately they were bonded by laughter. I'd already noted this duo's knack for getting the wrong end of the stick, so I interjected to correct the misapprehension.

'Ah. Not the creature per se, but some other little critters. We had a minor dispute.'

They both deflated in sullen disappointment. Nothing, it seemed, would have given them greater pleasure than if I had been trampled by a herd of stampeding ungulates.

Monty had by this time recovered sufficiently to stand and he joined our little quorum. His hair was tousled and he had lost his topi somewhere, presumably during target practice. He was dusting himself off, visibly shaken by the recent experience. I still had a fair stack of pressing questions to put to the chump, but before I could get a word in, Natalia took the first of them out of my mouth.

'What happened?'

He still appeared dazed.

'Someone coshed me,' he said, nursing the new bruise.

'I did,' she said.

'Huh.'

She seemed to feel that an explanation was required. Of all the extraordinary things I ever heard.

'I thought you were a crazy ruffian, hellbent on doing me a mischief.'

Monty appeared to be struggling to process this disclosure, so the Brigadier piped up, too.

'A reflex, dear Monty. You must remember that we knew only that Spencer had sighted the creature. Suddenly something leapt out from behind us. It's only normal Natalia should want to concuss you.'

For once the Brigadier and I were of one mind. Monty checked himself over and agreed that everything appeared to be intact and Natalia turned to me with a question.

'So why did you shout for someone to help Monty?'

I, not having been bludgeoned on the head by a rifle butt, was compos mentis enough to see that she had grasped the wrong end of yet another stick. Her question ran completely contrary to the actual turn of events. I politely refuted the charge, but this seemed to inflame them all the more. The Brigadier even gave a half-decent impression of me.

'I distinctly heard you say, "Please help Monty!"'

He was so certain in his convictions that it gave me a moment's pause and I tried hard to recall the episode, replaying events in their natural sequence. And it was while I was churning it over in my mind that a realisation dawned on me. Then it was as if Darwin's entire butterfly collection had come to life for a fluttering orgy in my stomach. I tactfully pointed out where I thought we'd come a cropper.

'With respect, Brigadier, what I said was, "Please help. Monty!"'

'Exactly!' he barked, his grip on the rifle tightening with irritation. "Please help Monty!"'

Natalia was also nodding in agreement with the Brigadier, and as I debated the merits of trying to explain to them the importance of dramatic pauses in English drama, Monty moved us onto more pressing business.

'Anyway, who was shooting at me?'

'Me, obviously,' said the Brigadier. 'I fired in the direction of your cries. They seemed to change direction after every shot, so I imagined that the hellish creature had you in its maw and was shaking you.'

Still scratching his head, Monty appeared to accept this and began recounting the experience.

'I remember becoming lost. Then Spencer gave his beastly cry and while I was leaning against a tree wondering from which direction it had come, a chunk of bark beside my head was blown off. I let out a cry and ran for it, but every time I dashed to a new spot another shot ripped off a nearby branch. By some stroke of fortune I ran out behind you. Things go blank after that.'

'I think you should both be jolly glad you're still here,' said Natalia.

I could think of other places I'd rather be. One look at Monty, who was still reeling from the aftershocks, led me to think that he felt the same. The other incontrovertible conclusion to be drawn from the affair was that this particular stage production from Monty had completed its one and only run and had proved an unmitigated disaster.

Chapter Eight

HOWEVER, if there is one thing that unites a fractious expedition party after a mêlée such as ours, it's the thought of a bit of scoff and something to swill, and on this note of zealous agreement, we sat down to the proverbial table with some haste.

Natalia, having decided to put Monty's attentions to some practical use, set him on the job of unloading the nosh, a task to which he leapt with the same relish as earlier. Though one suspects by the way he upended the food basket and a downpour of items scattered onto the ground, she wished she hadn't.

'Wait! Don't sit there,' he exclaimed, as she stooped to pick up a round of cheese. Tossing it aside, he unfurled a sheet and began flapping it wildly before laying it down with a gallant flourish that would not have been out of place on the plains of La Mancha.

Shaking her head in dismay, she turned to me.

'Spencer, perhaps you could rustle up a fire.'

'A what, you say?'

'Fire. You know. Whoosh.'

The mind boggled. She seemed to be asking me to do what man had been ordered to do since his earliest days. Then I remembered Uncle Cedric once saying, defeatedly, 'Stand idle while a woman busies herself and you've only yourself to blame, my lad.'

I glanced at the Brigadier but he was evidently preoccupied rummaging around the depths of the baggage with his proboscis, turfing out his own assortment of objects amongst which was a sturdy-looking axe. It caused me to gulp not a little, but steadfastly expunging from my mind what unspeakable uses he doubtless had in store for them, I tried to focus on the task at hand.

'Leave it to me,' I said, scratching my temple.

And after a moment of cudgelling one's brains, by Jove! I had got it. I scampered off into the densest area of wood that I could find and started blasting away at the branches until I was almost out of ammunition. Then, having scooped up the bountiful bundle, I sauntered back to the platoon and was feeling pretty chuffed with myself when I arrived to find them all standing bolt upright and rifles pointed at my waist in a beastly fashion. All except for Natalia whose aim was lower on account of the height advantage.

'Are you trying to send us into an early grave?' she yelled.

'Give me that!' snarled the Brigadier, snatching at my wood pile, and ordering me to sit down.

Then he took to sifting through the heap and, having tossed it all away one by one, he headed off into the woods carrying an axe and shooting me dark looks as he went. A moment later he returned with his own pile, which he set about arranging into the nest of a particularly untidy pelican before striking a match and holding it to the flimsier assortment of twigs. Having extended himself this far, he produced a tiny flame and went to sit down on a fallen log to catch his breath. Then he pointed to me and then at the pile. I thought at first that he was ordering me to lie on top of it, but I eventually interpreted his true meaning and blew on the thing. It extinguished the budding flame. Shaking his head and muttering something unintelligible to my ear, he bade me to stop.

'Stop what?' I asked.

'Just stop,' he said, resignedly. 'Go to the other two.'

I obliged with zeal, but as I fetched up to them, I saw that the table, as it were, had already been laid. Monty had been in charge of provisions and had, I must say, rather excelled himself.

'Decent spread, Monty,' I said. 'Don't you think, Natalia?'

'Yes, very nice,' she said. 'What is there?'

He read out a menu of sorts consisting of the items he'd requested from the scullery maid that he deemed essential for our survival in the wilderness:

Snacks/Starters
~ Quartered watercress sandwiches (crust removed as requested)
~ Scones (no jam or clotted cream, sorry)

Main
~ Quiche
~ Cured ham
~ Sardines
~ Asparagus and Jerusalem artichokes

Dessert
~ Roquefort

Beverage
~ Bordeaux (we didn't have any 1922 vintages, sorry)

(Please pack utensils properly before returning.)

On the popping of the cork all parties leaned forward and extended a sturdy goblet – all except Monty who'd brought his own sherry glass – but no sooner had I raised the glass to my lips than my arm was seized by Natalia.

'Spencer, it is important on such occasions for the *tamada* to give a toast.'

I am ashamed to say that I'd overlooked the etiquette of the moment.

'Oh, of course,' I said. 'What a blockhead.'

'Tomatoes?' said Monty, inspecting the menu again.

'Tamada,' corrected Natalia. 'It means the dictator.'

'Oh,' he said, becoming confused once more. 'And toast?'

She'd become lost, as so often happens when following Monty's train of thought.

'Right you are,' I said. 'Then let's be upstanding.'

Monty eventually got the message and as soon as we had risen to our feet, our full glasses held out in honour of the moment, I gave the Brigadier a gentlemanly nod. He simply looked askance at me, much as Sir Walter does to see if I've been at the vintages.

'Brigadier, your toast, if you please,' I repeated with a ceremonial wave.

'Mr Lockwood—'

'Spencer, please. No more of this Mr Lockwood nonsense.'

'Very well, Spencer,' he said, graciously, 'but *you* are to give the toast.'

I couldn't make sense of this fiddle-faddle.

'But how can I give it?' I said. '*You're* the dictator.'

I'd need Francis Galton on hand for a truly precise measurement, but I'd say that it took no more than a split-second after these words left me for an involuntary spasm of considerable force to rip through the Brigadier. Starting at his legs, it seemed to travel the length of his body and exit through the head. Such was the shock at being so described that he buckled at the knees and lurched violently forward, sending his claret spraying over Monty's chest; much like Uncle Cedric and the communion wine.

Now, when a military man who resembles an angry stork at the best of times bridles at what he perceives as a slur on his standing in the world, it is a sight to behold. Drawing himself menacingly up and glaring at me from his height of six foot four, it was clear that darkness was brewing in the man and what was uppermost in his mind now were thoughts of rearranging my body plan. Fortunately, Natalia intervened.

'Spencer,' she said, her voice filled with emotion, 'it means the master of the table.'

I was still drawing a blank, so she elucidated further.

'The giver of the feast.'

'Oh.'

I don't know why they hadn't just said so at the off. I was poised to try again, but broke off sharply as the Brigadier appeared to want the floor.

'Mr Lockwood, I have been a Brigadier of legions for over twenty years, serving as defender of my peoples and the government—'

'And a fine one, too,' I said, trying to get us off the subject. 'Anyway, we give this toast—'

'And never have I been called a dictator.'

Monty evidently found this too far-fetched to comprehend.

'Never?'

'Never!' said the Brigadier, scoffing at the suggestion.

'Not even a despot?' I asked.

And before I knew what was what he lunged at me. Upon my word! I vaulted with the spring of a jack rabbit and had only just evaded his clasp when his left boot came down on the fromage, sending it on a slide that would've twanged the ligaments of the most elastic gymnast. With a pained yowl he came to a stop. I looked back from twenty yards away to see he was bent double with legs six feet apart and his head inches from the ground. Any giraffes seeking tips on how to lap from a watering hole need have looked no further.

A frightened cry had come from Natalia during these proceedings, and she now sprang forward to right the Brigadier. Monty joined her a second later as he came out of his daze.

I returned somewhat circumspectly and, noting that the Brigadier's complexion had lost the beetroot tinge of before, offered my hand but he refused petulantly, snatching it away. He simply hobbled slowly towards the fallen log, lowered himself heavily down and began scraping the fromage off his sole. He cut a rather forlorn figure.

Some rather animated Georgian was exchanged.

'You've strained his groin!' cried Natalia.

'Oh, surely not,' said Monty.

I was still too nonplussed by the speed of events for thought.

'Have you brought any ointment?' she asked Monty.

He replied in the negative. Typically, on the one occasion that there was a genuine need for something medicinal, he had come without.

'Nothing for a sprain,' he said, but within an instant inspiration seemed to strike, 'but I think I saw some St John's wort round here. I think if he were to rub some, it might work.'

Who'd have thought it! Monty was on the cusp of redeeming himself.

'A capital idea!' I said, brightening at the suggestion. Suddenly I felt sorry for wronging the fellow. 'Point me towards it and I'll fetch it.'

'No, please!' pleaded the Brigadier. 'You'd probably return with a stinging nettle.'

For the next few moments all that could be heard was the laboured breathing of the Brigadier as he massaged the damage zone.

I, meanwhile, was given over to doing a spot of thinking and the conclusion I drew was that the Brigadier had been right. I, being the official host, should have been the one to mark the moment. It had been remiss of me not to suggest it in the first place. But never let it be said that Francis Spencer Lockwood Esq. would make such a blunder as to be an ungracious host. So, donning the proverbial hat of the dictator of the table, I fetched the Brigadier's goblet, thumbed the dirt from it and topped us all up. This had drawn their attention.

Then raising my goblet to the Brigadier, I addressed him directly, in the eye you might say, and with all the earnestness at my command issued forth a toast.

'Brigadier,' I said, clearing the throat, 'to your coffin. May it be made from a hundred year old oak tree and…' I couldn't remember the rest. 'Well, chin, chin.'

I took a step towards him to clink in the time-honoured tradition, but his goblet remained unextended.

I repeated the sage proverb in case he hadn't heard.

'May your coffin be made from a hundred year old oak tree. Chin, chin.'

But he was not in clinking mood. Far from it in fact. His moustache twitched rapidly and he got to his feet again, wagging a finger at me.

'Mr Lockwood, I see now from how Sir Lockwood Senior has spoken of your deficiency on matters of the mind that he is a master of the great British understatement.'

Well, I say! Try to strike a bonhomous note with the wrong sort of bird and see where it gets you. I'd understood it to be a toast to have originated in his part of the world, and I was rather expecting him to become teary-eyed and to embrace me, again. Here I would've welcomed a kindly embrace but he was obviously the type who preferred to spring it on you.

'Spencer,' said Natalia, giving a shake of her head in the manner of her father, 'I believe the toast you're trying to make is, "To your casket. May it be made from a hundred year old oak and may its seed be planted tomorrow."'

'Ah,' I said.

When you've just issued a toast that the elder man's resting capsule be as decrepit as he is, there isn't much you can say to cushion the blow. Monty put his arm round Natalia for comfort.

'I must apologise, Brigadier, for this Philistine.'

Now, I was more eager than ever to make amends, so I gave it one last go.

'Forgive me, Brigadier, please,' I said, 'but I hope that a man of your standing would afford me another try. At a different toast, I mean.'

A pregnant pause ensued and the tension was palpable. On his form hitherto, I wouldn't have credited it, but lo! his expression softened under that moustache. Beneath that exterior, it seemed, there was a man who could appreciate the plucky poet. Then it was his turn to give the courtly wave. And thinking it best to keep closer to my element this time, I stood up, cleared the throat again, and gave to.

'To newly formed friends,
Entering spinneys and fens,
Let them make merry,
Before it all ends.'

And by Jove! it worked. He leapt up smiling broadly and, with the clinking of our chalices, we struck a note of cheery comradeship. It was a touching moment. Monty and Natalia clinked rapturously and then all four of us united in the toast. Incredibly, in the blink of an eye the mood had become positively celebratory.

We sat down to feast. We'd been fools to let it wait so long. We scoffed our way through it without much in the way of chatter, but turning to the dessert, carefully avoiding the subject of the squelched cheese, I said I regretted the absence of any roly-poly pudding, but the Brigadier said it didn't matter and produced from his provisions a bottle of Ardbeg scotch. By George! Well, I mean to say, who'd have thought it?

'I'll pour,' said Natalia, beating Monty to the whisky.

And so it was that as we sat in a spirit of conviviality, helped along by the flow of wine and scotch, it seemed an opportune time to get more of the scoop on each other.

'So, Valerie, when did your interest in trophy hunting begin?' said Monty. 'Natalia says you have quite the collection.'

'It is true, our regional culture is rich in hunting tales that would grip the imagination of a growing boy. And that is when I first became fascinated.'

'Any juicy ones to tell of?' I asked.

He pondered for several moments as if sifting through the archives and then Natalia reeled off a few words of Georgian to deposit an idea.

'Ah,' he said, peering at me over his glasses. 'Indeed. That may interest you. It concerns a goddess called Dali. And she is in the throes of childbirth—'

I held up a hand.

'Is this story appropriate for adults?'

'Of course, you fool, we tell it to children,' said Natalia.

'Pray, continue.'

In our newfound rapport I was pleased to see Natalia extend herself into some playful joshing.

'Where was I?'

'Childbirth. Goddess. In throes of.'

'Oh yes. The child is born into the crags of a mountain, but little does Dali know that a wolf lies in wait. It snatches the baby and runs into the meadows.'

'That rotter.'

'Quiet, Monty,' said Natalia. 'Perhaps, father, I should tell the story.'

He waved a genial hand and she took up the mantle.

'This is witnessed by a hunter called Mepisa who was walking along a mountain ridge at the time. An honourable man, he resolves to retrieve the child.'

'I should think so,' said Monty, pouring himself another generous snort.

'Do go on,' I said, stifling a yawn, ruing the lack of my blindfold.

'Where was I? Oh, yes. He lies in wait for the wolf to approach the mountain pass. Outwitting the wolf, he rescues the child and restores it to the goddess. And in return for his bravery—'

'Hang on,' said Monty, 'what happened to the wolf?'

'He was killed,' said the Brigadier. 'It is not important. Continue.'

This struck me as a rather blithe attitude to the details, but given his earlier ambiguities, it was hardly surprising, so I said nothing. Natalia floundered again for the thread, so I provided the bookmark.

'One tot delivered on the double to a waiting goddess.'

'Oh yes. Curse your blasted interruptions, Monty. And in return for his bravery, she offered him one of three wishes. He could choose either to hunt one mountain goat immediately, or to take nine mountain goats from the month of September, or to lie with her.'

Another hand went up. We seemed to have moved away from the wholesome campfire yarn and onto some other bilge.

'I think,' I said, 'I know where this story is going and—'

'Go on,' said Monty.

'He chose the option of nine goats. The goddess granted his nine goats, but unbeknownst to him, she had transformed herself into one of the nine goats. One with golden horns.'

'Why?' asked Monty, gripped.

Her tone lowered to a sinister pitch.

'To lure the hunter. He took aim and fired at the golden-horned goat but the projectile ricocheted off and struck him in the head, killing him.'

Monty evidently thought this the epitome of underhandedness.

'But… but…' he stumbled, 'why?'

He was still pondering this perplexing denouement when Natalia suddenly whisked his glass from him and gulped the lot.

'That is for you to decide,' she said enigmatically.

'Who knows why women do these things?' said the Brigadier, sighing into his glass.

As this bewitching tale lingered in the air and Monty took to cuddling the whisky bottle for comfort, I found myself pondering this arcane riddle. It struck me as typical of the cryptic bosh guaranteed to send Monty's imagination into perpetual spin and he was in a deep reverie when he felt a sharp tug on the bottle which suddenly brought him back with a jerk. Releasing his grip apologetically when he realised it was Natalia, she set about topping up his glass.

'Allow me,' said Monty, gently taking the bottle back from her. 'It's like peas. Something you want a lot of or not at all.'

I'd never seen Monty abstain from either. By now it had struck mid-evening and with quite a nip in the air, the fire was a real boon. The party also seemed to have given up any prospect of duelling with hoofed creatures today, so the scotch kept flowing. Natalia, who'd been keeping up admirably in the high-spirited-whisky-sloshing, was soon sufficiently oiled to throw caution to the wind, and you might say we got to see her soft underbelly. Slouching up heavily against me she clinked my glass as if we'd just agreed a solemn pact. She'd also been bitten by a touch of curiosity, it seemed.

'Tell me… how'zee instute doing?'

'Ah, well,' I said, somewhat surprised that she should now want to talk shop. 'It's bound to be a bumper year. Upwards from here, I'd say.'

This was warmly received by our benefactors, obviously impressed at the institute's rising fortunes. I imagine it's the same in any field – all investors like to know the house is in order.

'Oh, yes, things are definitely on the up,' added Monty, jovially, sending another one down the hatch. 'I mean, Spencer's responsibilities have been halved, but I've been reinstated again. Swings and roundabouts.'

'The silver lining,' said Natalia, raising her glass for another snootful.

Monty obliged with a sub-measure.

'Cheers,' she said, wrenching back the bottle from him and adding the rest.

Here the conversation took a decidedly personal turn. Natalia sidled up to me again swaying somewhat and, settling down, looked up at me and hiccupped.

'Whidge of you is closer to Swalter? You or Monty?'

Well, of all the questions I might have been asked, never in a month of Sundays would I have predicted this. I scratched my chin, but Monty simply snorted like a hog.

'Ha! Between Spencer and I? No contest. Me, of course. Spencer's not the industrious type, you see.'

'Oh, yes,' said the Brigadier, reflectively. 'Lockwood's *favourite son*. I remember.'

'You said it,' said Monty, grinning broadly.

Natalia dashed back to sit with her father again and they set about another lively conversation in Georgian. The occasional English word pierced through, of course, but then things seemed to go from animated to heated and I'd have placed a goodish sum that they were quarrelling. Then suddenly Natalia stomped off into the woods saying she'd be back. Monty's curiosity had got the better of him, as it often does.

'Something wrong?'

The Brigadier was understandably put out by Monty's directness. He had the guarded air of a man asked to reveal the combination to his safe. Doubtless Monty was building up to that.

'Hmm? Oh. No. We were just discussing matters of the heart,' said the Brigadier, dismissively.

Monty and I laughed in unison, agreeing that it was always a heated subject.

'While we're on the subject,' said Monty, sensing his moment, 'has Natalia, you know, been scooped up?'

On what was clearly a matter of some delicacy for any father, the Brigadier appeared initially uneasy about revealing too much, but eventually decided the enquiry was benign enough.

'She wishes.'

'Oh, really?' said Monty, trying to contain his delight.

To him, these honeyed words signalled that the fixture was on. Retrieving the bottle, he topped up the Brigadier handsomely.

'You see,' continued the Brigadier, acknowledging the gesture, 'there are not many men nowadays who are keen to indulge in the fading practices which Natalia still holds in high regard.'

Monty tutted disapprovingly.

'What sort of thing, Val, ol' chum?'

'Well, like her friend, for instance. She was, as you say, "scooped up".'

'Absolutely top-hole,' said Monty, hanging on his words. 'All ran smoothly, I expect?'

The Brigadier gave a cryptic rocking of the hand.

Monty knitted his brow.

'What do you mean?'

'Her mother and I became worried when she didn't return for two weeks.'

'Honeymoon?' I asked.

'A honeymoon comes *after* marriage, Mr Lockwood,' said the Brigadier, bluntly.

'You mean they eloped?' said Monty.

'Exactly.'

'Is that,' said Monty, 'reason enough to be alarmed?'

'Well, it's more than the typical length of time for a girl to go off with her abductor.'

Here the wheels appeared to come off Monty's vocal apparatus while I spilt a full measure of good whisky.

'Ahh…' he said, fumbling for words. 'Ababawawhat?'

'You mean snatched?' I blurted.

'Quite.'

'As a sort of, well, a sort of conquest?' I said, incredulously.

'Why, of course,' said the Brigadier, relighting his cigar. 'That's how it is done.'

I'd encountered plenty of tommyrot through the years, but nothing of this calibre. This eclipsed everything. Of course, some cobblers is to be expected as the years advance and the hippocampus blows a gasket, or when one is so blotto that one can't tell the difference, but when I judged that the Brigadier had hardly touched a drop, it caused me no little befuddlement. His calmness about the affair made it all the more jarring. I found my mouth drying up.

As for Monty, something in the magnitude of this revelation had rendered him incapable of articulating much of anything. He wore the look of a chap who'd missed his early schooling and was feeling the strain of mastering conversation. The blowhole was opening and shutting but nothing emanated. Seeing that we were bereft of speech, the Brigadier pressed on. Elaborating, you might say.

'It's not everywhere, of course, but some quarters keep alive this custom where the unmarried womenfolk overtly refuse the romantic overtures from their romantic hopefuls while secretly delighting in them. It's to maintain their innocence. The idea is to be unattainable, you see.'

Natalia had rejoined the group and became quite flushed when she tuned into the topic of conversation.

'And the male, driven to frustration with desire, scoops her up and takes her somewhere to...'

'Form a union,' she said, demurely.

'Yes, yes,' her father said, clearing his throat loudly. 'Then they are betrothed.'

I'd composed myself sufficiently to try to make sense of this babble and there was something preying on my mind.

'But if one party, on the face of it, appears unwilling, isn't it terribly confusing for chaps to receive such mixed signals?'

'That's their problem,' said Natalia, without missing a beat.

'You have expressions for it, do you not?' continued the Brigadier, eddies of cigar smoke swirling as he spoke. '"Sweep someone off their feet", and "Playing hard to get".'

He looked at me expectantly, but I was too stupefied to do anything other than gape at the man. I couldn't picture it. I mean, how does one pull the thing off in the first place? Perhaps in the days of the Mongol empire this might have come off by mounting the Arab steed and lurking in wait for when the prized female emerged before breaking into a swashbuckling gallop, scooping up the kicking and screaming bundle and riding to one's lair, but what does one do in modern times? Wait till she's asleep before bundling her into a hemp sack and make off with a wriggling swag bag? Then what are the formalities once arriving at Journey's End? A braver man might have probed more deeply into these customs of yore, but I hadn't the gumption to prolong the discussion. Not only because sleepiness had taken hold but also because Monty was still looking as though he'd taken a straight left to the temple and had been rendered mentally deficient by the revelation. I wasn't far behind.

Thankfully, Natalia drew a line under these epithets of cultural exchange by reminding us that we'd reached that part in proceedings that would have had even the most ardent insomniacs calling for their beds. She'd read my thoughts.

There was a zing in my step as I set about fetching my things and I'll be jiggered if something didn't stir in Monty, too. He awoke as if a curse had been lifted. The Brigadier had already begun rummaging through his provisions.

'Come along, Spencer, Monty. Let us make camp for the night,' he said.

I froze in situ.

'Camp?' I said.

He nodded.

Just like that. Said in a throwaway fashion as if it were next to flopping on the mattress after a hard day at the mill. I was astonished.

'Sorry, Valerie,' said Monty, sheepishly, 'I didn't think to bring a tent.'

'Of all the rotten luck,' I said. 'We'll just have to return to the manor. Still—'

'It is no matter. We have a spare.'

'Oh,' said Monty and I in unison. Mine was a deflated vowel. His carried more than a hint of delight about it.

The time had come for a private word in Monty's ear.

'Monty, you can't possibly want to camp, do you?'

'As much as I want a vat of Mrs Caruthers' sprouts, my man.'

'Well then, let's go.'

'Not so fast. Surely you can see that this is a gift from the gods I can't pass up.'

He seemed to be proposing the unthinkable.

'You don't honestly propose to stay?'

'I propose exactly that, old fruit.'

Then placing a hand on my shoulder, he shot me one of those looks that pass between warriors on the threshold of the final hurrah.

'I have to.'

I considered the man's plea. It struck me as one of those binary choices one faces in life – traipsing back and possibly ending up inside the belly of the beast or sharing a tent with Monty rambling in his sleep. After some time I caved and as I stepped towards the equipment Natalia seized me squarely by the arm.

'Spencer, I don't think you understand. I think the idea is for Monty and I to share.'

I didn't quite take this in at first. Not until the Brigadier piped up.

'You will share with me.'

All of a sudden the trees began spinning around me.

'Spencer? Are you all right?'

Then, in a flash, everything turned black. Sometime later, as I started to come round, I perceived only a blurry outline of something above me. At first it appeared just a pale oval shape hovering overhead, but slowly my senses recovered to reveal a ghoulish spectacle above me. I howled at the gruesome sight. What was bearing down upon me appeared to be the harrowing vision of a skull, half-illuminated in the moonlight. Those dark cavernous eye sockets and smiling teeth gnashing together mocking me. In this doomed forest I had somehow crossed into one of the circles of hell. As if at once, I was being shaken violently by the fiend. With my arms locked to my side, morbid terror gripped me.

'Wake up, you sluggard.'

Then a series of explosive gushes of wind and a wet spray covered my face.

'Breathe, damn you.'

A wallop to my cheek brought an end to my mania and as if a switch had been pulled, I now perceived Monty's face, both eyes now dark from his bruising encounter with Miles and Natalia's well-aimed boot.

It was only an instant later that I realised Monty had been blowing on my face and I had taken in huge lungfuls of his foul breath. The noxious quotient of this made me feel even more likely to slip away again and I panted profusely to expel the stench.

Satisfied that I was back amongst the living, he rose and busied himself yards away. I lifted my head to see all three of them pottering around a pair of tents. It was not for another minute that I recalled what had brought about my lapse of consciousness – it was this wretched discussion over the sleeping arrangements.

The more I examined it the more I shuddered. I'd never given the matter much thought until then, but I surmised there must be plenty of chaps with whom I would be happily ensconced in friendly tentage, but this generalissimo ranked very low on the list. Besides, I felt that I deserved to sleep soundly and this cannot be done lying beside Brigadiers with a penchant for the surprise embrace. Oh, my word, no.

Fetching up to him, I made another appeal to Monty's senses.

'Monty, would you really have me billeted with the Brigadier?'

He glanced across at him.

'Why not? Seems a genial fellow.'

The Brigadier had already stripped to the waist. A fevered yip escaped from me.

'Monty, don't you realise you're leaving me to a fate worse than death?'

'Hard cheese, old chum, but it's for the best.'

Egregious. The cad seemed entirely unmoved by my plight. I tried a different approach.

'Well, you can't share with Natalia.'

'Who do you expect me to share with?'

I was astounded at the man's chuckleheadedness.

'Me of course.'

'You?' he said, incredulously. 'No fear!'

'You can't share with Natalia. You've haven't known her long enough.'

'Balderdash.'

'What if she rolls onto you in the night? Have you thought about that?'

A dreamy expression came over his face and I saw that I'd blundered. So, I scrambled for something unassailable.

'She'll take up all the bedspread. You'll freeze to death. Why do you think Shackleton never took female crew?'

'It's sleeping bags, not bedspreads.'

'She'll suck up all the air. You'll suffocate. Do you have some sort of death wish?'

'Enough of this clucking and squawking, Spencer.'

He pointed to the Brigadier's finished tent.

'Ah-ha. Your bed, sire. All that remains is for you to lie in it. Come on. Stop being such a crosspatch.'

I saw that it was futile arguing with the love-struck blighter, and I was resolved to give it up as a bad job.

'Very well,' I said, appealing to the crew at large. 'You leave me no choice but to return to the manor.'

There was no reaction. At first I thought they hadn't heard me. I appealed again, highlighting the inherent dangers in such a suicide mission.

'I'll simply have to trek through the dark forest and hope I'm not mauled, slashed, thrashed or gobbled up.'

I poured every ounce of emotion into this last-ditch effort.

'Perhaps, father,' said Natalia, 'Spencer is right—'

At last! Relief surged over me.

'A walk might do him good.'

'What!'

I'd been expecting Natalia's maternal instincts to yank me back from the brink, but it seemed that she was being governed by baser instincts. The Brigadier appeared to show just as much compassion.

'If that is your wish,' he said. 'Goodnight, Mr Lockwood.'

'Night,' said Natalia.

'Cheerio,' said Monty. 'Pass the mallet on your way, would you?'

I know what you must be thinking. 'What a complete shower!' And if you're not, I certainly was. I don't mind admitting, I was poleaxed. After the countless times I had borne Monty on my back, this flagrant dereliction of duty was the ultimate betrayal and it wounded deeply. I found myself consumed with animosity.

'Judas!' I said, handing Monty the mallet.

The breezy way in which he was prepared to see me venture into the lair of the beast was beyond all imagining.

Again we had reached an impasse and there was now only one route open. So, transferring hosting duties to Monty, I bade the company a bonne nuit and sallied forth into the darkness. I gulped deeply, for my wicket was as wet and sticky as any wicket has ever been.

It was a sour way to end things, I'll admit, but it wouldn't be on my conscience that Monty had spurned every lifeline I'd thrown him. Anyway, it was no time to be musing on the past when the night loomed large. I still had to make it back to the manor without getting lost, pecked, hoofed, scratched or chomped. And when one is stomping through the undergrowth at night with only donkey tracks and the glow of a battery-operated torch to lead the way, casting these malignant fates aside takes an iron will. I scampered along, nervously.

Before long it started to hail and this fool's errand set my mind racing. Soon I began to wonder what other brigands might be skulking in Winsbrook forest. What if a bloodthirsty savage were to suddenly lurch out and pail me on the onion? I even pictured my epitaph: 'Here lies Francis Spencer Lockwood. Perisher.'

I was in this morbid frame of mind when from nowhere there came a rustling. I flashed the light towards the spot, trembling.

'Who goes there? Show yourself, confound you.'

But after a few moments of the lower lip quivering and nothing to be seen, I scurried along and came to a clearing. It took a moment for the nerves to stop jiggling but thankfully I was able to pull myself together somewhat. I may be up against it, I thought, but the task that lay ahead was one of navigation. I need only chart a course. And so, imbued with this rather different mindset and steadfast outlook, my strides became more confident and I made up some ground.

Imagine then how I felt when I came across a signpost indicating that the manor was in the direction whence I'd just come. I couldn't fathom it. How could I have meandered so far off? I felt heat rising within me and I was in half a mind, when opportunity permitted of course, to write to the nearest Sign-Makers' Guild recommending that this particular sign-making Johnny be given a good thrashing, when I caught sight of the other alternative pointing to Bramley Hut, a hundred yards away.

'Skippers, by Jove! Of course!'

Lo and behold, it seemed that my trajectory had led me to a place of possible refuge. Bramley Hut was the name that Skippers, the gamekeeper, had given to his lodgings. He plied another trade elsewhere during the off-season and usually returned a few weeks into the commencement of the academic year. His empty chamber was only a hundred yards away.

The relief was overwhelming. I scuttled eagerly towards it, but when it came into view I stopped abruptly. Lit by daylight this charming wooded cabin represented an idyll in a tranquil setting, but late in the dreary night, seen from under a leaf canopy, rendered amid a black forest darkened further by a gloomy sky, its aspect was distinctly forbidding. I approached with caution and became more acutely mindful of the tiniest sounds. As I drew near I stopped again. What if I were to lift the covers and find a ruffian cradling an iron file? Or some other malingerer with nothing better to do than to roam forests at night.

But, courage is knowing what not to fear, I said to myself. This didn't help in the slightest, but unable to conjure anything comforting, I took a deep breath and, committing my soul to whatever grisly fate awaited me, I strode to meet it.

No lights shone, so I switched off the torch as I reached the door. I paused to listen to any sounds from within. Silence. Hand shaking, I gripped the door handle and, turning it slowly, poked my head inside. Then opening a little further, I shone the torch inside at all four corners. It was empty. Feeling round for the light, I flicked the switch but the room remained unlit.

I groped fruitlessly around in the hope of finding some candles until after some length of time and many drawers later, oh Fortuna! I found one and some matches. In the paltry light it provided I was able to discern the bed and a range of amenities including a scullery, stove, fireplace, a bathroom and lo! a cabinet of warming spirits. Everything I could possibly desire. I made light work of a generous snifter of Skippers' brandy and I was between the sheets quicker than a tyke hearing the footsteps of the house master. At first my chest pounded like a nervy timpanist but I soon felt the nightcap getting to work and, as it coursed through the bloodstream, a heaviness set in. This combined with the fatigue from my hike and I fell into a slumber.

The weather in the night worsened and I became aware of the patter of heavy rain on the roof and winds whistling through the woodwork. All of this made for a broken rest and after a time an uneasiness stirred within me.

I was cursing the abysmal conditions when I heard some heavy footsteps without. I sprang up and peered out of the window into the darkness. At first I couldn't see anything amiss but then I saw it – a shadowy figure skulking in the darkness. I froze. A beastly feeling gripped me. About the only upside I could see in this ghastly business was the absence of a cloak and large scythe, but in every other way, it was a goose-pimpling, skin-crawling sort of moment. The heavy rain and moonlight only enabled me to discern the general outline and movement of the figure, but I could see that he approached apprehensively. My throat became parched and a certain numbness had taken hold. I suspected that, whenever vacant, this hut must be a tempting refuge for all manner of brigands intent on fearful deeds, so I decided that the best course of action would be to issue a warning in the language of ruffianship by sending one into the ground at his feet. So, I yanked at the window and it screeched open. The figure paused, but, quick as a flash, I fired into the ground and he let out a shrill cry and fled. I listened to the sound of his footfall fading into the distance. There was another cry and a heavy thud, but the figure was soon on his way again. My heart pounded and after a significant length of time, I closed the window. Still panting hard, I helped myself to another brandy to calm myself. It was a while before I settled back into bed. I found myself wishing, of all things, for one of Monty's devilish concoctions he keeps in the lining of his jacket, but had to make do with the patter of rainfall on the roof for something soporific to induce me under. I held slim hopes that I would yield.

Chapter Nine

IT was no small wonder to me that the next time I stirred, it was on account of the daylight pouring through the windows. As I sat up blinking, scouring my surroundings and aching from the nocturnal romp through the forest, I was a bit delayed in piecing it together. Eventually, it was the sight of a rifle beside me on the bed that brought the events of last night surging back to me. This hut, my place of refuge, had drawn a hellish figure towards it and I suddenly remembered being called upon to issue something in the way of firm treatment to this tearaway.

But as I took in the full interior of the hut I noticed there was something amiss in its general aspect. My eyes came to rest on a second rifle and then fell upon a general untidiness that could not have been made through my fumbling for candlelight. Items of clothing that would be alien to Skippers were strewn about the place and the unkempt state of the table with leftovers of food suggested that some slapdash wastrel had been loitering just before I arrived.

Then a harrowing thought gripped me. What if the ruffian had been in the hut as I drew near and, hearing my approach, had abandoned it? Would he not harbour hopes to return? Could it have been the same brigand who had approached during the night? What if the evictee was now lurking without and was itching to do me a mischief? This was the clincher. A shiver ran up my spine and I leapt out of bed with zeal. Still squinting, I seized the rifle and had reached the door, about to scour the immediate vicinity, when I froze. The inherent danger into which I was walking was borne in upon me. I was on the cusp of emerging head first, in the way of a seal poking its muzzle out of the hole in the ice, when, for all I knew, lurking patiently at the aperture could be a half-ton polar bear poised to swat me.

Realising that steps must be taken, after a moment of pretty tense thinking I hit upon a ruse that was, I felt, sure to reveal the presence of any dastardly beings at large. Reckoning that it would make for a target so irresistible, yet small enough to be beyond the skill of any marksman, I extended a leg and, in the nip of the morning air, began invitingly waggling a toe. Silence. I alternated legs. After a moment or two I had a pretty good scissor action going. Some minutes later I deemed there was no imminent threat; at least nothing interested in my toes, so I put an end to this yoga.

Even so, it was with extreme vigilance that I stepped out with rifle in hand to secure the perimeter. Inching farther still, with rifle pointed skywards, I let loose two warning shots, which blew off part of the porch. No matter. More important was the lack of any return fire. Nothing came. Only then did I feel truly beyond any obvious peril and able to relax.

Returning indoors, I set about the first order of business of any self-respecting gamesman in the morning – tea. And it didn't take much foraging to unearth a stockpile of the manna.

The first cup generally has a transformative effect on most sluggards, but after a quick slurp and feeling a tingling sensation creep over me, I could see that this variety was something entirely new. At the half-way mark of this potion any polar bears who crossed the path of *this* seal would have been sorry they did.

As morning-rousers go, there was no question about it, this pick-me-up was a sensation. As the mind began racing under its effects, I couldn't help wonder if Skippers had gone off the rails and become a racketeer of mind-warping hallucinogens. It seemed to explain why there should be scoundrels guarding the booty throughout the night.

I was luxuriating in the solitude, savouring this probable contraband, making a point to mention it to Monty, when my mind inevitably turned to what had transpired the previous night.

Since wading into the woods, leaving the trio to themselves, I'd had little chance to reflect on proceedings, and here wallowing in the aftermath, special blend in the hand, I felt it somehow proper to dwell on it a little.

Doubtless, by any standard, the culmination of the day could manifestly be said to have been marred by unpleasantness, but, though I was initially disgruntled by Monty's blithe attitude towards my plight, completely ignoring my yeoman service in his drivelling histrionics in the woods earlier, I had lost the bitterness that ran through me last night.

As ever, a sun-kissed morning restores a sunny outlook and as I contemplated the state of affairs, running as they had to a fine kettle of fish, it seemed to me that we'd been the mere victims of circumstance. I mean to say, neither Monty nor I could abandon our posts without paying a price too staggering to contemplate. For Monty, this was the chance to snuggle with Natalia under a starlit sky to while away the night discussing the eternal questions of the cosmos, bringing their entities and souls ever closer together. I, on the other hand, faced the prospect of hitting the hay with a bushy-moustached Brigadier who likes to whisk you into a cuddle when the moment takes him.

Examined thus, our separate directions seemed almost fated from the first. It was in this way that I opted to let bygones be bygones, think no more of it and focus on the day ahead, starting with a shower.

With a crank of the lever there came a slight gurgling sound and after sidestepping the spurt of brown sludge, I was suddenly pelted by a blast of nipping coldness. After several seconds of floundering while jiggling the knobs and levers and being deluged by the prickling, biting sharpness, I eventually settled to simply enjoy the tingling sensation of life's essential force gushing over me. Lo! how it washed away all trace of any lingering anxieties. As I stood beneath the cold jet being slowly revived I came to feel a close affinity for those Japanese monks who immersed themselves under waterfalls. This lacked the thrill of slipping off a crag and plummeting to my death onto sharp rocks, but in every other way it had the same bracing effect.

It was in the same devil-may-care attitude that I reached above, arm fully outstretched, to fiddle with the flow to get the full monsoon effect, and as I twisted an uncooperative bit of metal the shower head snapped and clunked me on the head. Bouncing off the parietal spot, a torrent of water burst from the wall and started gushing as if from a hydrant. In my panic I placed a hand to stem it, but the water sprang out of the sides and sprayed the room liberally.

By the most extraordinary happenstance during this blizzard that engulfed me, while I was becoming light-headed from the blood loss, I had something of an epiphany. It concerned the Brigadier's quest for his next quarry.

After some frantic tampering with some other knobs, I managed to stem the geyser. As I watched the blood drain away I couldn't help feel that if divine inspiration only comes from being pelted by a sub-zero torrent and a generous clump on the two o'clock position, it might be best left to the enlightened thinkers of our day. Monty, I felt, though some way forgiven, could still use a falling metal shower attachment to the head.

Still, at least the general fogginess that had plagued me from the outset of this mission had now lifted and revealed to me, with clarity, what the Brigadier had seen and brought us here for.

The task ahead was to return to civilisation forthwith. And I determined that, when I next encountered the Brigadier, I would lay the facts before him in no uncertain terms. So, it was with no little pep that I collected my things and sauntered out. I had scampered some fifty yards when there came a loud rustling and some staccato articulations from the bushes.

A frightened yip escaped me and only added to the flurry of utterances permeating the air, but by some extraordinary fleetness of foot I found myself concealed behind the hut, peering round to see what was encroaching on this idyll. Through the dense thicket a large grey object appeared to be moving towards me. As it drew near, entering the more sporadic terrain of the hut surroundings, between the branches, just visible was the undercarriage of a large, four-legged creature.

Gadzooks! Suddenly, all the fearful visions from the day before resurfaced and began whizzing through my mind. And had I happened upon this sighting yesterday, I would certainly have scooted like billy-o, but this morning's moment of awakening in the shower had realigned the parameters, as it were, and caused me to see things anew. So, what rooted me to the spot more than dread was intrigue.

As it lumbered nearer and the vocalisations became more vivid I perceived that they were the discontented words of an adult male. A moment later onto the path emerged the shambling figure of a donkey. And slumped on top, resembling one of the wise men who'd been ditched by the other two, was Monty.

Following some way behind this cavalcade was a second beast of burden of, it has to be said, extremely disgruntled appearance. This was only to be expected for loaded onto its back, which sagged under the weight, was some drooping cargo that swayed like a pendulum as it plodded along.

How typical, I thought, that when the peace is suddenly shattered, it's a fair guess that Monty isn't far behind. I burned with curiosity to learn what he was doing here and this was to be my opening gambit when we began discussions, but as it happened, I never got the chance. Looking back, my sudden leaping out from behind the hut waving my arms and bellowing 'Monty!' was a trifle misjudged. The frontrunner, assuming it to be an ambush, bolted into a speedy trot in a perpendicular direction. In the process, Monty, who'd let his attention slip, was sent sprawling and landed face-first in a thorny rose bush.

'Gaargh!'

The cargo-bearer, meanwhile, who'd only just made the clearing and was breathing heavily, had stopped, presumably feeling that it had fulfilled the terms of its contract, and it was now time for some well-earned respite. As it stooped to chew on the long grass, it came to deposit on the ground what appeared to be a body.

Its molars had already got to work by the time it looked up to see the pacemaker standing some distance away, stranded in the rough. Then, as if from nowhere a third donkey – evidently the laggard of the bunch – sidled up to its load-bearing chum for what I imagined was a frank exchange of views on recent happenings.

I took this as my cue to do likewise and, fetching up to Monty, I wrenched him up.

'Ah, aah,' he said, opening his mouth awkwardly. In anticipation, seeing the upward lift of his hand, thinking it a peace offering, I took hold and began shaking it when he expelled a wet gale explosively on my front. It was a sneeze of epic proportions.

'What the devil…' I said, drying the features.

His face was now nicked with blood as if he'd been wearing a crown of thorns.

'Do you intend to pull my arm from its socket?'

The surly blighter began picking the thorns out. And no sooner had he performed this task than he thundered at me.

'What the blazes are you doing roguishly skulking round huts?'

He seemed primed to fire more questions when he spotted the lesion on the side of my head and brightened up immeasurably. With the Brigadier's claret from the previous day sprayed on his front he appeared to have been slashed across the chest. I acquainted him with the facts.

'I was not skulking. I was on my way to the manor and just happened by this little bijou hideaway—'

My words broke off because at this juncture a loud groan pierced the air and this brought my attention to the large object that had slid off the donkey's back and flopped on the ground.

Speeding over, I arrived at the spot to find the unmistakable sprawling figure of the Brigadier. The occasional snore emanated from the limp mass. Needless to say, this rather altered the course of the conversation. Monty came up beside me.

'Monty,' I said, struggling to know where to begin, 'the Brigadier appears to be lying on the ground. Or do my eyes deceive me?'

He looked down at the body.

'No. That is he.'

It was difficult to argue with the facts. There he was.

'Why?'

'Hmm?' he said, wiping the sweat from his forehead with the back of his hand.

'Why is he lying on the ground?'

'Oh,' he said, glad of a straight question at last, 'that's easy.'

'Well?'

'He's been that way since late last night.'

I leaned over the Brigadier for a closer look.

'Ill?'

'Not in so many words.'

'Tight?'

'Good heavens, no,' he said, as though that were a ludicrous suggestion. 'He's comatose.'

'What!'

'Away with the fairies.'

I eyed Monty keenly.

'Monty, don't take my next question amiss, but how much did you down last night?'

'Eh?'

'I mean, what is this tosh? Make yourself understood, please.'

'Don't adopt that sanctimonious tone with me, Francis Spencer Lockwood,' he said, indignantly. 'A fat lot of help you were last night, running off as you did, you bounder.'

I reeled. From the beastly look in his eye it was clear that he resented my buzzing off. And here I had been tying myself up in knots over whether to bury the hatchet. The brass of the man!

'So here he is. In the land of nod.'

'Asleep?'

'Still!' he said, as if he thought it very poor form. 'Not responding. I've tried everything. I had to bring him here so Skippers could take him to the infirmary.'

'Infirmary?' I cried. 'Just a minute.'

I clutched the brow trying to register this disturbing news and marshal the facts. I had established that the Brigadier was in some sort of coma so deep that he could remain unconscious while drooped over a donkey as it traipsed across dense vegetation on an unplanned expedition and, according to Doctor Monty Moreau, the one thing he needed more than anything else was hospitalisation. Now, as one who was officially charged with being the Brigadier's host, you'll understand why this ghastly predicament was setting my teeth on edge. And yet, the central pieces of information to this riddle alluded me.

'How?'

'Eh?'

I was starting to become peeved by this stage. This put me in mind of my conversation with the Brigadier yesterday, trying in vain to extract the salient information.

'How did he happen to be like this?'

'Oh. Well, why didn't you just say so?'

Checking first that we were alone, he unfurled the explanation.

'Well, sometime after you'd stormed off in a huff, I offered the Brigadier a nightcap—'

'Oh God—'

'To help him sleep and to allow Natalia and I some privacy, you know. But well, look at him. Tall as a moose and thin as a rake. I must've miscalculated the dosage.'

This first instalment was still ricocheting in the cerebral cortex when he heaved another complication into the mix.

'The thing is, Spence, I'm not entirely sure I didn't confuse the vials.'

'Oh, dear God—'

'He obviously needed more than the average chap, but not having any light, I may have poured in a bit of something else, too.'

'What?' I said, ominously.

'I don't know. But whatever it was, he didn't like it much.'

'How so?' I asked, dread beginning to set in.

'Well, he sent it down the hatch as directed. Then, after a moment of wild scratching at his temples, he emitted an earth-shattering cry, began dancing on the spot a goodish bit. "Why, that almost blew my head off!" he bleated when his breath returned.'

'Save me, Mother of God,' I said.

'He recoiled when I tried to comfort him, so I just watched the Brigadier retch a few times trying to dispel the stuff from the pipes. After a while he rose to full height, eyes red, where he remained a moment. And then he came crashing down in the way of a felled tree and began snoring like a buffalo. Natalia, thank goodness, was already asleep.'

'Oh, you didn't lace—'

'No, that girl sleeps like a log. It was a bit of a bust actually. We didn't get to talking at all.'

If I didn't know better, I'd say this was his foremost regret about the whole episode. He continued his distressing tale.

'Well, I dragged him by the heels into his tent and let him sleep it off. And this morning when Natalia saw that he wouldn't wake up, to calm her, I insisted on hastening back to the manor with him.'

'But what does she think is wrong with him?'

'I told her you'd laced his drink.'

'What!'

'Well, I couldn't very well say I'd done it, could I? I mean, think, old man. I could hardly step into the guise of rescuer otherwise, could I? We agreed to meet here so we can continue our tryst.'

'What!' I cried. 'You can't possibly be thinking of—'

'Of course we are,' he said, unequivocally. 'Now that the hunt is off, it leaves us time.'

He placed a hand on my arm and gave it a squeeze.

'I feel this could be the start of something, Spence.'

Well, I was lost for words. Now I'd heard it all.

'So, be a pal and take him with you, would you?'

I looked at the Brigadier, resignedly. There he was, a man of advancing years, twenty years of active service, lying pitifully on the ground in his voluminous undergarments. Monty hadn't bothered to dress the man. Well, there was no question that I had to taxi him back. The consequences of not doing so were too hideous to contemplate.

'Fine.'

He whooped, somewhat indecently I thought under the circumstances.

'Will Natalia find her way here?' I asked.

'Oh, yes, a real trooper, that one.'

And there it was. After enticing the donkeys back by promising they'd never have to endure any load-bearing hardships again, we hauled the Brigadier onto the same donkey and I, for my part, resolved that I'd need to think up something pretty special when my day of reckoning came. Monty, I reflected, had been a lost cause since birth.

I had straddled my donkey and was poised to set off when Monty came bounding from the hut brandishing a folded piece of paper.

'Make sure he reads this when he wakes, would you? It'll make him feel better.'

Only Monty could have the immortal rind to dose the blighter and then prescribe the antidote. I slipped it into his breast pocket and thought no more about it. I didn't want to be within a hundred yards of the Brigadier coming round, but I felt assured he'd see the note protruding from the top of his pocket.

'Oh, incidentally,' I said, reminded of a titbit of my own, 'the hunt is off.'

Monty appeared quizzical.

'Hunt?'

'Yes, you know,' I said, finally finding something to cheer about. 'The Brigadier's beast.'

Since my shower revelation a short time earlier, I'd been harbouring a longing to make some sort of grand disclosure, if you will. Of course, I ought to have been addressing the Brigadier since I held him primarily culpable for this ill-advised jaunt from civilisation, but the one thing I insist from my audience is that they be conscious.

Monty rolled his eyes.

'Well, of course, it's off. Until the Brigadier is compos—'

'Ah, there I must correct you. The state of intoxication of the whiskered one has no bearing on the matter. The answer struck me in no uncertain terms this morning, Monty. I had what you might call a revelation that shed light on this whole ghastly business. And I daresay, old man,' I said, lowering the registers, 'I think you should brace yourself.'

I stood back after this preamble to see a familiar faraway glassy expression characteristic of the man which foretells when he is totally uninterested in anything I have to say. But I was resolved to draw him into my flash of insight all the same. Now, it's customary, when one hopes to lift the lid on a tantalising mystery, to provide a short recapitulation, which I now did, starting with a few important particulars to our expedition.

'Do you recall the aim of our quest?'

'Spencer—'

'A yes or no will suffice.'

His glare may have, at another time, persuaded me to cork it, but he saw that I had the wind in my sails and would not be budged.

'Get on,' he said, begrudgingly.

'We set out on donkey-back to hunt a creature witnessed by the Brigadier lurking close to the Lockwood Manor, *n'est-ce pas*?'

He was making not even the slightest effort to stifle his yawns, so I hushed the fellow sternly before proceeding. There is a certain propriety in these matters, you know.

'The description he gave, which you were too embroiled in the throes of infatuation to hear, was, "Between a cow and a moose… tall… large flat feet… brown coat… long spindly legs". An oddity by any standards. Wouldn't you agree?'

He nodded, listlessly.

'So then consider,' I said, enigmatically, 'three days ago they'd have been setting up the grounds for the fête. Imagine the bustle. This on top of the usual droves of attendees swarming the estate. What sort of abomination would clop about amongst this menagerie? Think of the awful din that you and your ilk were making during rehearsals. How many ungulates do you know that take an interest in the works of the Bard? Was this Humbaba the Terrible we were pursuing?'

I examined the man's features. It was marked by a total vacancy of expression. And from the way he began tenderly passing a ladybird from finger to finger, I could see that this was failing to grip. I must say this got my goat to no small degree. When one is shedding clues, in the style of the master of deduction, what one really desires is an enraptured audience, biting their bottom lips and hanging on your every word. Instead of which, this blighter was making friends of the insect variety.

'Monty,' I said, my voice tinged with dudgeon, 'have you not the slightest interest in the revelation that has stunned me to my core?'

He straightened himself so as to be sure of clarity of diction.

'Spencer,' he said, pointedly, 'you have, in your usually perceptive way, picked up the general theme.'

'You would not care to know—'

'I would not.'

'That all this time—'

'I said not!'

'What the Brigadier saw—'

'Not!'

'Was in actual fact—'

'Shh!'

The rotter had stymied me. I was appalled. I may have been astride a donkey, but it was a mulish Monty that I was up against this morning. Monty has little patience for topics not of his choosing and here he was at his most bloody-minded. It's a galling feeling when the audience would rather you took to the road. Still, there seemed nothing for it except to stop dawdling and be on my way.

'Very well,' I said, resentfully, pointing towards the Brigadier's ass at my rear, 'then hand me the reins of the Brigadier and look snappy.'

As if feeling his own need to unburden himself, Monty suddenly seized my knee.

'Spencer,' he said, becoming solemn, 'you speak of revelations—'

'No more,' I said. 'Any thoughts in that line have been scuppered. Stop hogging the road and step aside.'

He positioned himself in front of my donkey, holding his arms outstretched.

'Not before you behold *my* revelation.'

I couldn't recall any stories of people being mowed down by donkeys, but after giving mine a heel in the ribs and finding it uncooperative, I rather wished that we'd come on elephants.

'Oh, Spencer,' he continued, drawing on his penchant for amateur dramatics, 'only by coming to this Eden, away from the myriad distractions, could I ever hope to see the virtuous and noble path. And last night as we basked in the resplendent glow of the fire, amid the twilight, how fitting that I should feel so clearly what I must undertake for Natalia to accept me.'

Monty's chuckleheadedness comes in many forms, each as stupefying as the next, but the two I find particularly intolerable are his propensity to twirl flamboyantly in public places on a whim and resorting to operatic ramblings that are indistinguishable from hogwash. And it seemed to me certain from this gushing outpouring that he had violated the latter of these sacred terms. I gave a bitter snort of the Sir Walter variety.

'Oh, Spencer—'

I raised a life-saving hand.

'Without the lyrical flourishes, please.'

He thrust his bottom lip out in disappointment.

'Philistine.'

'Just as you say.'

He fetched round beside me and had got as far as saying something about Cupid's bow when I, seeing he was about to buttonhole me with more of the same, issued the sort of swashbuckling 'Yah!' to end all swashbuckling 'Yah's'. And before he knew it, we were breezing along the terrain, the Brigadier's arms and legs swaying pendulously to the sides. Monty was left eating dust.

It felt so wonderful dishing Monty the just deserts after he'd given me such short shrift that I was too busy basking in triumph to concentrate on the task of navigation, so while I revelled the donkey just followed its nose – an arrangement with which I was perfectly content.

As the terrain whizzed by I found myself replaying the episode over in my mind. At times, I pictured myself holding aloft a victorious arm with the full-throated 'Yah' of a legionnaire on the battleground, while at others it was with the steel of a dispatch rider sallying forth with a coded message carrying the hopes of the nation. I deemed this latter vision to be closest to my own predicament. Though I couldn't claim to have the heart of a sovereign state resting in my dispatch, there was certainly one soul resting on it – mine. I mean to say, in all likelihood, the Brigadier would wake and have no recollection of this whole ghastly woodland romp, but what was giving me the most pleasure was the moment that I would reveal to him that all this time what he'd had us chasing was in fact two members of the cast of *Hamlet* in horse costume taking a shortcut through the grounds. I judged the humiliation would be too much for anybody.

Still, the thought that the expedition was now over put me in such a merry frame of mind that as soon as we entered a colourful spinney and happened upon an abundance of wild berries, I stopped our little convoy so the donkeys and I might enjoy this harvest. And so they did. It seemed a fitting final farewell to the forest and as I mounted the hardy beast again, noting how its ears no longer sagged and a welcome vim had returned to its step, I gave it a matey pat that ere long its ordeal would also soon be over.

Shortly after this, as I paid attention to my surroundings, it was borne in upon me that, left to chart its own course, my mount had gravitated towards Arkdale's patch of farmland where, I gathered, it must usually be left to pasture.

I dismounted so I could survey the scene and get my bearings. I knew that the farm was the proverbial short hop from the institute grounds, but the question was where. I hadn't yet formed a direction of travel when my attention became drawn to two blistering objects hurtling at full pelt in the distance and it was not until the other pasturing Equus hurried aside that I realised that Arkdale's two slavering shepherd dogs had been unleashed. These slobbering monstrosities, whose celebratory howls pierce the night air when they've fulfilled their duty by mangling a few trespassers, were bounding towards me at breakneck speed.

And so acrobatically did I leap in terror that I'd have landed squarely on my mount had it been there, but by the distance it had already covered down the flank, I judged that it had long ago assessed the situation and taken steps to avert the pending atrocity by deserting me, with nothing in the way of a chummy warning. Its companion, proving even more disloyal, was a half-step in front happily taking the Brigadier with it.

Another yowl escaped from my lips as I saw the Brigadier disappearing off to become at one with nature, but I realised that this was no time for dallying and, in a feat of acceleration that I wish had been recorded for posterity, I bolted hell for leather towards the perimeter fencing and hurdled over it with a spring that was close to flight. My piston-like legs didn't stop moving until I was back in the berry grove of earlier.

But for the lack of snarling hounds snapping at my heels I might have continued for some time. As it happens, I stopped for air, and, more importantly, to panic. With one catastrophe avoided, I was now able to devote the strength of my full faculties to the one that would truly matter to Magda and Sir Walter – my losing the Brigadier, and more importantly in their eyes, the sponsorship. I remember it was after several minutes of dancing on the spot that the real dread set in. The inevitable sense of doom that engulfs one when staring ruin in the face assailed me and I writhed as if tied to a burning pyre.

I was in this distraught and swivel-eyed state, hatching a plan to flee to Greenland, when from yards away, I heard voices. It's uncanny how earlier, when Monty was approaching, I was unable to decipher from his drawl that it was not some abominable creature, and yet, here, I could tell instanter that it was a pair of human voices. They were female, lilting voices, in a high falsetto. While I was lurching, panting heavily, the pair emerged from the foliage. A short moment ensued while we drank each other in, as it were.

Devilish slim and about medium height, both looked as if they were taking a hiking holiday. And what drew the eye especially, as I gave them the head-to-toe, besides the fact that they couldn't have been better outfitted for rambling if they tried, was the fact that on their heads, lo and behold, they wore the Lockwood navy caps given to all attendees. By Jingo! it was the equivalent of spotting a lighthouse in a dark swirling maelstrom. Not least because they could lead me, or direct me, to the estate.

I couldn't help notice that they'd blenched upon first seeing me, but after giving me a berth of some thirty yards, they had scurried on. They were now increasing it by some leagues.

I wasted no time.

'Yoo-hoo! I say!'

One turned her head back, but the other wrenched her arm to face forward and they hurried their steps.

'You there!' I bellowed.

This seemed to elicit a small yip of sorts, which I couldn't fathom. They now upped the footwork and were verging on a small jog.

'Hello, curse you,' I said, galumphing behind them.

I can't say that I didn't rather throw these words at them as I was finding this maddening. I was pretty exhausted and the last thing I wanted was another race for freedom, but I kept closing on them until both parties were locked in a scramble into oblivion.

'Are you heading back to the institute?'

I didn't mind that they weren't the type to stop and debate, I just wanted to know if we were going in the right direction.

But after some time shambling through the woods, pursuing them with a hunger, I came upon a glimpse of some familiar structures in the distance, and I could at least breathe a sigh of relief to be on my home turf.

There was a slight feeling of the wild animal yearning to return to captivity as I plodded my way through the grounds. A sea of mingling attendees parted before me. As I advanced I couldn't help notice the bewilderment across their faces, mystified how one so unkempt and slovenly could be allowed on the premises at all.

I spotted Quinton shambling between buildings, and as I caught up to him and tapped him on the shoulder, he recoiled violently.

'Waaahhllaaargh.'

His face contorted into a look of sheer horror and he began muttering absolutions.

'You've come for me, oh, my terrible God.'

I shook the man to snap him out of it.

'Quinton, shh! Pull yourself together.'

After a moment, the haunted febrile look seemed to pass.

'Thank goodness,' he said, taking a lungful of aether. 'It *is* you, Spencer. I thought you'd been possessed.'

First I assumed he'd succumbed to some sort of doddering fit and now his senses, such as they are, had returned, but this last utterance gave me pause for thought. A concern of the kind a great-nephew might feel filled my breast, so for a moment we just drank each other in, me judging if his pupils were still dilated and he transfixed by the lower portion of my face. Once he'd exhausted that he moved on to giving me a top-to-bottom inspection. My concern for him also lifted.

'Well, you seem to be all there,' I said, 'but don't repeat that to anyone, will you.'

He appeared deaf to anything other than my get-up, which he caressed between his fingers with an air of mystique.

'The habiliments,' he said, stooping to inspect the textured fabric of my lower half. 'Oh, heh-heh-heh. Phooey.'

Pleasant as it is to bring a little joy into an ageing man's day by the sight of my bare knees, time was pressing, so I got down to brass tacks.

'Quinton, I'm in a fix, and I have something to tell you. In confidence, you understand.'

This galvanised him as if he'd been reminded of a matter of huge import. Being one of the more experienced porters, Quinton often becomes a vessel for information, but, to extract this resource from him, one might as well pan for gold. I mean to say, he can be relied upon to divulge tiny fragments which, had they been assembled cogently, would be valuable, but sadly this latter half is often lacking.

'Ah, yes,' he said, breaking off to greet one of the more demure attendees skipping by, twirling a parasol. 'Lovely morning, Wilfred.'

Judging the distance to be sufficient, he continued.

'Now I hoped to run into you, you see. Magda wants a word with you.'

He couldn't have upended me more if he'd had a ten yard run-up. This bulletin brought on a sudden sickening feeling. Much as I tried to remind myself that the Brigadier's whereabouts hung in the balance, one has to recognise the greater threat.

'Good lord. What about?'

'Something about the Brigadier.'

'Oh God!'

'Whatever it is, son, look out. Here comes the memsahib now.'

He sped away and I felt an icy chill on the back of my neck. I spun around to find her so close that it was almost a clinch, but one look from her told me that this Magda was even less amenable than the one at the soirée. An apology from me was in the offing when it was literally wiped clean from my lips. Placing an index finger on my upper lip, she swiped in a downward motion, across my lips to the chin.

'Ah-bibble,' I said, as she began subjecting the remnants to an unremitting scrutiny with her beady eye.

So much for the pleasantries.

'Spencer, I have something to ask you, but first,' she said, showing me her index finger, 'what is this?'

There was an odd, crusty, crimson residue on her finger and it couldn't have been more than a moment later that it was borne in upon me that caked on my face, like a fruity compote, was the berry juice from my feast earlier, which to the naked eye gave me the appearance of the Transylvanian count after gorging on the innards of some forest-dweller.

'Oh my giddy aunt!'

This also went some way in explaining why the sight of me had led those ladies to flee in horror and also why Quinton had recoiled from me more than usual.

I could see from Magda's manner, however, that this was only the start of my troubles. Over the years I've come to discern some of the imperceptibly subtle signs when she's about to erupt, but here, even the most slapdash observer could tell by the way her head was bowed slightly when she glared, not bothering to lift a shard of hair that would otherwise have been slotted behind her ear, and from the way that her eye twitched, that this lady was in no mood to be paltered with.

I gulped hard. I don't know if you've ever mislaid a Brigadier in a semi-wild field – it was far from my métier too – but it's a reasonable assumption that the party who put you up to the job of ensuring his wellbeing won't take kindly to discovering that they've joined the ranks of another species for a better life.

It was while I was trying to decide how to approach the matter that she spoke.

'Spencer—'

'Yes,' I blurted.

'I have something to ask you.'

'Oh, yes?'

Beads of sweat were now bedewing my forehead.

'Yes,' she said, spreading her fingers and blowing on her nails, 'it's the Brigadier I wanted to speak to you about.'

'Oh, yes,' I said, my mouth quickly drying up.

'Where do you think he is?'

Now, veterans of the form will know of what I speak when I say that something in the way she'd asked the question seemed to foreshadow an imminent hazard. For the uninitiated, I shouldn't worry if you weren't able to spot it from the off. This singular ability passes in the womb from mother to daughter bypassing the male progeny entirely. Let me illustrate with the following example:

Question 1: Where's Rupert?
An inoffensive and harmless question from someone who's mislaid Rupert: I haven't the foggiest where Rupert is. If you know, please tell me.

Question 2: Where do you think person Rupert is?
This seemingly innocent query is a baited trap with a wholly different meaning: I know full well where Rupert is. You clearly haven't the foggiest where he is. I would like to see you wriggle and squirm.

It is a device commonly employed by the irate female, but what the many well-meaning volumes written on the subject lack is any meaningful instruction on how to contend with the irate female who poses it. This is where you are left to plough on clumsily.

'Ah. Well,' I said, thinking on my feet, 'he was enjoying himself so much that he decided to stay out there a little longer. Excited as a schoolboy to see the local topology and all that.'

'Topography.'

'The whole thing, really. All creatures great and small, you know.'

'That's splendid, Spencer,' she said. 'I knew you two would become chums.'

'Oh, yes,' I said, handkerchiefing the brow. 'Great pals.'

'Then, Spencer, would you care to explain how it is that the Brigadier was returned to us care of farmer Arkdale a short while ago?'

The strength of this revelation knocked me for six. And the next time I spoke it was in the range of a high falsetto.

'Did he?'

'Yes,' she said, cracking her knuckles, 'can you explain that?'

The glint of the sun was setting off the slight tint of red in Magda's hair and it reminded me how she belonged to that group whose inner self willed them, when a chap was holding up proceedings, to tuck those shapely fingers into a clenched fist and let him have it between the eyes. So, on grounds of safety, I shed the facts.

'OK, I'll tell you—'

'No, let me tell *you*,' she insisted.

She revealed how it had happened. Apparently, farmer Arkdale had been drawn to the commotion in the field and went out to investigate. Seeing me dash across like a highwayman brought on painful flashbacks of my youthful larks through his patch. Becoming enraged at this transgression of the neighbourly code, he unleashed his gatekeepers from hell to bring back my mangled carcass or die trying.

Then, as his hounds had moped back disappointed, he saw that one donkey appeared to have six legs. Going to investigate what looked to be a bag of swag tied to the creature, he found it to be a man strapped and draped over the animal's back. And judging this to be another egregious liberty by the landed gentry, he became stirred to the core and, taking up the cause of the common man, he bunged the fellow onto his cart, careered over to the institute entrance, flicked a switch and when the angle of elevation was just right, the Brigadier poured out onto the dirt. Were it not for one or two public-spirited attendees the Brigadier might still be lying spreadeagled at the foot of the gates.

I must say I received this with mixed feelings. I mean to say, I took it that the man was intact physically, which was all to the good, but at the same time, he had ended up in the infirmary, so I braced myself for the most fearful part – the medical report. I was expecting a catalogue of stomach-turning injuries, so when Magda reported that he was in with nothing more than a few broken ribs, I was elated.

'Well, blow on my buttons!' I yelled.

It's no exaggeration to describe my emotion at this news as euphoric. You could not have found a happier man in all of Winsbrook at that moment.

'Don't be indecent!' she snapped, furiously. 'Our benefactor ending up in a slag heap was not part of the plan.'

I was staggered at how we could both be at such diametrically opposed ends. It seemed to me that she was not seeing the full picture. So, before she ruptured a spleen or socked me on the jaw, I resolved to point out the silver lining.

'It's OK,' I said, in soothing tones. 'It's perfect.'

'Perfect?' she said, looking at me in disbelief.

I placed a gentle hand on each arm in the manner of a genial vicar comforting an unduly alarmed member of the flock.

'He's been drugged.'

'What!'

I see now that this was one disclosure too many. What also became abundantly clear was that she had only been teetering on fury. Her eyes now seethed with a wrath that might have inspired many a

Greek myth. In my panic, I quickly unloosed the fact that it had been Monty's doing.

'Right,' she said, clamping the jaw shut. 'Where is he?'

'In a tryst with Natalia.'

'Huh?'

I gave a hurried, and somewhat embroidered, account of Monty's exploits on the expedition, which I said had unnaturally culminated in a fledgling romance that outshone this slight mishap with the Brigadier and this seemed to quell the imminent eruption.

'Really?' she said, in disbelief. 'Monty?'

'Indeed so.'

This seemed to alter her entire world view.

'Monty?'

'Absolutely. No more corking chap will you find. I've always said.'

These assurances seemed to soften her somewhat. The features relaxed into a look of amazement; of the sort you might see on a careworn parent learning of a saintly act from one of their hellish brood. The gravity of the situation, put in its proper context, made for a much brighter outlook altogether. No longer was the sky above filled with the ominous clouds of ruin that she had initially imagined.

Having ameliorated things to this extent, I carefully returned to the thorny topic of the Brigadier, pointing out how ironic it was that he had managed to sleep through most of the adventure. It was clear she thought I'd taken leave of my senses.

'I see you've been struck on the head,' she said, spotting my shower bruising encounter, 'and I only wish it had been harder.'

'Don't you see?' I said, pleading the case. 'After a few days in stirrups—'

'His legs are fine,' she said. 'Yours on the other hand are anything but. I've seen flamingos with more meat on the bone.'

Feeling relaxed for the first time in these exchanges, I brushed this aside.

'Maybe,' I said, 'but in a jiffy he'll be waking up to a genuinely death-defying story to tell on the musical circuit. And this is more than can be said for the damp squib adventure he took us on.'

Somehow I'd lost her.

'What is this babble?'

'Magda, old thing, if you only knew what a merry dance he led us.'

The penny dropped.

'Oh, you mean the Brigadier's sighting.'

'Indeed I do. You'll never guess what it was.'

I was now dancing on the spot.

'Go on, take a guess.'

'No.'

'Go on.'

'Spencer, classes are in session.'

She seemed to be almost as indifferent as Monty. I resorted to a whisper.

'I'll give you three guesses.'

'OK, let me think for a moment,' she said coyly, finger on lips. 'Two men in horse costume from the repertory?'

'What!' I cried. 'You knew?'

She tapped me twice on the cheek.

'Sir Walter and I both knew. Only an imbecile would've taken so long to work it out.'

And with that she left me, reeling.

Chapter Ten

THE effects of this sleight-of-hand were still rippling through me and I was conflicted by a myriad of emotions as I trudged my way moodily through corridors and up staircases to my lair. I threw open the door with the entrance of a returning private from a tour in the trenches. It had only been a night, but when my eyes fell upon the centre of the room, I looked upon that silk bedding and fluffy pillows and I don't mind admitting that it was all I could do to hold back the tears. Stooping to kiss the pillow, I slumped onto the bed and immediately began reflecting on Magda's eye-opener. The nature of the campaign struck me as reminiscent of other past double-dealing I had come up against, and it rankled, in much the same way as Mrs Prenderghast's beastly swindle a few days ago.

The more I reflected, the more it seemed to typify the thankless sort of jiggery-pokery I am occasioned to undertake to fortify the coffers of the blasted institute. One never quite becomes entirely inured to it, of course, but Sir Walter never fails to remind me of my lack of contribution. Not content with my twelve hours of sweat and toil each week, he cleaves from the Spencer body or soul to make up the shortfall.

But at least, I told myself with a deep sigh, in spite of a few near misses, the tribulations were at an end. The task now was to consign the episode to history and restore the works; something I usually achieve by submerging like a satisfied hippo into the tank, or with a spot of slothful slumber. And since I'd already diced with the apparatus of the bathroom once today, I opted for the safer option and slipped between the sheets with a decided readiness.

It was only several hours later, though it seemed a mere eye-blink, that I found I was being roughly manhandled by the shoulder and I felt the bed sag under the weight of something hefty.

'Wake up, you wastrel,' said a resonant female voice.

When my head had stopped bouncing on the pillow and the faculties had caught up I strained open the eyelids to see the blurry figure of Aunt Beatrice who, by the looks of it, had come to rouse me.

'What are you doing sleeping at this hour?'

Without allowing a right of reply, she reminded me of what I'd been trying to forget.

'Gosh, what have you done to the Brigadier? Didn't you bring him back in one piece?'

I gave a languid yawn that would have shown our feline friends a thing or two.

'Shh.'

'Don't shush me,' she said with a rumble from her very depths. It had its intended effect and I sat up at once, but in those few seconds I'd forgotten the question. It came to me, in the nick of time.

'You want to know about the Brigadier?'

'Yes.'

'What would you like to know precisely?'

'His inside leg measurement,' she snorted, fixing me with a stern eye. 'He was out with you two – always a recipe for something. He's in the infirmary, isn't he?'

A mammoth yawn stifled my reply.

'Well, is he dead?'

I had to think a second.

'He'd be in the morgue, wouldn't he?'

'Well, what's he doing there then? Having a check-up?'

'In the morgue?'

'The infirmary, you chump.'

'Oh,' I said, having disentangled the thread. 'Fractured a few bones, but that's all.'

Her features all gathered in the centre as happens when someone describes splintered bones and torn ligaments. Then she swatted me firmly on the shoulder.

'And what's the idea of leaving Monty out there by himself? You should be ashamed.'

To others, I might have said that it was an act of goodwill to the human race, but doting mothers with goodly natures are apt to land a heavy flipper on the side of the head when their pride and joy is referred to in this way. So, I provided a short précis of the circumstances of Monty staying on.

'He's probably giddy with pleasure,' I said, rounding off.

She seemed content if not exactly pleasantly surprised.

'Right,' she said, getting up to exit. 'You're wanted down in the drawing room. You can tell me all about it there.'

I'll never know why it is that the sight of a chap getting forty winks during the day stirs an instinct in the opposite sex to rouse the blighter. It is one of life's eternal mysteries, but I buttoned it for now. The several hours of bliss had gone a long way to casting off the lethargy and as my thoughts turned to her proposal, I have to say, it tinkled in all the proper regions as just what the doctor ordered.

What a watering hole is to the great plains, the drawing room is to Lockwood Institute. In this kaleidoscopic hotchpotch one experiences the full gamut of Lockwood Life in all its splendour. Attracting as it does all species of the menagerie, staff and attendees alike, everyone is content to drop the formalities and swish the malted stuffs. And it seemed to me that some time marinating in its atmosphere was the perfect tonic to reinstate normality.

So, I charged across like a cub galumphing for its mother's teat. Along the way I stopped by the billiard room to get the lay of the land, as it were. As I opened the door for a peek, there was a clacking noise and the sound of a cue scuffing a ball. A loud, unforgiving cry of 'Damnations!' rang out. Blissfully unaware of the off-season rearrangement of the room, I'd entered through the wrong door and scuppered the shot of a chap on his back swing. And by the annoyance of the multitude, I guessed he was the people's favourite.

The onlookers eyed me as if I were an interloper at a secret coven interrupting a ritual sacrifice. I backed out to leave them in peace when I caught sight of the scoreboard and, becoming intrigued by the contest under way, I decided to take in the proceedings. It soon became apparent that I'd wandered in on a single frame knockout affair between Otto Wolff and Timothy Pickering. Otto had been a nose in front until my mistimed entrance levelled the score.

Though we were close pals and socialised freely, it was a rarity to find Timothy and I on the premises together as we took turns running amok as bursar, my putting in my unholy shift on Mondays and Tuesdays and he putting nose to the grindstone the remainder of the time.

Timothy's turn came and I found my interest piqued as I watched him survey the scene. He bent a little at the knees and, in the manner of a painter judging perspective, held up a thumb and closed an eye to consider the perfect line. Then, after doing the same with the other eye, he rubbed his hands together as if it were in the bag and realised he'd left his cue behind. Having fetched it he pitched up at an entirely different spot and repeated this rigmarole. Assured of the new line, he shuffled his feet like a golfer and, hunching over the table, thrust his behind high in the air and wiggled it like a cat about to pounce before spasmodically jerking the cue on his knuckles. His tongue jutted out from the strain of concentration.

To those who knew him it was clear this was a different Timothy. This wasn't the supreme thwack-it-between-slurping-drinks expert I knew. The tension on his face suggested much was riding on the outcome and when Otto left Timothy with a sitter, a young woman at the front yipped in excitement. She remained on tip-toe with her hands clasped together throughout Timothy's final shot and no sooner had he sunk the last ball than she bounded forward and flung herself into his arms.

The Wolff pack were still glowering at me when Timothy fetched up at my side beaming with gratitude. This seemed to defuse the unruliness.

'Spencer, you couldn't have timed your entrance better, old man.'

'Ah,' I said, as the multitude scattered, 'well, I seem to have put a few noses out of joint.'

'Oh, pish. They're probably just reeling from sinking a stash.'

'Eh?'

'I was on at six to one!'

'What? You don't mean—'

'I certainly do, comrade.'

This could mean only one thing.

'Who's running this syndicate?'

'Your father, of course. I'm doing the admin, obviously.'

I thought this spectacle for the masses had the hallmarks of a Sir Walter ploy. He'd been harbouring a desire to put a scheme of sorts into effect for some time. What surprised me, though, was how popular it appeared to be amongst the populace. The essence of it ran little short of turning the place into a casino where attendees could fuel their sporting appetites by betting on a variety of similar contests and thereby racking up losses on account, which were added to their fees. Even with the occasional payout, the operation looked a sure way to boost the institute's coffers. I gather this brainwave had originated with Timothy and had led Sir Walter to look upon the chap with a kindly eye. I also recall some stinging comparisons between us to boot with Sir Walter frequently remarking why I lacked Timothy's flair for devising wheezes. Still, as I reflected on the specifics of the operation before me, something needed fleshing out.

'But, Timothy, aren't you also the chap who is by way of setting the odds?'

'Certainly am, old fruit,' he beamed, his face still flush from victory.

I could see he wasn't following.

'Well, I mean to say, aren't you rather in the way of rigging it? If you're setting the odds, too, I mean.'

The penny dropped.

'Oh, that,' he said, dismissing the thought with a wave of the hand, 'that's OK. As long as the plates are spinning in Sir Walter's favour he's none the wiser. To tell you the truth, I only cottoned on to the fact that I might play today by chance.'

As I pondered what he was saying, I couldn't help feel awestruck. He had inadvertently stumbled upon a way to back himself using Sir Walter's wherewithal on odds he set himself against opponents of his choosing. And when examined thus, I had to doff my hat at the brilliance of the scheme. Here he was, a working man creaming off the knight of the realm who was creaming off the gentry. It takes a lot to out-diddle Sir Walter, so I felt my affection for the man reach new heights.

'Timothy, but that's brilliant!'

'I'll say it is.'

His face suddenly fell fearfully.

'You won't tell, will you?'

With the memory of my having been hoodwinked into a pointless forest excursion still fresh, it gave me great pleasure to set his mind at ease.

'My dear Timothy,' I said, embracing him warmly, 'you have my honest word.'

He beamed with the air of a man on the crest of an upswing in life; a thought which reminded me about that fan of his I'd seen earlier.

'Say, who was that enraptured young lady just now? Covering you in a warm embrace.'

'Francesca? Oh, yes, she's a spillover from last year and decided to stay on. She's the girl I'm going to marry all right. She doesn't know it yet of course.'

'Eh? You've asked her?'

'I'll tell her soon enough. Sort of surprise her, you know. I'm picking my moment to spring it on her. Traditional like.'

'Yes, well—'

I broke off when someone, slipping through the adjoining doors, had allowed a rather crisp Gershwin piano number with plenty of oomph to carry over to us and, before I knew it, the foot was tapping away. It seemed to warrant closer inspection so we breezed through to the music room for the full experience. We entered to see, amid the hubbub, two lissom, bouncy girls doing their take on the Charleston. They'd come nattily dressed for the part, too.

With a whisky apiece, Timothy and I resumed our confab and he began telling me of recently trifling times regarding his landlady. This brought the encounter with my own landlady to mind, so as you can imagine, I was agog.

'Trifling? You mean she was taking liberties?'

'Yes,' he said. 'Or to be more precise, no. Well, what I mean is lady luck has not been particularly kind to me of late.'

This seemed to be flying in the face of recent evidence, but I let it pass.

'I put it to Mrs Hesmondhalgh, my landlady, that things simply needed to change.'

'How so?'

'Well, "take a look at this coffee stained rug," I said. "How can anyone be prepared to put up with this?"'

'Sounds reasonable to me.'

'"But you spilt it," she said.'

'Typical,' I said, shaking my head. 'There's more?'

'Certainly there's more, old chum. She lowered her head to the floor in a defeated sort of way and muttered, as if they were her final words. Then she slumped in the chair and sobbed.'

'Sobbed? Good heavens. Why?'

'She said it had been the week to end all weeks. She took out her teeth and said she'd lost her set somewhere and she'd had to use an old pair belonging to a friend. This had left her writhing in agony. That same week her husband's side of the family had suffered a bereavement. Someone passing before their time.'

'Goodness. That's tragic,' I said, tutting.

'Tragic, indeed, old chum.'

On this point we were agreed. Things were tragic.

'And to whom should the funeral arrangements fall?'

'Not Mrs Hesmondhalgh,' I said, incredulously.

He nodded at the shame of it.

'In her state?'

'Afraid so, old man.'

'Well, of all the dastardliness I ever heard of in families,' I said. 'Those dashed rotters.'

Turning to the barman, I said, 'I'll have what he's having, please. On him.'

Two whisky sodas duly arrived and, after a quick clink, Timothy sunk his teeth into a sliver of lemon, winced and continued.

'Then two days after the first, the family suffered a second loss. That same day Chester, Mrs Hesmondhalgh's dog, had begun to display signs that he, too, would soon be shuffling off this mortal coil.'

'What!'

'Spencer, old man, I've been on the brink of emotional turmoil. Here I was asking this poor woman for money when all the evidence was that I should've been giving *her* money.'

I held up a hand.

'Don't do it, my man!' I said, fervently. 'It'll turn out that she's not related to any of them and it was all a ruse to bleed you.'

I felt strongly on the subject of landladies. As a breed, they're forever looking to rout you and I felt compelled to tell him about my landlady's recent sting operation. It opened his eyes. He thanked me for a lucky escape and vowed to look out for similar underhandedness in future. I've always felt that it behoves one to stop another unfortunate going the same way. He returned to Francesca a wiser man.

Here, Magda arrived to introduce the more freewheeling element to the dynamics of the music room. It's usually guaranteed to stir the attendees into summoning up a bit of national pride and this usually takes the form of some klezmer, wailing lament, lesser known folk melody or display of nifty footwork of some kind.

No sooner had she announced the billing than Nikola, the charismatic lead violinist of the Sabauri Chamber Ensemble, leapt into the limelight, obviously keen to show that his prowess extended beyond the fiddle. Taking hold of the accordion, he gave us a humble Ossetian folk song. This was, I felt, so much more his métier, I wondered why he'd inflicted the fiddle on us at all. After being swallowed up by the populace, the only glimpse I saw of Nikola for the remainder of proceedings was him feeding the Charleston dancing duo olives from his martinis. His humble ballad was, in any case, a nice way to start off the proceedings.

Next up, gambolled two Belgian twins with expressive faces to offer the multitude a revolutionary workers' song, originally intended, they said, to raise the spirts of the proletariat. With the tiniest of preambles, they launched into a lively and soulful rendition, in perfect key, which is not something one can often say about the music room. It was so warmly received that it seemed to define the zeitgeist, so to speak.

This, as it turns out, was the undoing of Henrik von Brandt, the third act in this spree. Magda introduced him as a high-ranking figure amongst the operatic elite who'd just composed a libretto in the style of Verdi, and he was proposing to play the prelude for us now. Then she sloped away to a safe distance so all eyes could feast on the von Brandt form, which to my mind was purpose-built for a blower-upper of children's balloons. It was only through the occasional flash of white through the facial shrubbery that I came to notice it contained teeth.

Seating himself at the piano with the hubris of a man treating the adoring masses to a world premiere, he started off with a few melancholic opening bars. He hadn't got far into it when I judged the atmosphere in the room sour. To me it made a welcome change from the usual polkas or thigh-slapping numbers, but I was evidently outvoted. The audience had begun carping and murmuring and, in spite of the fact that the majority of the populace stemmed from homes where this sort of din bounced off the walls most nights, little could he have known that he was surrounded by a rebellious youth who'd had their fill of the high arts and had been inspired by revolutionary ferment.

There was a time to revel in blue-blooded proclivities, but tonight, it seemed, was not it. The character and tastes of the music room were notoriously fickle and on another occasion the choice might've taken home the bacon, but tonight the masses seemed to embody the spirit of Everyman. The cause of the oppressed had spoken and it demanded one thing.

'I know others,' Henrik pleaded as he was being ejected by the staff. 'But I'm a rumba teacher from Hanover!'

It was no use. I was feeling for the fellow and reflecting on yet another example of what it's like to misjudge the mood abjectly when Aunt Beatrice socked me in the ribs.

I'd become so engrossed in institute life that I'd forgotten about her. Pulling up a chair, she joined me with a drink for a tête-à-tête of our own. She seemed to be the only one amongst the senior regiment in the place. There was no sign of Sir Walter, Kristina or Uncle Cedric to be seen.

'Uncle Cedric not attending?' I asked, looking around.

'You just missed him,' she said, 'for all the use he was.'

My acuities have never received much in the way of credit from the Lockwood or Fipps clans, as you may have gathered, but by her manner I'd say she was peeved about something. And it seemed to concern my Uncle Cedric and, so I discovered, Kristina. After my second whisky, I was able to discern that much.

'Well, she'd been due to get the populace warmed up with something of a soliloquy, you see.'

She'd lost me already. Kristina had been called many things, but warm was never one of them, so to expect an audience to bask in her radiant glow seemed fanciful to say the least. I probed deeper into the fog.

'The audience took one look at a ghostly emaciated figure appearing out of the shadows and immediately concluded they were seeing Act I of *Hamlet* again.'

'An easy mistake to make,' I said. 'I speak from personal experience.'

And I told her how I'd run into her, so to speak, in Sir Walter's boudoir looking as pale as a phantasm, only more gaunt looking. The ground-shaking roar of laughter that followed all but deafened the populace and drowned out the sorrowful ballad in progress.

'Was she heckled?' I asked.

'She'd barely started her soliloquy when the couple at the front began waving their table candle about and chanting incantations. They'd got half-way through an exorcism when Kristina dashed out. To join a witches' sabbath, I expect.'

'Good lord.'

'That sums up the popular sentiment perfectly,' she said. 'Your uncle was ushered in to banish the evil spirits. He came in swaying like a bishop and began christening Jafar.'

I was nonplussed.

'Who?'

She pointed to the chap with the clean-shaven dome in the front row.

'But he's a Buddhist, isn't he?'

She fixed me with a despairing look and shifted in her seat.

'That didn't stop your uncle pouring a few drops of water on his head and renaming him Hilary.'

'Great Scott!'

'So he was led out. I'll speak to him later.'

This struck me as rather harsh on the fellow. I mean, imagine it – after heaving a sigh of relief from another day of tending to the spiritual needs of your flock, you've slipped out of the robes and are just pouring yourself a double measure of something nourishing when you're summoned to work your powers in a supernatural emergency.

I was still reflecting on this business of Uncle Cedric being plucked from his blessed haven and deposited into Lockwood's swirling epicentre of theatrics when my attention became drawn to a familiar figure. Beckoning me from across the room, in a somewhat frantic manner it seemed to me, was Magda. So, bidding the aunt adieu, I answered the call from Magda who led me to Sir Walter's office – a place in which I'm never at ease.

'It's about Monty,' she said as we whizzed along the corridor.

By the severity of her manner, I concluded that Monty had made a pig's breakfast of something, but where to begin? He's such a versatile fellow.

'We've received a letter,' she said.

A complaint from one of the attendees, I thought.

'Oh, yes. From whom?'

'Monty, pinhead.'

'Ah,' I said. The effects of my indulgences were quickly beginning to wear off. 'What about?'

As she paced the room, she hardly knew where to start. It was the first time I'd seen her this rattled. Then she paused, as if summoning the strength to say the words, which by turns of conversation has to rank as one of the most stupefying in all my puff.

'He says he's kidnapped Natalia.'

She thought, by my silence, that I hadn't heard.

'He's kidnapped Natalia Sabauri,' she repeated all the louder.

And placing her palms together, she raised them to her mouth in the most frightful way, as if wishing that it weren't so. I struggled to make sense of this. For a moment, I kept expecting her to spring the punchline, but I hadn't known Magda's sense of humour to be anywhere near this warped.

'What?'

She spelled it out, growing impatient.

'Monty. Has. Kidnapped. Natalia.'

I perched myself precariously on the desk to try to make sense of these words, but the whole thing seemed unintelligible – beyond my comprehension, that is. I'd not heard anything so incongruous from her before, so naturally this set me wondering about her state of mind. Her present jitteriness led me to speculate if she wasn't experiencing some sort of breakdown. I mean, one hears of people snapping. There they are addressing the House of Commons in the afternoon and by tea time they're writing messages on the walls with chalk between their toes.

'Now, Magda,' I said, in my gentlest manner, 'don't take it amiss, but have those lovely Belgian fellows, by any chance, been plying you with absinthe? I know it seems harmless enough but—'

'He's ruddy well kidnapped Natalia Sabauri!' she bawled.

As she continued her pacing, I subjected her to a closer scrutiny. She appeared clear-headed enough, but I kept probing into her mental state, starting with the basics.

'Let's just be clear. You are referring to my cousin?'

'Of course! That blasted cur.'

'But surely, old thing,' I said, assuming a fearful mix-up, 'you don't expect me to believe that the chap who gambols waywardly into moving traffic to stroke a cat on the other side of the road has overnight developed the nature of a hardened thug, do you?'

I'd hit a stride, as they say, and felt compelled to put to her what I felt were the obvious flaws in her arguments. Namely the traits she'd overlooked that pushed the enterprise firmly beyond the bounds of possibility.

'Come now. I ask you to consider what you're saying about Monty. I mean, is the fellow dunderheaded? Innately. Is he excitable? As a toddler. Is he irritating? Like an insect bite. But malicious he is not.'

I ended this case for the defence with a downcast and disappointed expression suggestive of the absurdity of it. Some shard of doubt appeared to penetrate.

'Well, something has happened,' she said. 'The Brigadier is speechless.'

I simply couldn't accept it. The idea was repellent. Preposterous even. Monty was capable of many outrages and all of them before breakfast, but this was of an order that was simply unthinkable. I tried to unravel where there might have been a mistake, but ran dry. I remained convinced, however, that someone, somewhere, had boobed.

Dismissing this as the evident slop it was, I tried to recap the facts, starting with the letter she'd mentioned.

'Could it be fake? How do you know it's from him? Now, that Miles fellow strikes me as the sort of scoundrel that might—'

'I recognised his handwriting.'

'And you're sure it's his?'

'Certain.'

'Hmm.'

She seemed convincing enough.

'Where did you find it?'

'In the Brigadier's breast pocket.'

I sprang up from the desk.

'Come again?'

She repeated this morsel.

'You don't mean the note in the Brigadier's pocket?'

'That's it.'

'Just a second,' I said, the gravity of this dawning on me for the first time.

Throughout this ghastly conversation I had felt the memory start to loosen. But now, I had begun to feel wobbly on my foundations just as a building teeters before its imminent collapse. Then I thought back to the previous night in the woods.

'Oh goodness—'

'What, what?' she asked, in agitation.

'I just need a moment.'

I was trying my hardest to think back to the previous night.

'When we were in the woods the Brigadier mentioned some vestigial custom where girls are whisked away by chaps with matrimonial ambitions.'

'Whisked?'

'Snatched. Made off with. Scooped up. Nobbled.'

Closing the gap between us in a single stride, she raised my chin and eyed me gravely.

'What else?'

I gulped.

'Well,' I said, trying to collect my thoughts, 'the Brigadier seemed to describe it as the secret longing of many girls.'

'What!'

'In certain regions where this fashion is de rigueur, I mean. I paraphrase, but that was the essence.'

She turned away in disbelief. This seemed to send her into a deep spin. A faraway look came into her face and she became deathly mute. No doubt she was considering the implications of such an earth-shattering incident on the fortunes of the institute and on Monty, but in which order, I couldn't be sure.

I, meanwhile, slipped into my own reverie. As I replayed events in my mind, what may have transpired began to register and it was as if something within had been awakened and had begun hacking away at my insides. When I recalled the moment the Brigadier had described this quaint practice of yore from the more rustic regions I remembered vividly how Monty had been bounced into a sort of stupor. I wondered if it was from this fantastical realm that this loathsome scheme had sprung along with an internal voice whispering, 'Go on. Do it.' The theory squared with how he'd stood in front of my donkey for me to behold his beastly revelation.

Slowly, by turns, a sickening realisation began to settle that Monty, no stranger to flights of fancy, had put into action his own quixotic fantasy of whisking Natalia off as a throwback to this ritual elopement.

Pretty soon I was feeling the full force of this bombshell and, as the blood left my head, the room began to spin and I staggered, holding onto the desk to steady myself. At a conservative estimate, I'd say my condition was that of a man who'd sustained a wallop to the gut, a hammer blow to the head and whose sanity dangled by a thread. There was no question in my mind that of all the pitfalls and pratfalls in Monty's existence, this had to be the scale topper.

I explained my suspicions to Magda. Many questions remained, but this, I remember, was the moment that everything turned.

Chapter Eleven

WHILE the aftershocks were still reverberating through me I clawed to open a window and noticed two police cars parked on the grounds. I asked Magda if they'd been notified.

'Of course,' she said. 'When the medical orderlies discovered the note they called the local constabulary immediately.'

'So they know the position?' I asked, horrified.

She nodded gravely. I shuddered at the significance of this. It meant of course that Monty was now under police suspicion and officially a wanted man. Then an even more cataclysmic thought barrelled into me.

'Oh my God!' I said, my hand shooting up to my mouth. 'Does Sir Walter—'

My words froze on my lips because at this juncture Sir Walter's office door opened sending a cold snap pulsing through me. It was Sir Walter himself with his arm around the shoulder of Chief Inspector Bartlett. A contemporary of the Brigadier's in age, the chief inspector was a man whose entire mass appeared to be centred about the middle. Perched on top of the stalk-like neck was a comparatively small head dominated by an epic beak and finishing off the aspect were two sagging eyes, a grey, bristly upturned moustache and at least two chins. At the other end were two standard issue boots made to measure for a kangaroo with whopping feet. All of which meant that when they crossed the threshold together to enter the office their combined girth was too much and they became wedged in the frame. Eventually Sir Walter stood aside.

'I've put my best men onto her, sir,' said Bartlett.

'Yes, yes, yes,' said Sir Walter, irritably, 'but it is paramount to employ discretion. Think of the reputation of the inst—'

He broke off at the sight of me. But astonishment was succeeded by rage and he shot a beam of stupefying ire at me, his nostrils twitching in agitation. It was singularly unpleasant.

'Spencer,' he growled, 'if you've had anything to do with this—'

It was one of the quickest denials I've ever had to make.

'No, no, absolutely not.'

I must say that the suggestion that I might somehow be embroiled in something of this magnitude struck me as beyond the pale.

'Hmm...' he said, seeming to accept me at my word, which made a change.

'A nationwide missing person's case is to be opened,' continued the chief inspector. 'My officers are sorting through the photos now. We will shortly be informing the consulate.'

Sir Walter started violently at this news.

'Ah. About that, Chief Inspector, might I have a word?'

Putting his arm around the fellow's shoulders again, he led him to the corner for a whisper. Meanwhile, Magda, who had been asked to provide identifying photos, was now peering over the shoulders of the constables seated on the chesterfield to select imagery for the 'wanted' and 'missing' posters.

I wandered across, hoping we might resume our tête-à-tête, but she'd become drawn into this slice of police activity. Casting an eye myself, I was a little perplexed why they'd gone for one of Monty looking unflatteringly heavy-browed, but it seemed settled. They'd moved on to deciding in which photo Natalia appeared most like the Virgin Mary when Chief Inspector Bartlett stomped towards me.

'Now, you, young man,' said the official, 'we'll need to ask you some questions. Look at me, can't you!'

I snapped to attention and gulped.

'Me?'

'Yes, you. I'd like you—'

'This is all very pointless,' said Magda, rolling her eyes, 'but Constable Bartlett—'

'Chief Inspector—'

'Insists on another person to verify this is in Monty's own hand.'

She snatched a note from the chief inspector's hand and shoved it on my chest.

I squinted a bit and after clearing the old larynx I read it aloud.

'"Dearest Bunny, Long have been the nights since we last—"'

'Oooh,' he exclaimed, snatching it from my grasp. 'That's mine. This is Monty's.'

He handed me another note. It ran as follows:

Dear Brigadier,

You'll be pleased to hear Natalia is doing her family proud, resisting superbly with lots of wriggling about etc. etc. Looking forward to tying the knot.

Toodle pip.

Her unworthy captor,

Monty.

There was no doubt about it. It was a vintage Monty missive all right. I recognised his scrawl and the scribbled signature. When I had placed the note in the Brigadier's pocket I'd assumed it was a prescription that would restore the spring in the man's step, but by Magda's account, it had done the opposite.

Now, being asked to verify its provenance catapulted me into a crisis. Confirming it to have come from Monty's hand, to my mind, would be tantamount to pointing to him from the witness stand and crying, 'That's him, your honour!' On the other hand, if I denied all knowledge and it later came to light that *I* had placed the note in the Brigadier's pocket, would I not become the guilty accomplice?

My quavering was at its uppermost when the chief inspector jolted me.

'Well, stop dithering, man.'

There was nothing for it.

'It's the genuine article,' I said, with a heavy heart.

'Excellent,' he said. 'Sir Walter, if you won't be needing Spencer we'll take him away.'

'Eh?' I said.

'Hmm,' replied Sir Walter, looking up from his desk. 'No, no. Please yourself.'

As I was being escorted away Magda shot me a despairing look. Arriving at what I understood was to be a makeshift interview room, it was only at this point that it dawned on me that my identifying the note marked a mere preliminary in the beginning of the investigation. Now was to begin a deeper probe into the affair, starting with my role in it. This instantly brought home to me the youthful follies which had brought me into the path of the local precinct. But this ghastly scenario had all the makings of a felony, so when I sat down, it's no exaggeration to say that my heart was in my mouth.

I was joined by Inspector Fletcher, the official leading the operations. He stomped in and shot me a contemptuous look, kicked a chair out from beneath the desk and sank heavily into it, exhaling deeply. In his late thirties, he was a man who gave every impression that flushing out ruthless figures from woodlands was the perfect way to work up an appetite for the evening meal. Built on broad lines, he was a square-jawed fellow whose features appeared to have been moulded by a child's hand. With a bulbous nose, cauliflower ears and half the number of teeth of the average person, he was an oddity by any standard.

I had just begun picturing him clanging the bars shut and whistling jauntily all the way home for some well-earned pheasant, when my musings were cut short.

'So then,' he said, smiling through widely spaced bovine teeth, 'do you often consort with persons of a despicable character?'

'What!'

I was stumped right from the off. I mean, if this was to be the cut and thrust of things, this was shaping up to be a very one-sided exchange. Not least because it was a terribly difficult question to answer. With the sort of element that passes through Lockwood's doors on a regular basis, this sort of thing becomes an occupational hazard and I've always felt that it's a bit unfair to be tarred with the same brush by association.

The sweat had started trickling down my back in brooks and I was just beginning to wonder whether I should take up the right to a legal counsel when it was borne in upon me that I didn't have any. He flipped open a pocket notebook and began skimming its contents.

'Now, getting down to the p'ticklers of this diabolical outrage, let's start with the basics, shall we? Four of you, I see. Now, what was the purpose of your exp'dition?'

I'd begun to wish I'd curbed my visions of the man's evening proclivities and concentrated instead on fixing my story. After all, I couldn't explain that we were hunting without a licence. The fact that it was for something non-existent wouldn't, I felt, carry much sway. Then again, if I explained that we were on the trail of a two-man horse, I'd be in a padded cell before the week was out. I had to give some other pretext.

'Oh, we were taking a ride, you know.'

He referred to his notes.

'Donkey riding one of your pastimes, is it?'

It was beyond my capabilities to extol the virtues of the noble creatures, so I just nodded.

'I see,' he said, rising to his feet and standing in a domineering way over me.

'OK, now where is the little heathen?!' he cried.

The volcanic force of this left-field question floored me.

'What? Who?'

He sneered.

'Edgar Montgomery Fipps, that son of a,' he said, flipping a leaf of his notebook, 'Cedric and Beatrice Fipps.'

'Ah—'

'Cousin of yours, is he?'

I gulped. I gathered the golden rule is to say nothing on these occasions.

'Yes,' he said, scrutinising my features, 'I thought there was a resemblance.'

I'd heard these scoundrels often resort to personal insults. He placed his hands in the pit of his arms and exhaled. An essence of the man's onion soup lunch wafted over.

'All right,' he said, perching on the edge of the table, when did you last see them?'

'Natalia last night. Monty this morning,' I said, spilling the beans.

I couldn't help it. It just poured out of me.

'Ah-ha,' he said, scribbling while mouthing the words, 'and was Monty on his own this morning?'

Egad! This was another Pandora's box which had me in fits and starts. By mentioning Monty had lugged a man through the forest, lifeless and bound to a donkey, one might as well ask the fat lady to start limbering up. And yet, how else did I come to meet up with the Brigadier for our return journey together? I was in a state of complete disarray.

'Well?' he thundered. 'Was Monty on his own?'

I bit the bullet.

'No,' I said, swallowing hard, 'the Brigadier was with him.'

'Ah.'

He appeared fascinated by this titbit.

'Look,' I said, in stricken voice, 'if you're going to ask how the Brigadier ended up in the infirmary, you might as well know he was feeling unwell and preferred to sleep slumped on his donkey while I escorted us back.'

He looked at me askance and I squirmed under this penetrating stare for some time.

'And where do you think they are now?'

'The donkeys?'

A fist pounded the table.

'If you're not in helpful mood, Mr Lockwood, we could always award you the dubious honour of obstructing police enquiries.'

I gulped again. How anyone escapes police questioning without implicating himself, his relations and all known acquaintances was beyond me. The blighter began pressing me again.

'I'm trying to think,' I said, loosening my collar.

'Yes, I thought I heard the machinery at work,' he said, placing a booted foot on the desk.

Resting his arm on his knee, he held this most unflattering position, staring at the floor deep in thought.

'Until yesterday morning Winsbrook was a calm oasis. Then the four of you venture into the forest and the following afternoon all hell breaks loose.'

He seemed to view us as the four horsemen of the apocalypse come to bring ruin to a peaceful land.

'But where,' he asked rhetorically, 'would he take her, I wonder.'

It seemed to me that he was within a whisker of deducing their actual whereabouts, so I summoned all the composure I had within to try to throw him off the scent. It seemed the only way to help Monty out of this fearful spot without ending up in chokey myself.

'Well,' I said, trying to exude a concerned, but calm air, 'we remained on the fringes of dwellings and close to the road network, so for all I know Monty might now be in possession of a motor vehicle. I daresay he could be anywhere in the country by now. He used to speak fondly of the Lake District. A fan of Wordsworth and all that.'

'Hmm,' said the officer, inscrutably.

It was difficult to say whether he'd taken the bait, but after flipping his notebook shut he concluded the *interview* and warned me to stay nearby lest I be needed for further questioning.

I stepped into the corridor still a free man, for the moment. But the likelihood of Monty being able to say the same for much longer was an ever diminishing one. After my nerves had stopped jangling I scurried to Magda's office so we might resume our deliberations on this sordid episode. I brought her up to speed with my recent inquisition. She seemed surprised by one aspect of the business.

'You mean you know where they are?'

'Of course.'

'Well, why didn't you mention it before?'

I reflected on what I could remember of our earlier exchange.

'Shock, I expect.'

'OK,' she said, placing her hands to her lips as before, 'then there's only one thing for it. The hut isn't on the phone, so you must go there.'

'What!'

The woman whom I regarded as the doyenne of practicality, who attends to situations with a keen eye and ready assessment, appeared to have blown a gasket.

'You can't be serious.'

Magda has a tone which she reserves for special moments when a chap is disobeying clear instructions. It sits a good deal below contralto in the vocal range and she employed it to good effect now.

'I *am* serious,' she said, fixing me with an austere look. 'Deadly serious. I don't care what devilish fantasies Monty let loose, but you will go and bring that poor sap back.'

'Are you stark raving—'

One look at her searing eyes was enough to check me completely. She was clearly in no mood to brook any pathetic excuses.

'But it's dark outside.'

'Take a torch.'

'And Natalia?'

She appeared absolutely stunned.

'I'm *talking* about Natalia.'

'What! And what about Monty?'

She thought for a moment.

'OK, bring him back, too. But give him a good, firm punch from me.'

'But—'

'Make it strong.'

'But—'

'Now, shoo,' she said, hustling me towards the door. 'I overheard Bartlett say that the search will shortly be starting.'

'But—'

'But me no buts,' she said, shoving me out the door and closing it behind me.

She was becoming worryingly more like Sir Walter every day.

It was a hellish task, I could see that. But what was also abundantly clear was that this possible watershed carried the sort of term in stir that would've been enough to put the wind up even the most recalcitrant of jailbirds, so what else could I do?

'Fine,' I shouted through the closed door.

She opened it slightly.

'Don't forget this,' she said, showing me a clenched fist and slamming the door shut again.

A short time later, after breezing by the kitchen for some luncheon leftovers and stopping by Quinton's lair for a quick snort, a shadowy hunched figure might have been seen shambling away from the grounds in the night with all the appearance of someone doing a sneak.

Within minutes I was regretting passing by Quinton's den for some Dutch courage. I'd known that he kept a supply of tinctures, but the vintage I'd quaffed had quickly begun liquefying my insides. But this was, under the circumstances, a minor gripe about the ghastly predicament. I mean to say, when you've only just readjusted to quasi-civilised surroundings, whichever way you cut it, returning to the undergrowth in the dead of night when it will soon be crawling with the constabulary and other critters ranks as the ultimate in unfettered lunacy.

Still, there was no getting around the fact that Monty's fate hung in the balance and I told myself that if ever there was a time for a fellow to hold his nerve and undertake an errand of mercy, this was undoubtedly it. It didn't mean, of course, that with every step and misstep I took I wasn't foaming with recriminations. On the contrary, I had it in mind to tick the blighter off in no uncertain fashion when I reached him.

I tried to keep my spirits up by reminding myself that many others had embarked on similarly foolhardy missions. Most notably, there was that other daredevil of the wilderness, Percy Fawcett, who had set out, against his detractors, to unearth 'The lost city of Z' in the forests of Brazil, but when I recalled how he'd come a cropper at the hands of some tribals and his remains were never found, I sought to stop that line of thought. But it was too late. Soon my imagination was awash with grotesque and haunting figures and, before long, folkloric tales began to infuse with my thoughts. The foliage compacting underfoot seemed to feel like I was squelching the recently deceased, but after stepping out onto a familiar stretch of more solid earth, which I followed unerringly for some minutes, I found that I had the hut in my sights.

Just as before, its presence was a chilling sight. Not just for the sinister aspect the night bears upon bucolic settings, but because it brought back to me the memory of the marauder I'd encountered that dreadful night. What if he had returned to the hut while Monty and Natalia were inside? What would I be walking into?

I spent several tense moments in deliberation before I plucked up the courage to press on towards it. Keeping the windows in view, I approached as inconspicuously as possible from the flank. My tread softened until I was moving with a stealthy silence across the low grassy stretch. As I neared I could see, set against the light, the outline of a person sitting still by the window and another, shorter figure occasionally coming into view whom I took to be Natalia.

Well, I have to say, this ordinary glimpse of domesticity sent a rush of relief washing over me. I imagined Monty was seated by the window doing the crossword, oblivious to his troubles, so as I relaxed my gait and settled into a more leisurely frame of mind, I began marshalling my thoughts as to what I would say to him. The best plan seemed to be to extricate him from Natalia's company briefly and let him have it between the eyes, explaining that he was a prize chump who had landed himself in one of the foulest predicaments known to man. What's more, he was a sitting duck for the inevitable dragnet that was closing in on him.

With this established I strode on with the disapproving air of an elder cousin who was looking upon delivering Magda's message with lively anticipation when, having come within thirty yards, I glanced up again at the window and froze. A shudder ran through me. The impression that had so unexpectedly borne itself upon me was the sight of the seated figure. With his back to the window, his hands were hanging to the sides and his head remained perfectly fixed, looking away to the centre of the room. It was Monty. He had been bound and gagged.

Well, I mean to say, this unforeseen spectacle had me totally poleaxed. I don't know if you've ever been rehearsing a rollicking reprimand for a blighter and arrive to discover him trussed à la turkey ready for the oven, but let me tell you, your former livid position becomes pretty untenable. I tried desperately to make sense of the scene. There in the foreground was Monty and in the background was Natalia occasionally breezing into view as if enjoying a get-away in a rustic chalet.

A flurry of possibilities raced through my mind. First I speculated if it was simply more of Natalia's wayward larkiness carried too far. Perhaps she had pranked Monty into the chair under the ruse of some game and, when his back was turned, sprang the rope. I couldn't help recall the time she'd stepped out from behind some hiding place with her 'hands up' gag. Then I wondered if Monty might have boobed while trying to impress Natalia with a straitjacket escape in the style of Houdini. Given his avocations over the years, this wouldn't have surprised me in the least. I daresay, some might have viewed the scene as not a little on the sinister side, but my knowledge of Monty over the years led me to view these possibilities as the more likely.

I was still toying with these when Natalia disappeared into the bathroom. The sound of heavy metallic clanking and a low rumble of running water followed, which I took to mean she was running a bath. For fear of entangling myself in further conjecture, I told myself that the one man who could shed light on things was indoors taking an inert approach to life. So, I scurried to the hut and, with the nimble fingers of a cat burglar, turned the doorknob and peeked inside. I had barely poked in more than the beak when our eyes met. Well, I hadn't until then appreciated quite how much can be expressed through the eyes alone, but by the way the chap's eyebrows shot up, his eyes growing to twice their size, and through an incomprehensible mumble seeping from the gag, I recognised relief as never before. There was no doubt about it – hope was dawning in those eyes. If it had another aspect, it was that he didn't appear to be enjoying this prank all that much. So, with a finger pressed to my lips, I snuck in and undid his restraints.

'Thanks, old man!' he said, springing up and thwacking me on the shoulder with a force that sent me stumbling into the tableware.

I had barely issued a tut when I perceived a draught and upon turning round I found that I was alone. When I crossed the threshold I started violently. There in the middle distance, showing a ballistic burst of acceleration, was Monty bolting across the fen with the foot speed of a cross-country champion.

I don't know how it is that seeing a usually unathletic specimen galloping like a racehorse away from a spot has the effect of stirring the flight instinct in idle bystanders, but so primal was this feeling that before I had time to think, my legs, taking charge of the whole, unleashed in me a latent propulsion I didn't know I had. And before I knew what was what, I was following in Monty's slipstream, closing in for the romp along the straight. Another dozen or so strides and I'd say I was within a semiquaver of the fellow when from behind there came the screech of the window being wrenched up. And a gunshot rang out.

'Pwaaaarrggh-ahaarr-haar,' cried a panic-stricken Monty.

Another rapid succession of shots whizzed past prompting another frenzied 'boowaaaarrggh-ahaarrh' from the fellow. This strangled articulation from Monty had barely died away when the air was rent by the fervent throaty cries of Natalia going berserk. What irked her was unclear but never before had I imagined the human voice capable of emitting such feverish apoplexy over such vast distances. These frightful vocals propelled us across the open spaces and towards the cover of the trees. The frenetic pace of our footsteps had brought on a twinge in my sides and I begged Monty to slow down, and mercifully, once he felt out of firing range, he did. Shaken by the events that had just transpired and breathless, I hardly knew where to begin. This momentary pause was enough for Monty to steal a march.

'Spencer, old man,' he said, huffing and puffing, 'I'm as pleased to see you as the Brigadier was at the soirée, but what the devil are you doing here?'

I was panting the more heavily of the two.

'Putting a stop to your… fool's paradise.'

Alas, we'd got as far as this when we heard the cries of a pack of hounds closing in quickly.

'What the dickens…' said Monty, his alarm reaching new heights.

Just then a terrible thought occurred to me.

'Tracker dogs,' I said, aghast.

'Eh?'

I reminded myself that Monty's lapse from sanity meant he was not hip to developments.

'I'll tell you later. For now, scram!'

No sooner had we slipped into the undergrowth than from the vicinity of the hut sprang a disarray of shouting voices, beaming torches and barking dogs. Another female shriek carried over, this one laced with fear and shock, which I took to indicate the constabulary had swarmed the hut. With Monty following my lead, like brigands fleeing the scene of a crime, we hastened our paces to the seclusion of the forest.

Sometime later, when we had reached what we both felt was a sufficient distance away from the bedlam, we stopped for breath, but more importantly to give the recent happenings at the hut a full and proper airing. I was poised to do precisely this, but as ever, leave a gap, however small, and Monty will fill it.

'Spencer,' he said, much to my annoyance, 'there's something I want to get off my chest.'

I held aloft a hand to stay him, but given that we were speaking in total darkness, he missed it.

'It concerns this business of Natalia.'

For once we were of one mind.

'Go on,' I said.

'Spencer, before we go on, I think I should share with you that I've gone off the idea. I don't think I'm cut out for this sort of thing. I just wanted you to know that I don't hold it against you for badgering me into it.'

'I—'

'And you're probably wondering how it came to this, so I'll tell you. At first Natalia seemed herself – hornet-like and quarrelsome – so naturally I assumed things were normal, and then she shrieked to high heaven that there'd been a sort of massacre in the bathroom which she demanded I scrub clean. Well, of all the earthly sights! That Skippers must be a psychopath. I should speak to Uncle Walter about it. Then as soon as I slumped down to rest I must have nodded off. The next thing I remember, I woke up bound to the chair. As I came round, she lunged at me in the manner of Lady Macbeth and with a maniacal cackle thrust a gag in my mouth. I was dumbfounded. Positively stumped, my man.'

This made two of us. The last time I'd heard anything of this sort was at Rufus Oakley's bachelor's binge and even then it was considered to have been a dastardly thing to do. I hadn't gone, but had heard on the grapevine.

'I think on reflection, Spencer, that I prefer my engagements the conventional way. I mean, if this is what it amounts to, I shouldn't wonder so few chaps go in for it these days.'

I couldn't remember the Brigadier mentioning any shenanigans of this sort the other night. Not that I had plumbed the thing to its absolute depths, you understand. Monty's description of his experiences had given me pause and I found myself wondering if I had completely misunderstood the roles of captive and captor when the Brigadier had spoken the other night. Everything was higgledy-piggledy.

'You don't imagine you misunderstood the set-up and, in fact, *you* were supposed to be the captive, do you?'

'I haven't the foggiest, Spence, but I prefer not to think about it any further.'

'Because that's what it looked like from afar.'

'I can well understand it.'

'So,' I said, ominously, 'if that is the case, doesn't this rather mean that you're affianced?'

This didn't register at first, but after swishing and encircling that hollow mind for a moment, it struck with a force of several megatonnes.

'Oh, Heavenly Mother... what if we're engaged?'

'Alas, that would seem to be the implication, old fruit,' I said, consoling the fellow.

'But...' he said, struggling with the unfathomable, 'you don't imagine it was simply a different angle to the ritual, do you?'

'Well,' I said, reminded of a salient parallel, 'the nymph Calypso held Odysseus captive and he was already married. Still, that's women for you.'

This seemed to make him shudder all the more. From his breathing, which had become stertorous in manner, I gathered he was finding this idle speculation singularly unpleasant.

I, meanwhile, was feeling as if the good ship Reason had been whisked up into a maelstrom and everything was in a perpetual spin. I wondered if going back to an earlier point in proceedings might help.

'But just a minute, Monty. When you mentioned a revelation this morning, what was it?'

'For Natalia to be my captive of course.'

'I feared as much.'

I had hoped that I might have erred and misunderstood the thing completely, but no. He had indeed been acting on what he imagined was a true pippin of an idea.

'She had agreed to it, though, I gather, hadn't she?'

He appeared nonplussed.

'How do you mean?'

'You talked it over and such like.'

'Of course not! Did you listen to nothing the Brigadier said?' tutted Monty bluntly. 'The object is to preserve the female's modesty. One has to show subtlety, you barbarian.'

'So, why,' I said, rubbing my temples, 'the communiqué to the Brigadier?'

'Oh, that. It was to ask for the Brigadier's hand, of course. No, wait a minute,' he said, rewinding. 'For Natalia's hand, you ass. Besides, the Brigadier's turn for the worse this morning put paid to any lengthy preamble. She said that as soon as I got him some aid I should hurry back because there was a lodge we could stay in.'

'You mean Skippers' hut?'

'I suppose so.'

I couldn't help feel that the way the night was unfolding, things were now taking on a disquieting hue. I wondered if Monty shared my thoughts.

'Monty, how do you suppose that she knew the whereabouts of such a remote hut?'

He thought for a moment, but was just as fogged.

'I haven't a clue.'

'Hmm.'

After mulling this over some, I saw that the time had come to raise the more pressing matter at hand.

'Well, Monty,' I said, trying to find a tactful way to put it, 'you whisking Natalia off to your enchanted grotto has not, I'm afraid, resulted in the satisfactory ending you had hoped for. As things stand now, only a biblical retribution could eclipse your present troubles.'

I expected it would take a moment to sink in gently, but Monty does try the patience sometimes.

'Enchanted blotto? What is this gobbledygook, Spence?'

So much for the gentle approach. There seemed nothing for it but to put the predicament to him straight from the shoulder.

'Your prospects have been placed on a knife edge and you are facing a lengthy stretch in clink over this business. Your only option, as I see it, is to emigrate to Russia and grow a bushy beard to match your generally unkempt aspect.'

'What on earth—'

'From there, follow the sound of howling wolves until you reach the Caucasus and your new homeland of Georgia where they may accept you as one of their own. I shouldn't think it likely, but there it is.'

'Spencer, old man, will you curb this tommyrot and Old Testament stuff and tell me what you're talking about? My ticker is already palpitating erratically.'

'Very well,' I said, spelling it out for the man. 'Glossing over the fact that Natalia harbours the yet-to-be-named condition of longing to be kidnapped, the fact that she lured someone dunderheaded enough to take her up on it is the more pressing issue. Your note signed "her unworthy captor", found by the staff at the infirmary, soon reached the local constabulary and set off a detonation. They, unless you didn't know, take a dim view of holding people captive – for love or otherwise. I myself was interrogated by a man who has clearly forsaken family life for the cause and was, I suspect, amongst that search party now who entered the hut.'

By the heaving noises emanating from him, I took it that my words were taking effect and the gravity of the situation was beginning to dawn.

'Oh my giddy—'

'Oh, yes,' I continued, unveiling the full weight of the consequences, 'only this afternoon Chief Inspector Bartlett mentioned launching a national campaign, so as of an hour ago, I should think you are probably Britain's most wanted man.'

'Spencer!'

I was wondering if I'd missed anything out when he sidetracked my train of thought.

'Stop!'

'Oh, right you are.'

I began breathing meditatively, drinking in the air, and was just about to comment on the freshness of the forest at night when he piped up again.

'No, I mean, stop tying me up in knots. What am I to do?'

He rather had me there. My earlier thinking had concentrated entirely on letting him have it with both barrels; it hadn't extended to how to extricate him from the predicament. 'There you have me, old man,' I said. 'I was merely sent to give you the bleak news.'

He seemed stumped.

'So, you only came out to be the messenger?'

This seemed to me to sum up the gist perfectly.

'Like Hermes,' I said, 'only without the theft.'

'Sent by whom?'

'Magda, of course.'

He shrieked.

'Oh, that reminds me.'

'Ow!'

'That's from the lady herself,' I said, honouring the contract. 'And I'd say it's just an amuse-bouche to what Sir Walter will do.'

The air was rent with another shriek.

'You mean he knows?'

'Of course.'

'Well, trust you, Francis Spencer Lockwood, to land me right in it!'

'Me?' I said, staggered over the man's ingratitude.

'Don't you see what you've done, you blundering clot?' he continued. 'I would have been better off being discovered by the police. They could hardly have looked askance at the fellow when *he's* the one strapped to a chair.'

I bridled at first, but I pondered for a moment and I had to admit that there was something in this objection. But hindsight, as they say, is a wonderful thing.

'That's spilt milk under the bridge, old man. The more pressing question now is whether to take the ferry from Dover or hop on as a stowaway and dive out when you smell French cuisine. Or would you prefer the Emerald Isle?'

He began repenting for his sins and chanting 'Oh my God' like the dickens.

'Well,' I said, 'if you will insist on revelling in these Byronic fantasies—'

'Spencer!'

He spent the next few minutes pleading to a higher power and begging for a new lease if he promised to live a blameless life. In the process he confessed to an impressive tally of misdeeds that he'd racked up in his time, some of which came as a total surprise to me. While Monty was bargaining for his soul I drifted into the sort of torpor that can be found on the faces of the flock at chapel. And in this meditative, reflective frame of mind, I found myself going over the breadcrumbs of our recent exchange and there I stumbled upon a minor point we'd overlooked.

'Monty,' I said, interrupting his vows, 'there's a little something we glossed over in our recent conversation.'

He wiped the back of his hand across his mouth to stem the flow.

'Oh?' he said, stifling his blubbing. 'What?'

'Why the devil was Natalia shooting at us?'

It seemed to take his mind off his troubles for the nonce and he began scratching the side of his head at this conundrum.

'I mean, it's merely guesswork,' I continued, thinking aloud, 'but assuming that your being strapped to a chair and gagged was mere boisterous horseplay, some might feel that trying to ping one from long range was rather stretching a point. Wouldn't you say?'

He seemed to be reliving the moment in his mind.

'Yes,' he said reflectively, 'there was a certain coarseness that we could have done without.'

I agreed wholeheartedly. 'Contravened the bounds of acceptability.'

'Ungentlemanly of her,' he said.

'In the extreme.'

'Not cricket.'

'Far from it,' I said.

He began grinding his jaws as if stewing on this side of the affair.

'Do you know, Spence, well, I'll say it. The more I think about it, the more it was a beastly thing to do, what?'

'Certainly was.'

'I mean, we didn't even gag Rufus.'

'What! You were invited?'

The blighter ignored me.

'That was just innocent high jinks.'

For some moments after I tried to bring him onto the whys and wherefores of the thing, but he was now fixated.

'And to think I was considering toasting my chestnuts with that lady.'

He might've brooded indefinitely but far off in the distance we heard the teeth-chattering cacophony of the search and rescue unit approaching. Coming upon us like a rude awakening, we leapt to our feet and Monty began bleating about what we should do. Here, I felt we had come to an unpleasant cross-roads in our lives where our routes must sadly fork.

'Alas, Monty, I fear this is where we part.'

'Eh?'

'My kismet is to return to institute life, such as it is, and yours, I'm afraid, is to take refuge in the Kremlin. So long, old man. The few minutes' head start may prove decisive.'

An awkward silence ensued during which I was thoroughly expecting him to embrace me like a brother and thank me for everything over the years, but instead he took several deep breaths and spoke in a cold and measured way.

'Spencer, I think our paths are more entwined than you imagine. In fact, they are inextricably bound in law.'

'Huh?'

'If the constabulary make a complete pig's breakfast of the situation, as I expect them to, they will see your involvement at the hut as aiding and abetting my escape.'

I thought it typical that Monty should hurl such an artillery shell at one's best-laid plans.

'Then let's have no more of this moonshine,' I said, springing like billy-o.

He followed in my wake.

Chapter Twelve

By sticking to the fringes of the forest we were able to needle our way back through the thickets swiftly to the institute. I daresay Monty's idea of deflating the tyres of the police vehicles, which I thought unseemly for a gentleman, I now see was invaluable in keeping us one step ahead of the convoy.

As we fetched up at the grounds, I remember expecting to be greeted by an impregnable barrier of police officials standing on watchful sentry duty, but as we peered over the stone fence to the estate, it was clear there wasn't a single bobby in sight. If anything, the estate seemed much like any other night. Eerily so. Faint sounds of music and chattering voices drifted to our ears, no doubt from the usual rabble of merrymakers who had spilled out into the garden to enjoy the clement night.

Even so, standing on the perimeter, this taste of the familiar did little to settle our jangling nerves.

'Well?' said Monty, anxiously.

'Hmm?'

'What now?'

'Good question,' I said, pensively, for this is as far as my plan had stretched.

'Come on, man,' said Monty, tetchily, 'my insides feel as though they're rearranging themselves.'

'I'm hardly tickety-boo myself, old man,' I said. 'I'm thinking.'

With everything at sixes and sevens and us having to flee under the cosh, there hadn't been much time for meticulous forethought. Now we were poised to enter the belly of the beast without a clue what to do next. What seemed paramount to me was to get the latest information on the dragnet from Magda. That paragon of elbow grease and perspicacity provided the only beacon that I could see before us.

'Magda,' I muttered.

'Eh?'

'She's your best hope.'

'Mine?'

'OK, *our* best hope.'

'But Magda?'

'You know as well as I do that nothing gets put into operation without her being aware of it. After all,' I said, 'she's the keeper at this zoo. The steward of the estate. We must leave it to Mother. She'll set us abreast.'

'But she'll have my guts for garters.'

Magda never lacks for zip and ginger at the best of times, but during times of high emotion the most adamantine of men would do well to mark the exits and escape routes. Still, I felt, this was a storm which had to be weathered.

'Better than Inspector Fletcher, old man. Trust me.'

With the faint light of the estate bouncing off his features, I was able to take in his visage again and I could see he baulked at the idea of getting within throttling distance of Magda.

'Oh hell,' he said, his voice tremulous at the prospect. 'Why don't I stay here? You go in, speak to her and get the latest.'

Here I braced myself to let the man down gently. I mean, while most of our journey back to the estate had been spent in gloomy silence trying to avoid coming a cropper in the vegetation, truth be told, a certain inevitability about Monty's situation had begun to dawn on me. After all, even the most skilled fugitive, when it comes to evasion, is only operating on borrowed time.

'My dear fellow,' I said, speaking openly, 'how you have managed to boil the oceans I'm still unable to fathom, let alone explain. So, Magda must hear of your machinations from the horse's own mouth, so to speak. She will also lend a valuable female ear. Then you may know how to pull yourself out of the abyss.'

He gulped hard and steeled himself. An instant later he nodded.

'By Jove, Spencer, I believe you're right,' he said, patting me on the shoulder.

For the first time since he'd learned of his tribulations, I felt perhaps here was a glimmer of pluck and spirit.

'Lead the way,' he said.

So much for fortitude. Still, I scampered on into the grounds under the moonlight and we managed to edge round the tennis courts, across the lawn and past Dowe House without setting off any police sirens. Had there been any stargazers at Lockwood they would have stood a sporting chance of observing in their peripheral vision the sight of two hunched figures flitting between equipment shed, store house and tree trunks with one of them taking a toss over a croquet hoop along the way.

Encouraged at having come this far, we hared along the flank towards the terrace, the hubbub growing louder with each step. Slowing as we reached the shrubbery, the full effect of the attendees was carried over to us. My word! It seemed as if half the multitude had strewn themselves over the stone steps to while away the night. Someone with his back to us, just visible through the French window, was tickling the ivories playing a moody sonata.

I was scanning the populace for Magda when my eye was drawn to a flicker of movement in the upper storeys and, looking up, I perceived a set of bulging contours silhouetted on a window blind. There was something singularly arresting about the outline of the figure and I was within a whisker of uncovering why it held me transfixed when it shot up to reveal Sir Walter in his evening polka-dot smoking jacket with his irrepressible walrus moustache sprouting out of its netting, which I took to mean he was retiring for the night. But by the manner in which he thrust his balding dome out of the window to peer at the frivolities and contorted his face in disgust, even from a distance, one could see here was a man who was in total sympathy with my fellow rail companion that something ought to be done about this abominable generation. As he began tapping the ash from his pipe onto the revellers below as token of indignation, I felt a tap on the arm.

'I don't see Magda,' whispered Monty. 'Do you?'

'Afraid not,' I said, studying the masses. 'But duty never ends, remember, so if she's not here, she'll be—'

'In her office!' he said, as if uncovering the clue to a riddle. 'Come, Spencer. We can't sit listening to Chopin's Funeral March all night.'

And leaving me stunned at this rare show of mother wit, he scampered for the bushes for thicker cover and we circled round towards the fountain. I was growing pretty fed up of skulking about in the undergrowth like an undiscovered sub-species out of step with time and I had all but caught up with Monty, when an unearthly shriek shattered the quiet and he barrelled into me like a kangaroo tot thrashing to find its mother's pouch. We froze in horror at a veiled wraithlike female figure standing motionless beside the fountain, directing a piercing look in our general vicinity. A full-length dress hung off her skeletal frame. It was a chilling presence. I recognised it at once as Kristina. Standing beside her was a gentleman of somewhat broad aspect, his identity obscured by the outdoor lights behind them.

Monty and I held our breath, careful not to move a muscle and, save for the twitching of Monty's ear and the racing of our heartbeats, not a peep escaped us for the agonising few moments spent locked in those penetrating rays. Eventually, their bearing softened and, dismissing the rustling as a fox perhaps, they resumed their whispered conversation, which was inaudible to our ears.

Monty and I breathed more easily.

'Spence,' he said, 'who is this priestess of Hades?'

'Shh.'

Monty has never really mastered the art of whispering.

'That's Kristina.'

'What!'

This exclamation might've been enough to reveal us, so with a hand I cupped his mouth like an insurgent on enemy lines calming a comrade lest he give away our position.

The fountain was a picturesque spot long favoured by young hearts looking for somewhere to exchange sensuous little touches and giggles; and in every particular, it seemed that we had stumbled upon precisely that. But having seen Sir Walter only a few moments ago retiring for bed, I must say this sight greatly distressed me. It was no secret that I had never been what you might call simpatico with the old commandant. In fact, one might say that life was one long exercise in eschewing his ghastly wheezes and escaping his wrath in some fashion, but nevertheless, there was only one conclusion to be drawn from the beastly scene before me. And perhaps it was the little time I'd spent sleeping through the half-remembered sermons from Uncle Cedric, but I held firm views when it came to playing away. I was stirred to my core.

I was still contending with this emotion when the sudden lighting of a cigarette by the man delivered a jolt that made my blood run cold. This brief flash had illuminated the man's features. It was Nikola from the Sabauri Chamber Ensemble. The blackguard!

'What the devil?' muttered Monty under my smothering hand.

As we watched this spectacle unfold, with every fibre of my being I was willing Kristina to sling her champagne into the man's eye just as Eva had done at the soirée, but from the way she beamed over his attentions, I concluded that this was wishful thinking. He whispered sweet words and she giggled coyly while, hidden from view, I watched on with a sick fascination.

What with one thing and another, the mind positively boggled. Surely, I told myself, any right-minded person seeing his conduct at the soirée and the music room had to recognise that this violinist was a rotter of the highest order. I writhed at this torrid exhibition, but my dismay was outweighed by the curiosity that burned within me. I had to find out more.

Bidding the clodhopping Monty to stay still, I edged closer towards them and settled into a crouch to listen intently.

The odd word drifted over, but nothing of import or interest, and perhaps on account of the chill in the air or the late hour, they abruptly ended their tryst and walked away together briskly. For some time afterwards I remained rooted to the spot as though at the epicentre of some mind-spinning intrigue. With the toll of the past forty-eight hours exacting its full effect on me, my mind was now engulfed by a phalanx of questions. I ambled despondently back to Monty, my head hanging low, watching every step, when there came a loud rustling and before I could trace it I was dealt a heavy blow on the head.

I vaguely recall staggering towards the fountain and collapsing before everything turned black.

***

Sir Walter tells me you can't move in the metropolis for the blot of unconscious blighters littering the pavement. He maintains that the authorities ought to drape lengths of soft carpeting over the fellows to form a squidgy walkway for the weary traveller, but not everyone is so public-spirited. Born Samaritans would, I suspect, first attempt the folly of resuscitation using, amongst the many common methods of reviving the incapacitated, either a dose of smelling salts under the nostrils or a series of hard slaps to the face (if an actual fish tail isn't at hand).

But Magda has never much gone in for the common touch. No doubt that was why, on her nightly inspection of the grounds, when she discovered me lying prostrate beside the fountain the first thing she did, after kicking off her shoes, was to stand directly over me with the garden hose aimed squarely at my unconscious face, swivel the supply until a torrent gushed from it sufficient to reach a twelve storey window, and let loose several gallons of high-pressure jet at the spot. She stopped the flow when it came to her notice, through my spluttering and flailing, that I might be drowning. After this drenching, she dragged me by my arms to a spot that hadn't become a water-soaked marsh and gently enquired after me.

'Where the devil have you been?' she said, shaking me furiously. 'I've been looking all over for you.'

To hasten my recovery, she tried the other method of revival when people are deemed gripped by hysteria, and a few of these hard palms to the cheeks soon brought life stinging back. In her generous reflections, I've heard Magda say I babbled something which was the gurgle of a man whose faculties have yet to follow. During less charitable reflections, she recalls my articulations as those of a lowland primate.

'Argshqubewhmmm?'

She leaned down and sniffed.

'Have you been drinking?'

'Eh?'

'Come on. I'll take you to your bedroom.'

'Now, now!' I said, surging back to life. 'Steady.'

My head was throbbing and a tribal drumming of sorts had begun sharply in my temporal areas.

'We really must do something about your narcolepsy.'

'Oh, my—'

'What happened? Where's Monty?'

'Head.'

'What happened?'

I held up a restraining hand to stem the bombardment while I collected myself.

'What time is it?' I said.

'One o'clock in the morning.'

'What!'

I must have been out for some considerable time. Things were still foggy, but the mist was beginning to clear. I remembered seeing Kristina and Nikola enjoying a tryst, but given the delicacy of the situation, I refrained from mentioning it.

'Monty and I were coming to find you. Ow!'

'Go on,' she insisted, impatiently.

I gave a short précis of what had transpired at the hut and of how we had crept back to the estate, like members of the underworld, to find her.

'Monty and I were a few steps apart. Then there was a rustle in the bushes. I went back and that's all I remember.'

'You didn't see who hit you?'

'Besides you, you mean?'

I closed my eyes to try to recollect, but couldn't. Then I shook my head and immediately wished I hadn't.

'Urgh. Could it have been the police?' I asked, groggily. 'The urge to employ the truncheon becomes irresistible after a time—'

'Then they would hardly leave you where you fell,' she said, tutting.

I couldn't fault her on this point. It seemed in violation of all natural laws to cosh a blighter and not revel in the pleasure of booking the fellow.

'So, Monty knows his position?' she asked.

'Yes.'

'OK. Sit up,' she said, wrenching my upper half up. 'Where is he?'

I looked round desperately.

'I haven't the dickens,' I said, half-remembering an earlier conversation, 'but I think he mentioned setting out across the Russian steppes to start afresh for his adoptive homeland. So, perhaps he went to his room to get packing.'

'Well, if he did he would have run straight into Constable Simmons.'

'Eh. Why?'

'He's standing guard in case Monty returns.'

'Standing guard?'

'Yes.'

'Like a sentinel?'

'Exactly.'

I shuddered. The thought that the rozzers were camped outside Monty's room was a spine-chilling one that did nothing to improve his prospects.

'He was stationed on guard while the others went out searching for Monty and Natalia. I'm expecting them to pass through here to provide a report.'

I was unable to follow her reasoning.

'What for, if Constable Simmons is already on the premises?'

'Well, to inform the Brigadier that Natalia is safe of course.'

'Oh, yes, of course.'

I'd forgotten how the poor fellow must've been fretting over this Natalia business.

'OK. Up you get,' she said, grappling with my arms. 'Let's apply some dressing to your head.'

With a herculean effort I rose to my feet and we set off. I tottered at first, but after a short while, managed to stride, albeit gingerly. As we passed along the terrace Magda snapped furiously at the remaining stragglers, which sent them scuttling back indoors, and we had just turned a corner towards the front aspect of the manor when, just visible under the soft lanterns, she spotted something and bade me to stop.

'What's that?' she said.

'Hmm?'

'The church.'

She drew my attention to the faintest glow of light just visible through the windows of the church.

'Someone's inside,' she said, gripping my arm with alarm.

My first thought that it was Uncle Cedric making another raid on the communion wine, but it never does to wash the family linen in public.

'Probably another tryst,' I said. 'Everyone's up to it. Come. Let's not get distracted by sideshows. Let's press on indoors. You can dress my head and then we can search for Monty. Splitting up, we can cover more ground.'

Under the circumstances, I had outlined what I felt was a lucid and tactical plan of operation, which usually never fails to appeal to Magda's practical mind, but from her manner it became clear to me that she found it less than scintillating stuff. I guessed as much when I noted from her squinting into the darkness that she hadn't in fact been listening. Instead she was eyeing the church like a cocker spaniel spotting something twitching in the bushes. We both stood fixed to the spot in silence. She seemed unduly aghast and I stood yawning after a trying day.

'Spencer, do you have your torch from earlier?'

'Yes.'

'Would you help me if I needed it?'

I was taken aback by the question.

'Of course, old thing, you know that.'

'Good,' she said. 'In that case you can accompany me to the church.'

Egad! Visions of us walking up the aisle were sent soaring into my subconscious, which was more than my delicate state could fathom. The ground beneath my feet heaved like a boat on rough seas. Taking a firm grip she steadied me.

'We must investigate.'

The shock faded and I grasped her meaning. I recoiled from the prospect and put my foot down.

'No, I'm sorry, Magda, but Father Time long ago rang the bell on this wretched day. The body is pooped, the mind is sapped and my capacity to entertain another of your dizzying escapades at this hour is zero.'

I spoke strongly on the matter, but not, I felt, without justification. But when Magda has picked up the scent, she does not relent. And by the way she had begun clicking her knuckles, her gaze fixed on the church, it was clear there was something stirring her intuition and beckoning her.

'Spencer,' she said, once again dropping to her lower registers, 'we will return to the Monty question imminently, but at this moment, foul play is under way. I can feel it.'

'Well, we shall discover what it was in the morning.'

'You don't want to investigate?'

'I do not.'

After adjusting her shawl she glowered at me.

'Well, I do.'

I'd come to learn at an early age that beneath shawls usually lie sharp talons, but I held firm.

'Well, I do not.'

'You would send a woman alone? You should be ashamed.'

There it was again. The bane of my existence. This remark was now passing from her lips so readily that she had almost become a stepmother figure to me; and a perpetually disgruntled one at that. And I daresay I found this approach unbecoming and beneath her. Not least because I had seen Magda send platoons of rowdy layabouts fleeing simply by spitting on her hands and cracking her knuckles while fixing them in a death stare, so if she did stumble upon someone lurking in the church, it was the prowler who had my sympathies. But the man who sends women into dark buildings to investigate prowlers alone loses all claim to chivalry, so of course I relented.

'Fine. But first let me say that I see that you are a woman…' I said, yawning for the day's exertions had been brutal, 'of determination.'

I extended a hand so that we might swear an oath.

'So, let us swear that after this—'

She'd lost interest and gone.

I scampered after her and drew up by her side, but with each step I couldn't help feel that we were becoming needlessly distracted from our main goal. Monty's fate seemed to be slipping from stark to singularly bleak and here we were, torch in hand, creeping up on someone who in all probability had snuck into church hoping to see the light. It beggared belief.

We passed into the unlit churchyard when Magda halted suddenly, gripping my arm like a viper. She leaned in conspiratorially and spoke in hushed tones.

'Spencer, do try to curb your breathing. There,' she said, indicating the rustic wooden side door. 'Go on.'

The sight of it made my blood run cold.

'But, that's the Devil's Door,' I said.

At the time I'm certain she didn't know what this was, but not liking the sound of it one bit, she took up a position of safety behind me.

'Go on,' she said, shoving me in the back.

I knew only too well what it was. During our childhood Monty and I had been the sort of heathens that would play knock-knock-ginger on the Devil's Door and the subsequent strife that had come our way since had convinced me of the curse we had wrought upon ourselves. So, the thought of asking el diablo for 'the same again, please' was a bone-chilling one. There was also a part of me that wondered if Monty hadn't, on reflection, decided to steal away for his new Soviet homeland and as I faced this grisly prospect before me, I began to envy the fellow. At least he wasn't being asked to rattle the cage of Lucifer.

'But you can't,' I protested.

'Spencer!'

Magda has never been one to brook objections, however well-reasoned the argument. So, gulping hard and with my teeth chattering, I ploughed on and we skulked across the unkempt grass. Glancing up at the bell tower, I couldn't help reflecting on the desperate souls who, over the ages, had retreated to this place of sanctuary. We surmounted the small stone wall and trod carefully along the unused footpath until we arrived at the door.

'Now what?' I whispered.

She shooed me aside as if I were an undesirable obstructing the box office. Then with the lissom wrist of a house-breaker she began turning the doorknob and, with the tiniest of clicks, it opened. I'd been expecting a peal of thunder and a sinister voice bellowing from the clouds cursing me for eternity, but nothing came. Only a bomb disposer hearing the ticking stop could have surpassed my ecstasy at that moment.

I was still basking in it when, from within, an arm suddenly wrenched me inside and a hand with long fingers cupped my mouth, just as I had done to Monty. As I writhed in panic, my hand fell on its face and I had just discerned a familiar nose when down came a set of teeth and nipped my finger. Thank heavens. It was only Magda.

'Shh,' she whispered.

We leaned perfectly still against the wall, holding our breath and standing underneath about a foot of porch. Beyond us just visible in the darkness was the altar and around the corner of stone wall was the nave. As my drumming heartbeat hushed I discerned footsteps pacing along the south side of the church and the occasional shuffling noise. Whoever it was who'd snuck in to cleanse their soul, I thought, must have a lot on their mind.

Judging the noise to be sufficiently far away for a glance, we each took a deep breath and dared to peer round the corner. Nothing could have prepared me for what I saw. The sight that had seared itself upon the retinas knocked me for six and it was all I could do to remain upright. Pacing nervously around a dim oil lamp was the Brigadier. He was holding a gaming rifle and beside him seated on a nearby pew bound and gagged for a second time tonight was the forlorn figure of Monty.

Well, I mean to say, I was dumbstruck. And from the way Magda's head jerked back, I suspected that a definite shockwave was passing through her, too. Upon my word, I never knew a man for getting himself in such a knot.

My first thought was that the Brigadier, having run into Monty on the grounds, had given in to rage and was exacting a retribution for dosing him and tying him to a donkey for rough passage across miles of forest. Many folks, I reasoned, would've needed much less provocation. I, for instance, having experienced the former of these first hand, could certainly sympathise with the goal of his campaign even if I found his methods slightly over the odds. Doubtless the Brigadier had decided it was time someone acted in the public good and dealt with this menace.

I was still laying the particulars to this conjecture, wondering where it ranked amongst Monty's exploits, when, against all imagining, from the south entrance, the door opened and there on the threshold stood the eerily thin, shadowy outline of Kristina. Catching the Brigadier as his back was turned, he spun and yowled in fright at this sudden apparition intruding into his vigil. Then as she seemed to float in the darkness towards him he cowered with the terror of a man who sees in the spectre before him an agent of doom. A moment later, the spell was broken when through the open door stepped Nikola.

Perhaps I'd sustained one too many blows to the head, but I couldn't follow these scenes. For a fleeting second I imagined that the Brigadier was going to dust off the cobwebs of the church organ and these ear-torturers were planning to inflict an infernal rendition upon their captive audience member, stopping only when his shrieks gave out through exhaustion, but after checking without, Nikola closed the door and Kristina shuffled forward into the glow of the lantern. From the waist up, she, too, had been bound and gagged.

Had I come upon this ghoulish vision afresh, without the mind-bogglingly peculiar happenings before it, I mean, the cold shock might've pushed me into full-blown hysteria, but coming after a series of mind-warping phenomena meant I merely teetered on the brink.

As for Magda, I had been standing close enough to her that every so often her untameable mop of hair would tickle my nose, but now,

I was conscious only of the heat rising off her, no doubt from the turmoil and rage surging within her. We looked on frozen by this harrowing sight.

'You took your time,' said the Brigadier, clearly agitated.

'You'll never believe this,' said Nikola, uneasily, as if this was entirely against expectations. 'But I just saw Natalia in the lobby.'

'What!'

'There were two police constables with her.'

'But—'

'Don't worry. They've gone. They wished her good night and left. I asked her to meet us here. She'll be here any minute.'

'Thanks God,' said the Brigadier, lighting a cigar, his hands beginning to tremble. This seemed so at odds with the aura of gravitas he'd exuded throughout our forest mission that it heightened my growing unease over what was unfolding before us. Nikola also lit a cigarette and soon the nave began filling with smoke. We passed a fraught few moments in this disquietingly murky atmosphere. For the Brigadier, the strain of waiting appeared almost unbearable. He was pacing the floor with the air of a caged animal awaiting some reckoning when the door opened again and someone else entered. It was Natalia, looking flustered and dishevelled.

'Thanks God you're here,' said the Brigadier.

Well, I mean to say, what! This was all too much. The last time I made such little sense of something was a production of *The Canterbury Tales* at the Old Vic. My vision had adjusted enough to see from Magda's contorted expression that she, too, was not following the programme. They all embraced with the relief of parents reunited with their estranged child after an ordeal and no sooner had the greeting concluded than all three of them began speaking over each other. The effect was a chaotic indiscernible din. Waving his arms to stem the emotions, Nikola brought an end to the madness. It was clear that things between them had somehow come to a head.

'But he's here!' said Natalia, goggling at Monty's presence. 'Where was he?'

The Brigadier was cut off before his reply had got going.

'Quiet!' snapped Nikola. 'I want to hear from Natalia first.'

She, meanwhile, had the air of someone who had just passed through her own trying experience.

'What happened?' asked Nikola.

'Well,' she said, trying to arrange her thoughts, 'I was at the hut, in the bathroom, and I heard a disturbance so I took a look. When I emerged he was fleeing.'

'Alone?' asked Nikola.

'No. Someone else was with him.'

Nikola snorted with a ballistic force I didn't know was humanly possible.

'That cursed Spencer again, I expect,' he said, bitterly. 'He arrived at the hut unexpectedly last night. My God! We're here because of you two. We would've been fine if you hadn't let the imbecile roam free and stumble upon it.'

The Brigadier and Natalia exchanged embarrassed looks.

'We wanted to be rid of him,' said the Brigadier.

'Where did you pick up Monty?' asked Natalia.

'Nikola saw him lurking in the gardens,' said the Brigadier.

'I was with Kristina by the fountain. I saw him so we left. I told Valeri to bring him here.'

'And Spencer? Where is he now?'

'I left him lying on the ground over by the fountain,' said the Brigadier.

Nikola curbed these digressions with a petulant 'pah!'

'He is not important. What happened with the police?'

Natalia was evidently astonished at the turn events had taken.

'They found the hut! I was still undressed when they burst in. I was petrified. I screamed the roof off. They asked me where Monty was and I said he'd disappeared moments ago. "Clever swine," one of them said. Then they kept patting me, saying, "there, there" and what a "frightful ordeal" I'd had. They dropped me here, told me to sleep well and to go to the station tomorrow to make a statement. Goodness knows what for.'

The Brigadier offered the explanation.

'The police arrived to *free* you,' he said, 'not arrest you.'

She appeared unable to follow this train of thought.

'Free me? From what?'

'From this knave,' said the Brigadier, directing a few frothy oaths at Monty in Georgian.

Natalia knitted her brow again.

'But why?'

'Well, for abducting you of course,' said the Brigadier.

Her expression now deepened to one of concern for her aged companion, as if she feared that senility had set in and twisted his words into some unintelligible hogwash.

'Abducting me?' she said, studying their faces sedulously.

Then she turned to Monty.

'When did he do that?'

A stunned expression passed over their faces, as if the rug was being wrenched from beneath their feet.

'The reprobate said he did,' fumed the Brigadier, 'in his note.'

'What note?' she said, becoming more mystified by the second.

What Magda made of this fiasco only she could tell – we've never discussed the finer points of this experience in great depth – but what seemed abundantly clear to me was that this ensemble had been reduced to a wreck of discombobulation. And in ways that escaped us all, Monty was the catalyst.

The Brigadier lunged towards Monty and began frantically undoing his gag. I didn't think it was possible for him to be stirred more than the time we'd called him a dictator, but I stood corrected.

'What was the meaning of your beastly note?'

'Well,' said Monty, clearing the larynx and flexing the vocal cords, 'it was to ask you for her hand, of course. As happened to her friend, just as you told us. In the time-honoured tradition and all that.'

This disclosure seemed to hang in the air for an age. It was just as well because, from the way the trio traded glances first of bewilderment, then denial and finally disbelief, it was clear they needed these precious seconds. So far, the mood had been one of cloak and dagger seriousness, but when the full implications of Monty's admission had been through all its necessary stages of impact, what began as a seep of air from Natalia was followed by an involuntary expulsion from Nikola, and with more synchronicity than they'd managed during past performances, all three erupted into a chorus of spleen-rupturing laughter that any self-respecting clergy would warn was likely to wake the dead. And in the middle of it all was that chucklehead Monty, his shoulders bouncing, laughing along with them, caught up in the infectiousness of it all. Only Magda, Kristina and I were left in limbo wondering what Monty's epic clanger had to do with the rest of it.

Magda and I stood watching this exhibition with the sickening sense of déjà vu having already come upon this revelation, but at a glance, I must say, it seemed a lot more diverting to them than it had to us. As the hilarity dwindled and the trio collected themselves, it was the Brigadier who spoke first. The thunderous laughter had evidently had a cathartic, uplifting effect on his spirit. His struggle to contain his amusement was such that when he now spoke, it was almost in the soprano range.

'And all this time,' he said, barely holding himself together, 'we've been trying to abduct *you*.'

This sparked the loudest single roar of laughter of the lot, with the Brigadier's deep bass baritone shaking the church to its foundations.

While the trio were splitting their sides, we four struggled to comprehend the skulduggery that had just been unmasked and I, for one, was feeling as if I'd been sitting on a powder keg and the Brigadier has just lit the fuse.

We were still reeling with this detonation when Natalia brought the conversation round again with her inquisitive note of earlier. This time she was interested in Kristina.

'What's she doing here?'

'Insurance,' said Nikola.

'Hmm?'

'Monty, Lockwood's famous *favourite son*,' he said, with a grand wave in Monty's direction, 'is now a disgraced kidnapper. So, there is no chance that Sir Walter will pay a ransom for him. She is our alternative.'

He looked pitifully at Kristina, who had been sitting meekly, sobbing through her gag. Unlike Monty, her fearful eyes were enough to convince me she was under no illusions. Somehow she had become a bargaining chip. This proved the final straw for Magda. An involuntary spasm sent her hands into the air and in a split-second, seeing her struggle to contain this ripple, I silently manoeuvred her out into the open. She'd been rocked to her absolute depths.

Chapter Thirteen

WE scrambled to a safe distance and in the few seconds we spent gasping from the shock, the brisk night air helped align the pieces and I formed a view as to the grisly events that had befallen us. Events that spanned as far back as our expedition, which I now suspected had been a ruse to lure Lockwood's *favourite son* under his own steam away from the confines of the institute grounds and eventually towards the hut with the express purpose of holding onto him to extract a fat pile from Sir Walter. I remembered how blithe they'd been when I insisted on returning to the manor at night. No doubt, I'd been an interloper ever since our campfire chat had established that Monty merited the dubious title more than me.

What the trio hadn't bargained for, however, was Monty excelling himself. Since framing himself as Britain's most carefree abductor – the daredevil who leaves a calling card – he had not only precipitated a manhunt for himself, but his value as a hostage, like a stock on Wall Street after Black Monday, had tanked completely. No upstanding and reputable knight of the realm, or even Sir Walter, would pay a ransom to recover a self-confessed kidnapper. Hence poor Kristina had become embroiled in this mesh.

I endeavoured to set Magda abreast, but she checked me in no uncertain fashion.

'Shh. I followed everything. This is no time for dithering. You just keep an eye on them. And don't fall asleep!'

Picking up her shoes, she raced away as if she were a parliamentary guard who's stumbled upon the Gunpowder Plot. I was left holding the fort. This was not the time, I felt, for division. Sticking together was why I wanted us to take an oath.

As I sneaked back to our earlier place of concealment to watch the clique, I was a deeply troubled man. As I tuned in, I found

Monty ungagged and trying to arrange the disparate threads. Uppermost in his mind seemed to be the elopement ploy for which he had lost the taste, while Nikola was rubbing his temples with the air of a man coming up against the Monty faculties for the first time.

'So, we're not engaged?'

'No!' shouted the trio in unison.

Monty brightened as if the royal order for his execution had been rescinded.

'Oh, my good lord, I say. Heaven have mercy, what? I mean, gosh.'

This seemed to bring him onto his present position, which he evidently still hadn't grasped.

'Well, if you no longer need me—'

'But we do need you.'

'But I thought you said it all amounted to nil.'

'Monty,' said Natalia, trying to get the message across, '*you* are the hostage, not me.'

He gulped as if trying to swallow a golf ball. An awkward moment ensued.

'But why,' he said, 'if we're not tying the knot?'

I studied Nikola's countenance and to this day I believe he was thinking it would be easier for all concerned to just throttle Monty.

'Mr Fipps,' he said, impatiently, 'you are a wanted man. That is not our doing. That is your own genius. And you would be arrested instantly. But this presents a wonderful opportunity that we would be mad to pass up.'

'It is a gift horse,' said the Brigadier, kissing his fingertips.

'Suppose,' said Nikola, 'Natalia's kidnapper, while at large, takes another victim…'

He turned suggestively to Kristina. The malevolence of this surged through me like an electric current. One look at Monty's gormless countenance was enough to convince me that he hadn't realised the dastardly consequences – he would be implicated for a second abduction. And while the police scoured the four corners for serial abductor Edgar Montgomery Fipps, this trio would, in all probability, slip through the net with their ill-gotten gains, leaving Monty squarely in the frame. The despicable cunning inherent in the suggestion floored me.

Lockwood had long been held as an establishment to send whippersnappers who were thought to be lacking somehow in the necessary sheen, so it stands to reason that there should be the occasional reprehensible character passing through its doors, but never had I imagined it to be possible that degeneracy of this magnitude might be perpetrated in our midst. Nor had anything occasioned me quite so much anguish.

'Valeri,' barked Nikola, 'fetch the transport.'

He hopped to command and, after passing the rifle to Natalia, exited hastily.

Magda had gone to fetch the cavalry, so I could only hope she returned before they absconded with Monty and Kristina writhing in torment in the back of a vehicle.

And yet, all the while, Nikola's manner remained gentle.

'Don't worry,' he said, smiling with the assurance of a family clinician, 'no one will harm a hair on your heads. You have my guarantee. It is purely a business transaction.'

He reapplied Monty's gag. The minutes passed in an excruciatingly interminable wait for the moment they would be whisked away to some dreadful dungeon. And I – a bystander to this purgatory – had never before felt such a helpless fool.

The stifling atmosphere hung heavy around us. I had never been what you might call religious, but the fact that this wickedness should be perpetrated in a church struck me as the ultimate sacrilege. In my inertia my eyes came to rest for a while on the altar and my mind feasted on happier occasions that had brought Monty and me here in the past. For a time I became lost to this reverie.

It was these precious few moments that engendered a shift in my outlook. How I longed to put an end to the vicissitudes in which we had all become enmeshed. I had been harbouring bitter, loathsome feelings towards these bounders, but my thoughts now moved beyond this primary emotion towards something more conciliatory. I found myself looking beyond their brutish methods and began to examine the motive – the wretchedness that had driven these roughnecks to pilfer and extort. If only this gaping, even maddening desire could somehow be quenched.

It was during this contemplation that I experienced an intense whizzing sensation pass through me. It was quite overwhelming. I found myself thinking back to the fête and that fellow with the cartouche giving the sermon on the crate about mutual understanding being the bedrock to progress and all that claptrap. It suddenly dawned on me that, as bursar of the institute, I was in the perfect position to broker a resolution to this ghastliness. With institute finances at my disposal, I had the resources to completely overturn this beastly scenario. Nikola had described it coldly as nothing more than a transaction and when I examined it in that dispassionate light I found that I, of all people, held the key. I merely needed to hammer out a deal. The only question remained whether I had the gumption for it. Well, one look at Monty and Kristina in their pitiful state was enough.

Summoning up as much fortitude and resolve as I could muster, I shone the torch on my face and emerged from the shadows with a loud 'Ho!'

They started violently and what emanated from them were some of the ripest expletives that Malta and Georgia have to offer. With hindsight, I ought not to have illuminated my face before stepping out into pitch blackness. The sight of a disembodied head suspended in the air is always guaranteed to startle even the most ardent of churchgoers.

'Who is it?' said Nikola.

Natalia recognised me at once.

'You again!' she said, aiming the rifle at me. 'Why do you so stubbornly refuse to go away?'

I felt this was a trifle thick considering it was my family home and all that, but putting that to one side, I got down to brass tacks.

'It is I, Spencer,' I said, from the shadows, 'and I have what you want.'

In my heightened nervousness, what emerged from my lips was not the voice of authority taking command of a situation, but a croaky, high-pitched plea.

They exchanged fevered glances, their minds running amok.

'How do you know what we want?' asked Natalia.

'A lump sum as a ransom for Kristina,' I said, clearing the throat. 'I know everything.'

They shared glances again and began shuffling nervously, even desperately.

'But you're going about it all wrong,' I said, approaching slowly, arms still aloft.

I had gone half-way when the south door opened and the Brigadier reappeared. Upon seeing me he staggered in the most overwrought manner and stumbled backwards over the step. Perfectly understandable of course. Nobody likes to nip out for a moment only to find the place is filling up with people one dislikes. Least of all the Brigadier, judging by the menacing look he was giving me.

Nikola ordered him to search me and, within an instant, he was upon me frisking me with none of the old warmth of past occasions. He rejoined the ranks and I lowered my arms. Brows furrowed and confusion seemed to abound. I could follow the trajectory of their thoughts. In the blink of an eye an interloper had materialised from the shadows who not only had an intimate knowledge of their detestable schemes, but had the effrontery to suggest improvements.

I was now standing amongst them. In a move I hadn't anticipated, Natalia raised the rifle muzzle to my chin.

'Speak.'

A rifle muzzle thrust into one's chin has a tendency to stifle the fluency somewhat and it was only after an uncomfortably long delay that my power of speech returned.

'I'm the bursar to the institute.'

'So?' she sneered.

So bitterly had she dismissed the insignificant fact of my daily crust that it put the wind up me no end and there came into my demeanour a renewed determination.

'Well,' I said, taking the bull by the proverbial horns, 'cast an eye at the estate. Take a good look. Decrepitude abounds. Imagine the upkeep. Do you seriously imagine there's enough working capital for such a lump sum? No, no, no, no. But there is an alternative.'

Nikola sniggered and the Brigadier snorted scornfully, which put me in mind of Sir Walter whenever I say I have a whopping idea.

'And,' I said, addressing Nikola, 'you strike me as a man of the world.'

'So, what is it you propose?' he said, derisively.

'A counter-offer.'

I paused for a moment to let this sink in.

'I can see to it that you regularly receive a sum that will accumulate to the capital sum you seek now.'

'Tcha!' said Natalia, flicking her hand contemptuously. With the exception of my inner circle and old tutors, never before had I heard disgust expressed so succinctly. To this female nothing I ventured contained an iota of merit. The Brigadier was also viewing me with the suggestion that I ought to be thrashed for making such a contemptible offer. And no doubt he'd deliver a few extra blows for his aggrievances accumulated during our expedition. Only Nikola let show the merest scintilla of interest. His eyes, which before were fixed on me as though I were a blot on an otherwise pleasant evening, softened. His countenance now was one of intrigue.

'Go on.'

'Well,' I continued, 'I'm sure I can conceal things so this regular outlay does not arouse suspicion and I'd happily keep a standing appointment to meet someone of your choosing until we reach the desired amount.'

Nikola looked at me askance and then at his companions, wondering how many screws I had loose.

'Provided,' I continued, 'Kristina is released unharmed, of course.'

Monty began writhing about and stamping his feet loudly.

'And Monty, too, I suppose.'

'But—'

'And, finally, Natalia absolves Monty over this foul business of her abduction. The police are expecting a statement tomorrow. You must simply tell the truth. That you had no knowledge of any abduction.'

She frowned in concentration along with the Brigadier, who was putting the scheme through its paces and examining it from all angles.

'And what's to stop Kristina running to the police?' he asked.

'Well, I'm sure she would do everything in her power to prevent the news of her tryst with Nikola becoming known,' I said, 'especially to Sir Walter.'

The rather shamefaced Kristina nodded frantically.

'And Monty?'

'As you already recognise, Monty would not elicit any sum from Sir Walter. And the police would hardly believe a wanted kidnapper raising the alarm about financial goings on at the institute.'

Nikola gulped. 'And you? What is to buy your silence?' he said.

'Well, I could hardly do that, could I? I would be revealing myself to be the insider responsible for embezzling institute funds. So, as you see, you have a free hand to leave with exactly what you want. And we can avoid all this unpleasantness.'

I could see he was giving my proposition serious consideration.

'How can we guarantee the payments?' he said, dubiously.

'You have my word.'

'Pah!' exclaimed Natalia.

In spite of Natalia pooh-poohing me at every turn and Monty and Kristina both looking at me with disbelief, I was now exuding confidence.

'I tell you,' I said, assertively, 'you will receive nothing by your futile plans. Sir Walter stands to profit much more from Kristina's demise than anyone. The life insurance payout would be a godsend for a man in as much debt as he is.'

I paused to let this chilling fact register.

'So, it's that or nothing, I'm afraid. Think about it,' I said. 'That is my final offer.'

This lingered in the air as I settled back on a pew, basking in what I felt was a masterclass of negotiation. And considering the widely held view that my efforts in this beastly direction sit well below 'mediocre' on the score board, I considered this rare feat nothing short of miraculous. Finally, I had prevailed in this dark and mysterious art. And at the centre of this uncharacteristically bravura display had been a meticulously argued and persuasive case. It prompted the trio to enter into another of their incomprehensibly muddling three-way bouts. I gave up trying to follow the ebb and flow of the debate after a few seconds, but if body language was any indicator, I ventured to believe that Nikola would emerge imminently and extend a hand by way of signalling his acceptance of my proposal. But life, I've found, has a way of putting the boot in when hope reaches its zenith and it was while I was reflecting on my recent effort, wondering, when all was said and done, if this high point in my career entitled me to a peerage and what Sir Walter would make of calling me Lord Spencer when from the sides thundered a familiar gruff, stentorian voice.

'Stand still!'

Of course, everyone leapt out of their skins, but I took the record by a fair margin, with good reason. Sir Walter had entered our presence. Both Natalia and the Brigadier yelled something in their native Georgian while Nikola, their chief negotiator, simply sighed under the weight of yet more complications facing him.

Sir Walter advanced towards us threateningly with gaming rifle extended.

'It's OK, Sir Walter,' I assured him, 'we've struck a deal.'

'Yes, I was listening,' he said, snorting with contempt. 'Deal my foot! There won't be any deal.'

'What!'

I could imagine no more crushing entrance than this. Sir Walter's forceful nature, especially when he gets the bit between his teeth, can pulverise the spirit like a juggernaut flattening a ceramic pot, but little could I have expected him to demolish all hope as spectacularly as this. Truth be told, I resented the intrusion. I mean to say, put yourself in my shoes. My tussles with Mrs Prenderghast and that stall merchant at the fête had left me inauspiciously viewing the art of negotiation as an insurmountable mountain. And I'd been feeling mighty chuffed to have shown such pilgrim's progress at having brokered a peace when he loomed out of the darkness. And he lost no time kicking sand in our faces, or at least mine. I shrivelled at the sight of this formidable form glowering at me so malignantly.

'Remind me,' he snapped, 'how much was the settlement?'

'Eh?'

'How much did you agree?'

He had me stumped from the off. I'd been so busy seeing to the other loose ends that I hadn't given any thought to the trivialities, so I turned to the trio for support.

'Uh, I think we said a sum of your choosing, didn't we, chaps?'

'Indefinitely?' he asked, glowering at me.

Now, I am no stranger to receiving a public dressing down from Sir Walter, and I'm always the first to admit when I've done something to deserve it, but it seemed to me that he was getting warm over a deal which anyone could see, when properly examined across the annals of time, was the equal of Thomas Jefferson snapping up the state of Louisiana for an absolute song.

'I hardly think this is the time for specifics, Sir Walter.'

'Don't you see what you're proposing, you clot?'

I was fogged. He was looking at me as if I were some half-creature pathetically attempting to imitate the ways of humanity.

'You'll ruddy bankrupt the institute!'

'Oh, come now, I'm sure they wouldn't. I mean…'

And before I could finish the thought, the penny dropped.

'Oh my sainted aunt!'

I was still grappling with the mortifying implications of this when Natalia gave me something else to think about.

'I think you mistake the gravity of the situation, Sir Walter,' she said, her rifle now at full-cock and firmly embedded in my cheek.

Upon my word! Things were escalating in the most deplorable fashion and I broke out into a cold sweat.

'Do it!' barked Sir Walter.

'Verrhwhat?' I said, peering desolately in his direction. This is hard to do when a rifle is pressed against your cheek.

Well, I ask you! I don't know if you've ever had a rifle muzzle wedged tight against your cheek by a homicidal female of small but robust form when your father gives the order to let rip, but let me tell you, it cuts deep with a chap. The knees lose all rigidity and a darkness begins to descend. I had barely opened my mouth to say that now was no time to taunt this infernal wildcat when the blood in my head, sensing there may soon be nowhere in which to circulate, began thundering southward and I teetered. A split-second later, as it coursed downward, I felt the rest of me descending with it and, as I grew limp, I became inextricably entangled with Natalia who let off a shot as we came down together in a lopsided crumpled heap.

It was during this that I discerned, through fading faculties, Magda manifesting herself from the Devil's Door with rifle extended. An instant later, in my semi-consciousness, I was aware of Natalia groaning and wriggling beneath me, but also at ground level appeared to be Sir Walter fuming with the most colourful dockyard English that I imagine had ever graced the church in its history. It completely eclipsed any frothy Georgian recently directed at me.

As my senses recovered and I peered through the cloud of smoke engulfing me, I perceived Sir Walter writhing on the floor in throes of agony having been unfortunately placed when Natalia's rifle rang out. He'd taken a loose one in the foot. The Brigadier and Nikola, thinking better of this turn in the odds, were standing with their hands aloft in a picture of confusion and despair.

'Where were you, blast it, when I said "Go on!"?' Sir Walter demanded to know.

Apologies poured out of Magda at an impressive rate.

'I'm so sorry,' she said, her gun still pointed threateningly at Nikola and the Brigadier. 'I moved as fast as I could.'

'Aargha-uh-uh-ah-arrgh-haar-aarghow-argh,' Sir Walter seemed to be saying while Magda issued comforting words to soothe his pangs of distress.

My faculties were still dazed and stunned, but what was sweeping over me at this moment was an array of conflicted emotions. While the commandant thrashed and flailed with his leg in the air, I winced in discomfort at his evident pain, but I was also mightily relieved to understand that far from being the order to dispatch me cleanly, this 'Go on' instruction had been the cue for Magda to leap out brandishing the second weapon, thereby tilting the odds in our favour. And had Natalia not toppled over and fired the cannon into Sir Walter's big toe, it would have been a perfectly worked bit of by-play, so I was admiring this turnaround in fortunes in evident astonishment when a penetrating order came in my direction.

'Spencer!' snapped Magda. 'On your feet. Untie them.'

I gathered up Natalia's rifle and, moving unsteadily, untied Kristina. No sooner had she been released than she scuttled across to burnish Sir Walter with kisses, finding expression in her native Bulgarian along with some first-rate sobbing with each passing step. This seemed to stay Sir Walter's peals and soothe the fellow immeasurably.

'Just stay calm, my darling,' said Kristina, in an affecting show of genuine compassion.

Meanwhile, Magda turned her attentions towards Natalia.

'Go on,' she said, gesturing with the rifle that Natalia should join Nikola and the Brigadier. 'Slowly.'

Having risen to her feet, Natalia now hobbled silently in a defeated sort of manner towards her companions. No words were expressed between them.

Still moving gingerly, I unshackled Monty and he, being a man of unending medical avocations, rushed to administer aid to Sir Walter with something in the style of a tourniquet.

'Here!' he said, clamping the injured extremity in a vice-like grip.

Sir Walter's howling reached a new stratosphere.

'Haar-aarghow-argh-for-God's-Sake-you-son-of-a-barrghaaaha!'

Having received a mighty wallop to the back of the head from Kristina so as to leave Sir Walter in peace, Monty trudged back to me, a little hurt by this rejection of his services, but he quickly brightened coming upon me.

'I thought you showed first-rate sangfroid, old bean,' he said, heartily patting me on the shoulder. 'Shame your wheeze was a stinker.'

He straightened his back and unloosed the frame with the euphoric air of a man released from devilish restraints and he was in the midst of this flexing of the joints, savouring his freedom, when his attentions became drawn to the forlorn-looking trio and he paused these amateur gymnastics. Now, if there is one thing that sullies a dignified moment it's the act of putting the boot in, and this turnaround in our respective fortunes seemed to unleash in him the pent-up aggrieved feelings of a man who's recently been strapped in bondage. I'm only thankful that Sir Walter, having passed out from the pain, never got to hear it.

'Well, *Brigadier*,' said Monty, massaging his wrists, 'if that is in fact your real name, I feel entitled to put it to you that you must give up this lark instanter.'

The Brigadier looked up with a defeated sort of incredulity. I could see that he had resigned himself to no further discussion for the evening, so being drawn into what you had to call 'idle discussion' when things had reached a fait accompli must have struck him as a jar to the senses.

'Lark?' he said, nonplussed.

'I had occasion to observe that dismal racket you were passing off as Chopin earlier, and as a musician myself I say that it was unfit even for the lawless badlands of the Caucasus from where you have no doubt been banished and with good reason. I should think the hurdy-gurdy is more in your line, my man. And while I think of it, as for this other business, well, all I can say is that you have as much calibre for an enterprising wheeze as Spencer has a head for business. It proved a bust and your efforts would've been better spent in tireless practice. Still, the confinement awaiting you should provide ample time to master the basics.'

From the way the Brigadier's jaw muscles began flexing and his complexion appeared to be taking on a distinctly rouge hue, I would have placed a significant sum that he was poised to lunge at Monty and clasp his hands around his throat in the manner Nikola had fantasised about earlier, so I sought to stem this ill-advised taunting.

'Monty,' I said, trying to exude a certain chumminess of manner, 'I think we've passed that, old man—'

'Balderdash, Spencer,' he insisted, resuming where he left off. 'And as for that diabolical, unmelodic dross you inflicted on us at the soirée, well, you would do well to leave that where it originated – as a tune hummed by your toothless gypsy grandmother who I can only imagine was kidnapped by Blackbeard himself. As for the diabolical family tree that resulted, well—'

I daresay that Monty was just warming up when the door flew open and suddenly four police constables trooped in carrying lanterns. It broke the flow. They took one look at the Brigadier, perching menacingly on a pew as if ready to pounce on Monty, and they rushed forth. In an instant they were upon him. After a swift but futile struggle of flailing arms and legs and raised voices, on went the bracelets. Natalia and Nikola were dispatched with more ease, putting up little or no resistance, and from beginning to end, the whole caboodle was over in a blur. Never again will I question the efficacy of the local constabulary. Natalia was the last to be led out.

'Inspector Fletcher for you, Miss Emin,' said the apprehending constable. As he and Natalia stepped out, in clomped Inspector Fletcher. Seeing Monty, his eyes lit up under the glow of his lantern like Shere Khan spotting Mowgli wandering alone.

Suddenly, a chill ran through the place.

'Miss Emin—'

'Yes, I know, Inspector,' said Magda, apologetically, 'I know we agreed that you would apprehend as they left the premises, but there were complications.'

'Yes, we heard,' he said, eyeing her rifle. 'You can put that down now.'

She did.

'Mr Lockwood and Miss Emin, given the hour I won't ask you to come to the station now, but you will need to come first thing for a statement.'

'Eh?' I said. 'What for?'

'So, we can get everything clear.'

'We'll be there,' said Magda.

He turned to Monty.

'Well, Mr Fipps,' he said with barely concealed relish, 'what a pleasant surprise.'

Monty hadn't the foggiest idea what was about to befall him. His shoulders relaxed and he shone as if greeting a long-standing fan of his work.

'Very kind of you,' he said, extending a hand. 'The pleasure's all mine.'

And in the blink of an eye the inspector slipped on a cuff.

'Now, it's mine.'

Before we barely had time to register what had happened the inspector launched into the handbook preamble and began hustling

Monty out over loud and vocal protest. He was led away in between accusations of brutality and crimes against the innocent.

Owing to my loss of consciousness moments earlier, the rest of this eventful evening remains a blur.

Chapter Fourteen

THE next morning, as my bludgeoned senses struggled to cope with the events of the night before, I stirred with an inescapable feeling that while passing too close to a pneumatic tube, I had been sucked in and carried vast distances through a labyrinth and ejected with considerable force. Besides my aching limbs, there was a dull ringing between the ears, as if someone had snuck in during the night and banged the dinner gong beside my ear canal. This, coupled with a parched throat and generally nauseous feeling, meant that it took several minutes of staring up into the blankness of the ceiling before the constituent parts of me started to function as one again.

At first what sprang to mind was just a sense of disarray and half-remembered fragments. The trio. The church. The arrival of the local constabulary. These disparate images seemed to defy all worldly explanation. Eventually, the appalling events began flicking through my mind like a carousel of moving images and it all came back to me. I shuddered as I reflected on what had transpired.

For reasons that may never be understood, Monty had fallen head over heels for Natalia. And upon hearing a campfire yarn of some fading custom of yore that appealed to the inner swashbuckler in him, he had put a scheme into effect which must surely rank as one of the worst brainwaves since the dawn of civilisation. And in the process he had tied his own noose for the abduction of Natalia, who, unbeknownst to us all, along with her nefarious companions, was doing her bit to shanghai him and hold Sir Walter to ransom. What a shower! The culmination of all this being that last night all four of them were pinched.

Natalia had been led meekly away like the little girl facing a roasting for splashing about in the pond. Nikola, too, had been escorted away with his head drooping on its stem as one who is regretting his life choices from childhood. Only the Brigadier had to be subdued like an escapee from a wildlife reservation.

Needless to say, my waking concern was of course for Monty's predicament. Ever since I had first learned of it, a trepidation had got in amongst me. And with Monty now in clink, I felt it even more keenly. I mean to say, when a cousin languishes in durance vile under a charge that would make the Victorians settle into armchairs for the long haul, the gloominess soon sets in. But then as I probed deeper into the affair, I came to the view that it was the trio who faced the real conundrum in this torrid affair. Natalia, by her own admission, hadn't the foggiest clue about Monty's sweeping gesture, and the manner of her departure last night suggested she would come clean, which would automatically absolve Monty from any wrongdoing, restoring his reputation, such as it is, to its former self. On this reflection I felt my spirits rising and a general lightness of mood started to return.

If ever there was a morning where I felt I had earned a lie in, this was it. The mind was lingering on this thought when a maid rapped on my door with considerable vim.

'It's a quarter to ten!' she bawled.

This jolted me back into the land of the living. I couldn't remember having ordered an alarm call last night, so I presumed it was one of Magda's minions put up to the task of rousing me. It had come just as I was breathing a sigh of relief that I didn't have to unravel these interwoven threads when, of course, it was borne in upon me that this was precisely what Inspector Fletcher had asked Magda and me to do this morning by way of making a statement.

So, at ten o'clock, having only had half my quota of shuteye, I breezed down to catch the last serving of breakfast before Magda and I set off on a walk for the station. En route we discussed the whys and wherefores, starting of course with a report on the convalescing commandant who'd been stretchered to the infirmary last night by a couple of beefy lifters. Considering that Magda, having the stronger constitution between us, had accompanied Sir Walter last night while I tooled off to bed, she appeared remarkably bright and zippy this morning. I apprehensively set about instituting enquiries.

'So', I said, clearing the throat, 'well, I mean to say… gosh, I mean, how is the old fellow? No lasting damage, I trust?'

When I considered the possibilities, each more sickening than the last, I must confess, I was already turning a shade of green and wincing before I'd finished the question. I mean to say, when one imagines the loss of a toe, for instance, the public's reaction is usually a glib air of acceptance, as if it's bound to turn up eventually. But linger on the visceral and grisly truth for a second and it's enough to harrow the mind, trigger convulsions in the solar plexus and bring water to the eyes. I braced myself for the worst.

'Nothing that won't heal over time,' she said, matter-of-factly. 'He'll be in a cast today, of course.'

Well, the elation at this news lifted a weight from my shoulders like Sisyphus humping that boulder up the hill for the last time.

'Spiffing news!' I said, relief pouring over me. 'Phew. Thank heavens for that. For a moment, the mind turned to… well, turned to… well, never mind, Magda, old thing. That doesn't bear thinking about. Not when you consider it was a lucky escape in the end. Come to think, it was a close thing in many ways, what?'

She looked away dismissively, making no reply. It was an uncomfortably awkward moment and it gnawed at my better sensibilities. Reading between the lines, I'd say that I'd dropped rather markedly in her estimation after what she perceived as an abdication of responsibility for one's forebear, and doubtless at other times, the circumstances being different, I might've agreed, but she hadn't endured the day I had had. I dared not mention this, of course, for fear of rubbing her up the wrong way and tarnishing what ought to have been a corker of a day. So, we walked on for a few minutes in this strained silence. The morning, after all, was clement and too good to pass up over anything as sour as spilt milk.

Breathing deeply through the nostrils while gazing up at the gently swaying treetops, I found myself without a worry or concern in the world and it had been some time since I could last say that. I found myself musing over Monty's prospects and this brought a smile to my lips, which she spotted, and this produced a smirk on her face. This combined with these few moments of restful relaxed walking appeared to engender a swing towards the more upbeat and lighter frame of mind in Magda.

'Ah,' I said, stifling a yawn, 'yes, it all turned out for the best, what?'

'It will.'

I took this laconic reply to mean she had already turned to the unfinished business of reckoning for the trio and clearing up this frightful mix-up with Monty and Natalia. As to the former, I was a little sad that we could not come to terms, but be that as it may, I firmed my resolve that justice must, I suppose, be done and there I was content to let the matter rest without another thought. But when my own thoughts turned to fraternising freely again with Monty, I found myself gripped by a fever of anticipation and of a heavy burden lifting – not surprising given the weighty fraternal responsibility for the chap that has come to rest on my shoulders. Besides which, I hadn't seen Aunt Beatrice or Uncle Cedric since the Monty crisis had engulfed us and I shuddered to think of the distress they'd been under, so I was expecting the mood later to be one of end-to-end celebration.

'Yes,' I said, my thoughts turning to the upcoming revelry, 'by supper time this evening, I should think he'll be home scot-free.'

'With any luck.'

'Of course, I don't expect you'd agree—'

'I do.'

I stopped in my tracks.

'What?'

She had carried on walking so I caught up to her, trying to match her long stride.

'You mean you agree?'

'I do.'

'With me?'

'Yes.'

'Let me get this right,' I said, eager to ensure no doubt, 'I say that the dark cloud that once hung over Monty's future has disappeared. Do you mean to say that you also subscribe to this view?'

'I do.'

I wished she wouldn't keep saying 'I do'. It does nothing but jar on a fellow. But as to us finally seeing eye to eye, by Jove! you could have knocked me down with a feather. As a rule Magda puts as much stock in my judgement as can fit on the head of a pin, so to be of one mind over such an issue put the cherry on the parfait. We would, I imagined, soon see a chastened Monty joining the league of free gentlemen having narrowly avoided an eye-watering term in the jug. It would be pretty rough on society, admittedly, to have Monty rejoin the ranks, but I fully expected him to emerge a reformed man after this near miss. I inferred from Magda's confident strut that she, too, was brimming with the right stuff this morning. After her fearless display of Boudicca spirit last night, this morning she exuded the aura of a woman who has vanquished the foe and is basking in triumph. It certainly became her.

'Well,' she said, with raised eyebrows.

'In fine fettle, thank you.'

'No. I mean, aren't you going to thank me?'

At first I thought I'd fallen into a reverie and had missed part of the conversation.

'Eh?'

'For arriving when I did.'

'At breakfast?'

She rolled her eyes.

'No, you dolt. Last night.'

'Oh,' I said, getting the gist. 'Certainly. Bravo. Spiffing work.'

'It was nothing.'

'Au contraire.'

'You're too kind.'

'It was a much welcome token of redress.'

She clutched my arm with the grip of a boa constrictor.

'Redress?'

'Yes.'

'Explain.'

'Well, far be it from me to tarnish an impeccable record, Magda,' I said, 'but it was *you* who sent us into the arms of those thugs on that doomed woodland mission in the first place. Fraught with danger would just about describe it. You're cutting off my circulation.'

She released her locking grip and crossed her arms in a belligerent sort of way.

'Oh, really?'

'Indeed. Did you know I was shot at?'

'Sir Walter was shot, Monty was shot at, you were neither. All you did was keel over onto Natalia, causing Sir Walter to get shot in the foot.'

It was typical of Magda to split hairs in this way.

'Ah-ha. Have you forgotten, my expert of operations, that when Monty and I both fled... that is, when I rescued Monty, Natalia went ballistic and began spewing bullets into the open on some spree?'

'Yes, surprising that none of them struck such a big head.'

'Plus, did you know the Brigadier lunged at me with murderous intent?'

'I can well imagine.'

'Did I mention that I was almost savaged by Arkdale's monstrous beasts?

'Well—'

'And,' I said, finding momentum, 'did you know I was almost stung by a battalion of bees?'

'Weren't you?'

'No.'

'Shame,' she said, wistfully.

'I just escaped by the nap of my – what?'

'I'm sure it'll be written up into an epic tale and song.'

'What will?'

'Your odyssey.'

I paused. If not careful, there comes a point in conversations when it becomes clear that one side feels the next course in the debate is to bosh the other with a heavy object and it was borne in upon me that we might soon hit upon that moment. Clearly, in Magda's mind, I hadn't been as unstinting in my praise as perhaps as I ought to have been. So, I took up a more conciliatory line. After all, she had shown considerable aplomb.

'Still, you're right,' I said, 'you did put on a valiant show. And you were right, there was something as foul as the ninth circle unfolding in the church. So, that thanks goes to you.'

Her glare softened into a radiant smile and for a moment I thought I'd overdone it as she hooped her arm into mine. Then she set off again and for a while we walked in step together with the aspect of a happy couple taking a routine stroll to the police station to make statements.

'Actually, it was your father's brainchild,' she said, picking up the thread again. 'I'll have a word with him. I'm sure he'll find a way of putting things right.'

Huzzah. This long-overdue measure sounded just the ticket to me. A word from his number two might just put an end to his crackpot wheezes and make the world safer for all.

'Yes. Do.'

As we continued at a leisurely pace, taking in what was a gloriously sweet summer's morning, I returned to our earlier point.

'Still, we excelled ourselves, didn't we? Were it not for us—'

She brought us to a halt again, rather sharply.

'Us?' she said. 'We?'

Her map clouded over as if I were speaking a foreign language.

'Yes, you know,' I said. 'Us. Nous.'

'Please don't mention nooses.'

'Oh, yes, sorry.'

'Hardly, Spencer.'

'Hmm?'

Now I was fogged.

'Thanks to the intervention from Sir Walter and me things ended without costing the institute a penny. Left to you they'd be milking the institute dry forever.'

I had an inkling she'd bring this up.

'Well,' I said, feeling it was indecorous to rake up the dirt, 'of course, last night there was scarcely time to explain. My intention was to dupe them.'

'Do what, pray?' she said incredulously.

'Dupe. Them.'

'By offering them how much they wanted, when they wanted, for as long as they wanted?'

Magda has a coarseness of tongue that can flay a carcass.

'If you must know, yes, that was the gist of it.'

She patted me on the chest and guffawed so violently that passers-by crossed the road to avoid the maniacal lady exploding with hilarity. I pressed on.

'It was a ruse to establish trust, sell them a fantasy and pull the rug from under their feet. Just as any bona fide businessman would.'

'Your father didn't think so,' she said as we entered the police station.

Chief Inspector Bartlett emerged from behind a door and, locking eyes on Magda, struck up conversation.

'Ah, Miss Emin, I understand you've made representations to the Home Sec—'

'Thank you,' snapped Magda.

'Well, I should like to say—'

'Let's discuss this in your office,' she said, abruptly.

Having been stifled in no uncertain fashion, for a moment, the chief inspector simply fidgeted nervously with the bristles of his moustache as if in the presence of a superior officer.

'Very well. This way, miss,' he said, beckoning her to follow him.

'See you back at the estate, Spencer,' she said, amiably.

I made nothing of this encounter between them, except perhaps that it was Magda's propensity to put officials in their place whenever the mood took her.

'Pip pip,' I said, with a carefree tap to the head.

A moment later, while I was merrily casting my mind back over this saga, a heavy hand landed on my shoulder.

'Ah, Mr Lockwood,' said Inspector Fletcher, materialising from nowhere. 'Here for your statement, I pr'sume. Follow me.'

He escorted me to an interview room and try as he might to be workmanlike about his civic duties, he exuded the air of a man who, having brought home the bacon, was looking forward to receiving a hero's distinction. With flashbacks still permeating my mind, I'd be the last to deny him if he were to rid us of these reprobates.

I sat down expecting to thresh out the epic from beginning to end, so I was surprised and not a little disappointed to find that the facts were largely already understood. I was simply asked to examine Magda's version of events, which I corroborated exactly. Evidently, she had marshalled events with her usual unerring deftness last night to the constable on guard outside Monty's bedchamber when she left me during those hairy moments to summon help. So, after adding a few morsels of my own to the details, with this formality briskly concluded, I got onto the burning question.

'So, when is the uncaging?'

He furrowed the brow.

'I beg your pardon.'

'When will you be releasing Monty?'

'Releasing?'

'Or hurling on ear. However you care to put it is all right with me.'

An internal tussle appeared to be going on in his mind whether I was merely unhinged or whether there was something more deeply wrong with me.

'Mr Lockwood,' he said, matter-of-factly, 'I feel it's my duty to inform you that Mr Fipps will be facing trial.'

'What!'

The man seemed to be speaking through the back of his head.

'What for?'

'For abducting Natalia Sabauri.'

'But, Natalia—'

'I can't go into her side of things. All I'm prepared to say is he has confessed to it.'

These clipped words barrelled into me with the force of a cricket ball hurled by a spindly tyke with gifted timing.

'What?' I said, rubbing my temples.

'He has confessed.'

The turpitude of recent events seemed to pale into insignificance in light of this dynamite revelation. I don't know if you've had the plug to your world yanked out to any great extent, but when someone has detonated a shock in this beastly way, you begin to question if the person making you feel dizzy isn't doing it for thrills. One look at his grave expression assured me that he wasn't.

I rose and tottered out of the door, thunderstruck. As his words ricocheted around the cerebellum, I sat on a seat in the waiting area to help me cope with the aftershock of this bulletin. I was groping helplessly to make sense of it. Amid a haze of myriad possibilities, one thing stuck out by a mile – it was the inviolable truth that no one can grasp defeat from the jaws like Monty. I fumbled to work out how this feat might have been achieved and came to the conclusion that it simply bore out what I've often said – once you eliminate the impossible, whatever remains, however dunderheaded, is what Monty will do.

I demanded to see him right away and found the blighter reclining on the issue bench as if glad of the rest.

'Spencer!' he said, rising to his feet.

From bow to stern, he had the dishevelled appearance of a man who's spent a night in the coop, but in other respects, he seemed robust and forthright, almost as if it had done him a bit of good. Aunt Beatrice had often said one day we'd experience these just deserts and that it would do us good, but until now I wouldn't have believed it.

'You, you…'

I could hardly bring myself to say the words. He held up a hand and took me through what had transpired. I must say, he appeared quite resolute, under the circumstances, and I soon learned why.

'They asked me to unburden myself, whatever that means. "Comes easily to you, this kidnapping lark, does it?" one of them asked. Uncouth swine. I'll tell you, Spencer, I've never met a more intrusive bunch, but since they'd brought it up, I gave them a piece of my mind.'

'Good God,' I said.

'"As it happens," I said, "I can't see what business it is of yours, but if you must know, yes, it was my first time, actually."'

I closed my eyes, pinching the skin between them. His words, which usually enter one ear and whiz straight through the other, had now become lodged and were causing me a throbbing pain.

'It was the most extraordinary thing, what they were asking, Spence. "Have you always had these sordid appetites?" Inspector Fletcher asked. "Don't you have any remorse?" the other one asked. I mean, can you fathom it? I said I regretted not having more experience, certainly. One of the blighters banged the table, calling me a "damned sadist!", and left the room, blast it.

'Well, I mean to say, this all seemed to be getting a bit near the knuckle, so I asked Inspector Fletcher why, for goodness sake, they were so interested in what I liked or disliked and he told me to shut my disgusting trap and showed me my note and asked if it was my handiwork. I said, "Of course. It seemed the civil thing to do." He was stumped, positively stumped, I say.

'I said I couldn't fathom why they were making such a fuss over it all and he called me a degenerate and other things I won't repeat and terminated the interview saying I'll be in here awaiting trial, the blighters. Then they cooped me up again. Well, Spencer, I tell you, I refuse to cooperate any further.'

If this was Monty's definition of cooperating with the authorities, it was just as well he'd decided to cork it when he did.

'Monty, you blockhead, don't you realise that you have provided them with all the rope they need?'

'Eh?'

'They've now taken your witless drivelling and your note as a confession for willingly and knowingly doing the dirty deed.'

'What deed?' he asked.

'Kidnapping, you witless chump!'

'But…' he said, the gravity of the situation hitting the densest of regions in the galaxy for the first time. 'Good lord!'

All of a sudden, his feet seemed unable to stop dancing. He started babbling and burbling in agitation from the realisation of what it all meant. The enormity of his predicament had at last come to him in no uncertain fashion. An officer came to bang on the bars to quell the hysteria and I was led out for disturbing the prisoner. Monty just about managed to shout something over my shoulder about enlisting 'Humph'. This was double Dutch to me at the time.

'It'd be capital punishment if it was up t' me,' snarled the officer, ejecting me onto the street.

I lowered myself gingerly down on a bench outside the station in a state of befuddlement after this encounter. In a perverse twist in fortunes, Monty appeared to have sealed his fate. A trial now loomed. And when I thought back to how Monty had a constitutional knack for muddling situations, the outlook filled me with dread.

With the refreshing air breezing over me I found myself whisked back to the time that Gerard de Bouza, a mature overseas attendee with a trusting and avuncular disposition, had attached himself to Monty. His wife, a religious sort of cove, thanked the heavens he'd made a friend of sensibility. It was only when Monty mentioned to her that Gerard, hitherto an abstemious teetotaller, had sampled the devil's brew and had become so dashed stimulated in merriment that he was 'guzzling as if he were dying of thirst' that the horror began to set in.

'Goodness knows what tyrant forbade it!' said Monty, sloshing her on the back and pushing off.

This short reminiscence stirred me to the core. His situation may be bleak, desperate even, but it was not a fait accompli; and I couldn't let this be Monty's lot. Oh, my word, no. The task that lay ahead was to secure the best defence in the land, by which I mean a legal bird loony enough to risk career suicide on this case. As I wondered who might possibly want anything to do with it, Monty's last words came to me – Humphrey. He'd been referring to the practice of Cornelius Humphrey Ponseby, the only barrister I knew who was still prepared to engage with Lockwood Institute in some capacity. There wasn't a moment to lose, so I pitched up at his none too salubrious chambers to speak with learned counsel.

I'd barely rapped the knocker when there came a heavy pounding tread and the oak door swung open and I was enveloped in a cloud of cigar smoke. It cleared enough for me to discern a stocky form of kindly appearance in his late forties wearing a smoking jacket. As I dithered on the doorstep an outstretched arm seized me by the lapels and, before I knew it, I was yanked into the dank corridor.

'Delightful to make your acquaintance,' said the baritone figure, vigorously shaking my hand.

'Ah,' I began, nervously. 'I suppose I'm looking for Ponseby. But perhaps Flock or Cromby will do.'

'All three? Good lord, what have you done?' said the old bird with a wheezy laugh that seemed it might be his last. 'My dear fellow, my associates Flock and Cromby have taken up new lines as it were. Can't be helped, can't be helped. How can I assist?'

'Perhaps I should speak to a solicitor to instruct you properly.'

'No, no need, young sir. I can direct you to just the fellow afterwards. He'll be only too happy to oblige with a brief. You can save me the trouble of reading it. Now, please sit down,' he said with a tap on my chest and plonking himself heavily behind the desk. 'Ponseby at your service.'

As I sat down he disappeared behind another grey cloud, entirely comfortable in this miasma, which is more than could be said for me. I remember feeling more than a little disconcerted to learn what remained of this renowned trio. I couldn't help feel that it was roughly equivalent to arriving at the quarters of the three musketeers to find it consisting of only Porthos. Still, I ploughed on and put the matter before the genial fellow.

'I'd like you to represent a chum of mine in a case—'

He held up one of his mitten-like hands.

'Aren't you Sir Walter's boy?'

'Afraid so,' I said, adding hastily, 'I mean, I'm afraid what I have may seem a somewhat grisly case.'

'Delicious,' he said, popping a bottle top and generously splashing some whisky about. 'Enlighten me.'

'Oh, well, if you insist,' I said, accepting a swirling measure. Goodness knows I could use it. 'You see, it concerns a case of whisky, er, kidnapping.'

He tutted at some length at the very inhumanity of it.

'Wretched business. Still, have no fear,' he said slinging back the dose. 'We'll make sure the degenerate rots behind bars for eternity.'

I admired the man's gusto, but clearly I hadn't made myself clear to the genial fellow.

'Mr Ponseby, you mistake me. I'm seeking a defence.'

'Eh?' said the weighty lawman as if this went against the grain of all litigation wisdom. He leaned his bulk forward on his elbows, the desk straining under the weight as he pondered this.

'Oh well, have it your way,' he said, lolling back in his padded seat and pouring another measure. 'I'm not much cop at prosecution anyway. So, leave it to me, young Lockwood, there's none better in establishing they've got the wrong man so rest assured—'

'But that's just the thing, Mr Ponseby,' I said. 'He did do it. And he is the right man.'

His cigar drooped sullenly at the news.

'Come again?'

'He did do it. Officially, that is. He's already told the police as much, but…' I trailed off, trying to cudgel the bean in desperation for a way to put it to him. 'He didn't appreciate the ramifications, if you follow me.'

I fretted at how to explain to this bird that I was cousins with the sort of chump who gets it into his nut that shanghaiing a young woman is the height of romantic expression. Naturally, he strained to understand and, seeing my unease, suggested we start from the beginning.

'Who, pray, is the client?'

'Edgar Montgomery Fipps.'

He deflated visibly.

'Oh.'

It's never terribly inspiring when the counsel for the defence asks you the name of the defendant and, at the mention of it, sinks disconsolately back in their seat in a defeated manner. Hope starts to haemorrhage. This turn for the unexpected clearly put a different complexion on matters.

'Reverend Fipps,' he said, clearing his throat, 'is known to the firm, you might say, and I have had occasion to hear of some of young Mr Fipps's exploits, but enough of family traits. Now, you say, he admitted to the act, so the police have a confession that he did it, but he doesn't really believe he did it. Is that so?'

I swallowed hard and cursed Monty.

'Yes, that's it.'

He rose to his feet and, judging by the frown lines and pained expression on his dial, he was the one who now seemed in a state of confusion. He began pacing the room.

'And where is this young lady?'

'Natalia? She's in chokey for kidnapping Monty.'

A heavy heel thudded the floor and he just caught himself from over-balancing.

'Come again?'

I gave him a précis of the imbroglio. Then in a slow and measured way he sat down, fixing me squarely with a grim sedulous eye.

'Forgive me for asking, Mr Lockwood, but is your friend compos mentis?'

Realising that these terms carry particular connotations in legal circles, I hesitated.

'How do you mean?'

'Mr Lockwood, I mean is Monty of sound mind?'

'Oh, I see,' I said, feeling a fool. 'Good heavens, no.'

He started.

'And why not?'

Well, of all the googlies that have come careering my way, none have double-backed and struck me repeatedly on the occiput like this one.

'Mr Ponseby, the list of possible answers occurs to me as so numerous that I fear we might both expire of old age before the end.'

'Very well, allow me to shorten your answer. Was there a single factor that might have caused Monty to commit this act?'

'Ah,' I said, adopting the argot of the man, 'you're referring to the real culpus, what?'

'Not exactly, Mr Lockwood. Perhaps we should stick to English. What might've been his motive?'

'Oh, well, that's easy. Because he's cock-a-hoop over this Natalia sort.'

'Now we're getting somewhere,' Ponseby continued, slurping another whisky and tutting disapprovingly. 'He was inebriated.'

'No, no. More like punch-drunk, I'd say. Bowled over. Smitten, if you follow me.'

I was glad to see the farthing drop.

'Ah, you mean he was in love.'

'Well,' I said, shifting uncomfortably, 'if you want to put it crudely.'

'Now, do you think Natalia would uphold this allegation by interpreting Monty's actions as he has?'

I harked back to that evening when the Brigadier and Natalia had coyly revealed to us Natalia's secret longing. All of a sudden my heart began racing. I hadn't considered this aspect to the affair and the more I pondered, the more plausible it seemed that her account might align with Monty's side of events. This would be the final nail in the sarcophagus.

'Yes, quite likely,' I said, draining my glass.

'Ah,' he said ominously before rising to his feet and pouring us both another doleful measure. 'Well, in that case, Mr Lockwood, I have no hesitation in recommending a plea of insanity.'

'What?'

'Moreover, I should propose to argue that Monty had been afflicted and entered into a beleaguered state of mind that rendered him unaware of his actions – ergo that his state of infatuation itself was, nay, *is* a debilitation of the mind.'

'Mr Ponseby,' I said, trying with difficulty to grasp the nettle, 'do you mean that he'd become intoxicated?'

'Delirious.'

'As if gripped by some insidious agent, you mean?'

His eyes beamed with radiance and the eyebrows rose an inch upward.

'Do you mind if I write that down?' he said, scribbling on his pad and rising quickly. 'Indeed, I do. With a progressive deterioration of mind. Intoxicated to oblivion, Mr Lockwood, intoxicated to oblivion. It's a potent force.'

'I see,' I said.

He reached for the last remnants of the bottle and, the effects starting to become abundant, poured it two inches left of his glass.

'Blast,' he said, mopping up the spillage with his handkerchief. 'Mr Lockwood, the instant I saw you I knew we were of one mind.'

I must say, this was troubling for many reasons. Not least because I could imagine nothing that would whip the general populace into a rampaging mass of dissent quicker than the suggestion that the ungovernable force of union commonly known as love is, in reality, a malign affliction that saps all reasoned judgement. In any case, as far as I know nobody in their right mind has stood in a court of law to assert that it is one stop on the road to the sanatorium. I stirred in my chair with every intention to leave.

'Pardon me, Mr Lockwood,' he interrupted, 'I shan't detain you long, but allow me a moment before you decide one way or another. Now, the validity of this line of argument rests with how well it stands up to scrutiny by the opposing side's cross-examination in court. So let us imagine it.'

By this stage I had begun to see that there was much in the thinking of Athos and Aramis when they had opted to do without this bassy compadre by their side. Monty may not be the full shilling, but to a jury with even the slightest romantic stirrings, this heretic was positively certifiable. Setting aside that this cuts unshakeably close to the truth is one thing, but suggesting that the scientific explanation for this curious phenomenon of pining hearts and the poetry industry is in fact a virulent pandemic that renders rash acts to go unchecked, it naturally follows that the only responsible course for responsible governments is to halt the spread of the contagion with a vaccine. The net result? Societal meltdown. Civilisation collapses and anarchy reigns. I was still gripped by these ghastly visions when Ponseby brought me back to his mock cross-examination.

'Had Monty been rendered unable to think properly?'

'Well,' I said, trying to think of the last time he ever had, 'he is easily boggled.'

'Hmm… but does this constitute a loss of reason?'

I considered the reason for his infatuation with Natalia and, well, I was hard-pressed to find any.

'Yes. Total loss of reason.'

'And would you say he was exhibiting this mental derangement at the time?'

When I considered that Monty had voluntarily chosen to stay in the woods in the black forest at night with Natalia and the Brigadier after our series of near misses and mishaps, it was clear to all thinking quarters that these were the rash actions of a deranged mazzard.

'Completely.'

'Well, if what you say is true, I should advise this plea on grounds that he was not of sound mind. Would you say these behaviours were characteris— actually, no need to answer that.'

I rose with the intention of making a polite exit and had got halfway across the room when I paused. It struck me that leaving without engaging this man's services might have catastrophic consequences itself – Monty may be compelled to make his own defence. Heaven forfend! This could have only one outcome – Monty would end up inexplicably boosting the case for the prosecution. After all, if ever there was an ace for scoring own goals, Monty was indubitably that man. When I weighed the outcomes I retook my seat.

'Mr Ponseby, putting the question of insanity to one side for the moment, could you not put up a defence?'

He seemed flummoxed.

'I don't follow.'

'I mean, plead not guilty.'

'Not guilty?' he said, darkening his brow. 'I thought he has already confessed.'

'Ah, yes, but I mean Natalia had consented to meet Monty at the lodge. He told me so.'

He lolled in his chair, looking at the ceiling.

'Well, Mr Lockwood, did you witness this arrangement to meet?'

'No,' I said, disappointedly. 'There were no witnesses.'

'Well, then each side would be relying on the word of their client. Monty would of course maintain that it was voluntary, while the prosecution would claim the opposite. Then there is the question of whether Natalia was willing to remain or not.'

'Oh, I can answer that. She was. I saw her.'

He surged his enormous bulk forward, leaning on his elbows, and another cloud of smoke billowed from him.

'Come again?'

'I saw her prancing around freely.'

'And Mr Fipps?'

'No, he wasn't prancing.'

'What was he doing?'

I hesitated to vouchsafe too much.

'He was,' I said, clearing my throat, 'sitting stationary for the most part.'

His eyes now sparkled with interest.

'And Mr Lockwood, would you take to the witness box to reveal this?'

'Certainly.'

And with a heavy thump of a palm on the table, he rose suddenly as though his soul had been transported to the clouds.

'Finally! A case I can get my molars into. How I've longed for…'

Here his expression fell into a sullen gloom; the light of wonder in his eyes extinguished like a flame. I'd never seen a man go from bombastic to crestfallen so quickly.

'Oh dear.'

'What is it, Mr Ponseby?'

'Dear, dear, dear.'

I repeated myself anxiously. He lowered himself gingerly into his chair with a defeated manner as if his dreams had just been obliterated. Strength seemed to ebb from him.

'No trial, alas.'

'What?'

'Without evidence that Natalia was induced or forced to go to the lodge the case is rocky enough, but if it can be shown that she remained of her own volition, the case stands very little chance of ever making it to trial.'

Here he sighed and stared dejectedly into the inkwell of his desk. As I took in the sight of the sunken figure and realised what a considerable boon the case would have been to his practice, I confess, my heart went out to the desolate fellow. It's always dashed awkward when you've just witnessed a chap's hopes be crushed and he sits before you in pieces while in your breast you're harbouring a secret euphoria. It makes the business of edging away all the harder. Thankfully, I saw an upside to our meeting.

'Well, Humphrey,' I said, remembering the upcoming case against the trio, 'don't despair. I'd say it's merely a matter of time till you are called upon for a different case, old man.'

With that glib remark I left the dispirited legal eagle and, after startling a few pedestrians by giving an unrestrained 'Whoopee!', I broke into a brisk step along Winsbrook's main thoroughfare with the singular goal of bringing this life-saving bulletin to the prisoner languishing in durance vile.

I arrived windswept and wheezing to find myself facing the same officious blighter who'd ejected me and it was only after learning that I was acting in the capacity of Monty's legal scout that he acquiesced. I don't know why putting one over on any doorman provides such uplift but it does. It was a euphoric moment.

Having tackled the ogre at the gate, I strode purposefully along with an all-conquering spirit regarding myself, justifiably I think, like an emissary on the wings of justice, but when I fetched up to Monty's spartan residence, I found that he was far from the demoralised wreck I'd imagined him to be. If anything, he seemed to be in his element. He was lying down on the plank bed, sloth-like, with his head resting against the wall, tongue jutting out, inscribing something in a notebook as if doing the crossword.

Such was his ease that I was reminded of our youth when he and I would be ordered to Headmaster Rotherham's office for the customary lash. Even at the time it struck me that there was a dividing line between those whom the courts would come to know on a first name basis and those who've simply been caught up in events. Now, seeing him take this spell in the jug in his stride, part of me wondered to which camp Monty belonged.

As I came to a stop he held up a patronising finger lest I ruin his concentration. He didn't look up. I stood there silently like a dispatch rider arriving at the court of Henry VIII with a message from the Pope only to find the 'do not disturb' sign on the door. It was more than a little galling.

Eventually he noticed me.

'Ah, good lord!' he said, brightening amiably. 'I thought you were one of the fuzz. You stomp just like them.'

Bursting as I was to spill the beans, you'd imagine that I would've uncorked the news without delay, and I would have done so, but curiosity had got the better of me.

'Doodling to pass the time, I see.'

'Hmm? Oh, no, no. Just writing a letter.'

Gadzooks! That Monty should look to take up letter writing again so soon after landing himself so spectacularly in the cart was typical. But Monty is nothing if not pugnacious, so I let it pass.

'Who are you writing to?'

'The Director of Public Prosecutions.'

'What! What for?'

He rose to his feet.

'You don't reach those heady heights without being a man of the world and I'd hazard this is one of many parallels in our lives. So, he's bound to be a decent egg and see things my way, what?'

The passing of events being what they were, I freely admit I was not at my quickest, but even so, I wasn't following the thread of this bilge.

'Why?'

He eyed me as if I'd gone off my chump.

'To intervene in my case, of course.'

I was flabbergasted. This rolled off his lips as though he were expecting the director to take one look at his illegible scribble, recognise a cry of help from a long-lost brother and come bounding over jangling the keys.

He showed me the letter. It ran as follows:

Dear DOPPS,

I had to write over this ghastly Natalia business. I expect you've heard of it, have you? Well, as man-to-man, these dunces at the constabulary are barking up the wrong tree, you know. Keep insisting on a beastly trial. Anyway, I was cogitating over it when I remembered (a lesson from school) that if I were ever to find myself wrongly cooped up in the jug that I ought to write asking for Habeas Corpus. I can't quite put my finger on what it is exactly, but it sounds just the ticket, so I'd be awfully obliged if you could dispense it, as it were. Don't linger too long over it, old man. I can be reached at the Winsbrook Constabulary, Suffolk.

Toodle pip.

Edgar Montgomery Fipps Esq.

Obviously I'd arrived in the nick of time. Far be it from me to deny a man every effort when he's up against it, but if one must invoke a centuries-old doctrine to ensure one's liberty, it's best not to evoke the impression that you're asking the director if he might manage to tear himself away from the putting green. When it came to impudence, Monty had entered a different league.

'Monty,' I said, suddenly gulping hard, 'there is no need for such a chit, old man. I bring cheery tidings. While you've been lounging, I've been busy getting the inside scoop.'

'News?' he said, sceptically. 'What news?'

'Your freedom is assured,' I said, with a grand wave of the hand. 'I heard it from Humphrey's own lips.'

'Spencer, don't toy with me. Is this the usual claptrap that I have come to expect from you or is there something to this?'

One who has been at their wits' end in the service of a chump trying to steer him clear of calamities might have bridled at hearing their efforts being thus described, but so topping did I feel that I barely noticed it. One must make allowances, I felt, for the opinions of the incarcerated male to sink to new lows.

'It carries the assurance of Humphrey Ponseby himself.'

He brightened immeasurably. And in a few minutes I summarised my conference with the lawman, laying the facts squarely before him.

'So, there you are, old prune. Your position is unassailable. You need only wait patiently and at the stroke of midnight you will hear the keys jingle, and in a few short hops you shall rejoin the league of free men again.'

And from the way his eyes welled up and his lower lip quivered, I was reminded again of that batsman with whom I began this volume and took it that, in much the same way, just the right spot had been hit.

'In that case, Spencer, old fruit,' he said, his voice tremulous with emotion, 'you couldn't bring me the crossword, could you?'

Chapter Fifteen

I ignored Monty's request for a diverting time-filler in the slim hope that the slower passing of time might allow him to reflect on his recent actions and when I got back I reported directly to the tsar's office. This was to be my last duty, I resolved, before slinking off for a well-earned siesta. I entered Magda's lair expecting her to be the epitome of stolid application to the demands of her duties, but as I stood in the doorway to find her staring into space, twiddling with a pen and grinning to herself, it gave me a moment's pause. Here was a lady exhibiting all the signs that it was a mighty fine day.

My entrance seemed to break the spell and no sooner had I finished furnishing her with the news regarding Monty than she bounded forward and folded me in an embrace, much like I had done to her at the soirée.

'You astound me, Spencer,' she said, enfolding me in her arms. 'You'll become a man of worth yet.'

'Not if I have anything to do with it,' I said, shuddering at the prospect.

She babbled something about a family meeting at eight o'clock in Sir Walter's study, but I beat a hasty retreat from her office.

Later that evening as Uncle Cedric, Aunt Beatrice and I assembled in Sir Walter's study awaiting Sir Walter and Magda for an extended family briefing on developments in the Monty affair, the ambience was, I'm forced to admit, strained to say the least. They, Aunt Beatrice and Uncle Cedric, that is, had blown back from visiting Monty in clink and lost no time in levelling the charge of irresponsibility I'd been expecting at me.

'How could you let this happen, you congenital blockhead?!' she bellowed, rattling the windows.

She was, I discovered, just limbering up. For the good of this volume I've refrained from repeating the coarser means of expression which now fumed out of her, but suffice to say that it was ripe stuff. In those few moments my ears were assailed with more tang and zip than the Brigadier had managed throughout.

Just as Aunt Beatrice had stopped for breath, Uncle Cedric became vocal, with altogether different concerns.

'Beatrice, I may as well tell you that if I get any letters from the Archdeacon over this Monty business, I'm going to say that I'd always suspected his true parentage and direct him to you.'

'What!'

They bickered for some time over whose example Monty had followed all his life, as if that could possibly explain the Monty phenomenon, and my polite interjection to remind them of his imminent release did little to raise their spirits. A decided froideur remained in the breast of the aunt. Uncle Cedric, meanwhile, seemed to fall into a reverie and began reliving some of his own hair-raising antics in his youth which seemed to be the embodiment of the Monty spirit.

We were sitting in an atmosphere of frosty silence when we discerned a faint rhythmic grunting, clacking and stomping coming from the corridor. We ignored it at first, but it grew louder and when it seemed almost upon us, we twisted round in unison to see Sir Walter grimacing and breathing in a laboured sort of way while standing in the doorway with his foot in plaster and crutches under each armpit. He advanced ponderously towards us, six inches at a time.

'All rise,' whispered Uncle Cedric, gently elbowing me.

I was standing in respectful attention of the incoming commandant before I realised it was Uncle Cedric's way of trying to lighten the mood. I must say, the sight of Sir Walter already mobile, albeit aided with supports, came as quite a shock to the system. I'd been expecting him to be laid up long enough such that he emerged a wiser human being for his experience and showering kisses to all of earth's creatures, particularly relatives, but to come upon him active so soon, obdurately sticking to the programme, it seemed to me that he'd foregone the most essential step in the healing process. I regarded him with a distinct weariness. Directly he sank into his chair he lit a rare scented cigar and beamed at us with the air of resolute triumph. Worryingly, he seemed more like his old self than ever.

Magda followed and appeared buttoned-up and sphinx-like, but also carrying a certain glint in the eye. She perched herself on the corner of the mammoth-sized desk.

'Now,' said Sir Walter, getting down to brass tacks, 'this wretched business with Monty. Foul business, what?'

'Very foul, very foul,' agreed Magda.

'And not to be presumptuous, but I understand that there is no case to answer,' he said, jabbing me with a crutch. 'Isn't that so, Spencer?'

'Huh?'

Never before having been asked my views, I usually made up the silent minority in these briefings, so I was rather caught out by the question. He pressed on, leaving me flailing to catch up.

'So, then there remains the question of this Safari Chamber Music Trio—'

'Sabauri,' I corrected.

'What?' he said, losing his rhythm. 'Well, dammit, who cares what this sodding outfit call themselves? The fact is that they are out of our hair.'

I looked up at his shiny bald dome and was relieved to hear it.

'What do you suppose will happen to them?' said Aunt Beatrice.

'Nothing less than purgatory if I had my way,' said Uncle Cedric, crisply.

'Cedric,' said Aunt Beatrice, kindly patting him on the arm and lowering her voice, 'do try to be a clergyman some of the time.'

'Don't worry, Mr and Mrs Fipps,' said Magda, 'we have taken steps.'

'Can't we throw them in the crypt?' said Uncle Cedric.

'I'm afraid not,' said Magda.

'Why not?' said Aunt Beatrice, warming to the suggestion.

'We couldn't do that, Mrs Fipps,' said Magda. 'The expense. No, they'll be returned to Malta and Georgia.'

'By Jove!' said Aunt Beatrice. 'The speed of the diplomatic machine astounds me. Who says it's not like the olden days?'

'Extradited?' asked Uncle Cedric, perking up.

Still contending with this instalment, I carried the silent air of a redundant committee member.

'Does that mean Monty and Kristina will need to go to Malta and Georgia to give evidence?' asked Aunt Beatrice.

I looked around and noted for the first time that Kristina was absent.

'What for?' asked Uncle Cedric.

'As witnesses for trial, of course.'

Sir Walter began swivelling in his voluminous desk chair.

'No,' he said, blowing smoke rings. 'Because there won't be a trial.'

'What!' said Aunt Beatrice.

'Straight in the jug and throw away the key?' said Uncle Cedric, enthusiastically. 'They know how to handle these rotters in Algeria.'

'Malta and Georgia, dear. Anyway, who are these bounders that they can just waltz off after such a reprehensible showing?'

Beatrice spoke with considerable feeling and stared unremittingly at Sir Walter. He pursed his lips under the piercing glare of the elder sibling and, I think, showed some contrition over throwing his lot in with the ghastly trio. It was left to Magda to provide the footnotes.

'They are known by some governments to operate under various guises and tour the international circuit seeking out hotspots for the wealthy.'

I became interested in where Lockwood Institute fared in their touring calendar, but before I could extract more details, Sir Walter took the floor.

'But,' he said, emphatically, 'their gross misjudgement lay in believing Lockwood to be a soft touch for such an enterprise. They learned a very sore lesson. Ha! Their tails are as firmly tucked between their legs as any have ever been.'

He delivered this rhetoric with a defiant flourish suggesting, to anyone who didn't know better, that his strategically placed trap had seen off the reprobates exactly as intended.

'So,' said Magda, intriguingly, 'we've come to an agreement.'

'With whom?' asked Aunt Beatrice, taking the words from my mouth.

'With the Home Office,' said Sir Walter, proudly.

My ears suddenly pricked up at this. With my offer having been so firmly squished and pulped, you'll forgive me for wanting to know more about this.

'What sort of agreement?' I said, apprehensively.

Magda glanced at Sir Walter for a by-your-leave. He unplugged his cigar, studied its glistening end and nodded.

'The embassies wanted to avoid it turning into an international scandal,' said Magda, 'and Lockwood can't afford the publicity of a cause célèbre.'

'So?' said Aunt Beatrice.

'So,' said Magda, taking a deep breath, 'in exchange for the trio being handed over, their embassies have guaranteed us a set number of visitors to Lockwood for the seven years they would have served.'

'What!' all three of us said in unison.

Several moments of stunned silence ensued in the wake of this depth charge. I received this diabolical announcement with incredulity, but when I came to reflect on the exalted circles into which Sir Walter had inveigled his way over the years, it became quite credible. When I considered that it was so often the striplings of the political classes that made up so many of the repellent specimens who infest the premises most seasons, it was almost inconceivable that those strings would not have been yanked in the style of village church bells.

Aunt Beatrice and I exchanged distasteful looks and, to my mind, there was no clearer manifestation of what someone once called 'the subtle designs and united cabals of ambitious citizens'. She patted my hand reassuringly, but it was Uncle Cedric, who had his heart set on punishment, who was sickening most of all.

This also served to magnify the other gulf separating us. I mean to say, for Magda and Sir Walter, inhabiting as they do a world of offers and counter-offers, this chicanery and promise of largesse amounted to a triumph and would have been lauded from the rooftops at the Chamber of Commerce, but there was something ineffably in the character of this Faustian pact that struck the three of us as just a little bit repugnant. And when it came to judging which breach of the code acted on me more – the injudicious actions of this ghastly trio or these serpentine dealings – I must say I'd be hard-pressed to choose between them.

Magda, perhaps sensing the mood plummeting, excused herself and beetled off. It was during this singularly glum moment that Monty drifted in looking more ruffled than his usually scruffy self, but otherwise unharmed for his ordeal. Had he arrived a few moments earlier he may have been swept up into the loving embrace of his parents and showered with kisses of relief, but the sour taste left in the mouth resulted in him receiving an avalanche of rebukes and reprimands at the hands of Aunt Beatrice.

As for me, taking my cue from Magda, I slipped away and scuttled to my quarters with every intention of banishing this ghastly episode from mind with a spot of refreshing repose, but as I slipped in between the sheets I found myself wondering, what if this marked merely the appetiser to the season?

THE END

{Please read the note from the author overleaf.}

Note from the Author

Dear Reader,
If you enjoyed reading this novel, please do leave a review where you purchased it and recommend it to like-minded friends. It would help me enormously. Thank you.
Yours faithfully,
P.S. Rover

Amazon UK	Amazon USA	Amazon India
https://amzn.to/3xgmOT4	*https://amzn.to/3924lR3*	*https://amzn.to/3Q1HZzK*

Other links:
facebook.com/fortefiction

To receive signed copies of books, free giveaways and enjoy author musings, discover more at *psrover.com*

Printed in Great Britain
by Amazon

87175355R00154